MW00352841

BETWEEN THESE SHEETS

BETWEEN THESE SHEETS

Devon McCormack

Other Works by Devon McCormack

Romance
Tight End
Filthy Little Secret
Weight of the World (with Riley Hart)
Faking It (with Riley Hart)

Dark Erotica
Bastards

Young Adult Titles
Hideous
When Ryan Came Back
The Night Screams
The Pining

1

Jay

"You want to start something?" Tyler asks.

"You already started it," I say, balling my hands into fists and stepping toward him.

I've only been here a few days, but this guy's been grating on my nerves ever since I began working at the factory. He's another packing associate, but for some reason, he thinks he's superior because he has a little seniority. I was fine with the attitude and him calling me Blue Jay to get on my nerves, but when he tripped me as I was heading to the loading dock, I was finished being cordial.

Glass is scattered across the floor beside the box I dropped. He could've seriously injured me.

"It was an accident, man," he says. "Not my fault you don't know how to use your goddamn feet."

That's it. I spring forward, fists flying. His jaw tenses, and he comes at me, rage in his eyes.

This is what he wanted. This is what he fucking asked for, but he's gonna wish he hadn't when I break his nose. I'm about to lay into him when a force hits my shoulder and knocks me to the side. I turn to the guy who pushed me and punch. The blow knocks him to the ground.

When I see who it is, I'm horrified—it's my boss, Reese Kline. The guy who interviewed me less than two weeks ago. The guy I practically begged to give me the position.

The right leg of his jeans is hiked up, revealing a dark gray metal rod. A prosthetic, I assume. Some of the guys in the office had mentioned he'd been in Iraq. The way he limps slightly, I assumed he'd been shot. No one said anything about him missing a fucking leg.

Shit.

His face bright red, his eyes are on me, and I don't see the friendly man who greeted me when I first got here. I see something darker—like I flipped a switch and now I'm facing off with the Hulk.

He rises to his feet, slowly, steadily, and I back up against the wall. Normally, I'd be game for challenging him, but the moment I saw his leg and the expression on his face, my guilt dissolved all my defensiveness. I want to tell him I'm sorry, but the words are stuck in my throat.

He approaches, but stops before reaching me, breathing heavily, his hands trembling beside him. "My office in fifteen minutes. No sooner. No later." His words are like bullets. Short. Quick. Frightening.

He walks away, leaving me in the middle of the small audience that's collected around me during the commotion. "Clean it up, Tyler," he calls over his shoulder, and I notice his limp more than I usually do—now understanding the reason for it.

The guys aren't even looking at me—not even Tyler, who I figured would be thrilled about me getting into trouble. We crossed a line with Reese, and I doubt that's something he's proud of. From what I know, the guys respect Reese. He's on the level with them, and he's a fair supervisor. Doesn't treat us like we're inferior. Doesn't condescend. It's hard as fuck to find a boss like him in this line of work. Typically, guys on the floor are talked down to by their superiors like we're too stupid to know the sky is blue. Reminds me of being a kid. Of my asshole father shouting at me like I was fucking nothing.

Tyler heads off to get shit to clean up the mess while I continue with my work. My co-worker William had dropped one of the packages off the forklift when he was moving them onto the loading dock, so I was helping him clean up the mess when I had my run-in with Tyler. I continue helping William, dreading this meeting with Reese.

I keep my eye on the warehouse clock uneasily. It's taking for-fucking-ever for fifteen minutes to pass.

After how I humiliated him in front of the whole warehouse, he's gonna fire me. That's all he can do. Guys like Reese have egos. Big ones. And they won't tolerate insubordination...or even worse, humiliation.

I've been in town less than a month. I thought I was lucky to have found a new job as fast as I did, but now I'm gonna have to pack up and head out.

Doesn't feel fair. But I'm the only one I can blame for this. It was one thing to lose my temper with Tyler. It was another to turn it on the guy who was friendly enough to give me a break after he called one of my references and discovered I'd lost my job because of my temper.

"One shot," he told me. "That's all you have. Got it?"

Shot blown.

I won't be groveling for my job. If he wants to get rid of me, I won't humiliate myself over mediocre work at a glass bottle factory. I can get a crap job like this in any town.

As the clock reaches the ten-minute mark, the suspense itches at me like a rash. Finally, the time comes, and I head to his office.

He's sitting at his desk. The cement walls behind him are lined with bookshelves and a few filing cabinets. He keeps his office clean.

His face stern, he rests a trembling hand on the table. "Close the door," he says as I enter. I obey and take a seat in front of his desk as I did when we had our first interview.

His bright blue eyes sparkle in the room's fluorescent lights, which casts sharp shadows beneath his cheeks. His tense jaw is covered in a dirty-blond beard that matches the tufts of his bangs, which wave to the side. His massive biceps shape the sleeves of his short-sleeved button-up. He's hot. The kind of guy I wouldn't mind rolling around in the sack with after a few drinks. The sort of guy I'd want to fuck. Hell, I'd let him inside me—let him take me, make me feel good. If only because there aren't enough moments like that in my life.

His gaze doesn't waver as I sit before him. He glares at me like he's two seconds from hopping up and beating the crap out of me for the spectacle I made of him in front of all his employees.

"Do you not understand the concept of one shot?" he asks.

This is the part where I'm supposed to defend myself. Tell him that Tyler started it. Go into the same long-ass monologue I would have gone into in the principal's office when I was a kid. But all I can think of is how much I've disappointed him. I don't know why that even matters. I guess because there are few guys who would have hired me after they found out from one of my previous employers that I was a troublemaker. But hell, no one ever checks my references for work like this, so I wasn't thinking he'd call anyone. As a packaging associate, you either can or can't do the job. It doesn't matter what sort of trouble you might have gotten into in the past. The fact that Reese took some time out of his day in the hiring process makes me respect him more.

A shame this is the last day I'll be working with him.

"Are you just going to sit there and stare at me?" he asks. His hand still noticeably shakes on the desktop, and as I gaze at it a little too long, he pulls it back and slides it under the table, never taking his eyes off mine.

"Mr. Kline, I'm sorry for pushing you," I say. I'm surprised by the sincerity in my own words. Typically, I'd be a dick. Maybe offer some facetious apology to piss him off even more, but I didn't mean to show every guy in the warehouse his fake leg. I didn't mean to expose his vulnerability. I wouldn't want that for myself or anyone else.

Although that must be one of only a few vulnerabilities a guy who's built like a pro-wrestler has to worry about.

Reese presses his tongue against his cheek. His gaze trails off, as if he's lost in deep thought about something. I can't imagine what. He just needs to tell me I'm fired and to grab my things out of my locker. Get the hell out of here. I can pack my bags in the room I'm renting and get the fuck out of town in no time. Move on like I always do.

Those blue eyes are on me again. "I've seen how Tyler's been treating you all week. Yeah, he's been a bit of a dick. He's gonna be that way because I technically brought you in to handle some things that he couldn't. He was shitty, but I don't need you making things worse during a tricky situation. That's what I'm here for. The guys give you crap, you come to me. My job is to take care of that."

Wait. Is he seriously letting me off the hook?

I'm so thrown by his words I can't even think straight. But as soon as I regain my composure, I say, "I don't need anyone protecting me from schoolyard bullies. I can take care of myself."

"If they're going to act like schoolyard bullies, then I'll discipline them like schoolyard bullies. That's my job, not yours."

The feeling of having an ally eases my tension.

"I catch you throwing punches or making a scene again," he adds, "I'll have your job, got it?"

I nod. "Yes, sir."

"It's Reese. Not *sir*," he says through his teeth.

I'm too stunned to say anything else. This can't be happening. Reese is the only boss I've ever had who would have tolerated that kind of behavior, especially when it resulted in such a humiliating incident.

"Now, get out of here and finish out your shift, okay?"

2

Reese

I'm still shaking from when Jay knocked me down.

I was on my way to the loading dock when I saw him and Tyler getting into it. I figured I'd just grab him. Get his attention. But then he turned on me, and the moment his fist made contact with my face, I was transported back into the heat of battle. It was a good thing he knocked me down, because if I hadn't had that time standing up to regain my bearings, I'm not sure what I would have done to him. With my adrenaline high and my body convinced I was facing an enemy, I could have laid a few blows to his head. Maybe severely injured him.

I haven't had an episode like that in a long time. I still have the usual ones. I'll never be totally fine, but I don't normally lose it. I might feel the impulse…Every muscle in my body might urge me to spring to life and kick some ass as every thought in my brain echoes the sentiment, demanding I act, but I've learned how to soothe those thoughts—at least enough that I'm not afraid of going apeshit on an employee.

Today was close.

Too close.

I've already been on edge recently. I'm hanging onto my sanity by a thread, and if I'd done something to Jay—hurt him in any way—I never would have forgiven myself. Not just because I'd lose my job and potentially have to deal with a lawsuit, but because it would mean that all this work—every group session, every therapy appointment, every month I spent working to find the right cocktail of pills—would have meant shit. I've worked too hard to get to this point. Too hard to live a somewhat normal life, even when the thoughts and emotions feel like they're too much to handle. Even when they overtake me to the point where I'm not sure I'll make it through the day.

I fought in the field, and now I fight in my mind. It's a battle I'll never win, and experiences like what just happened in the warehouse remind me of that.

When Jay leaves my office to return to his shift, I rise from my chair, adrenaline coursing through my veins. I'm waiting for this to pass. For my nerves to settle. But they're still overexcited.

Raging. Screaming at me to run for my life. Reminding me that if I'm not shooting, then I might wind up shot.

A weight presses down on my chest, making it difficult for me to breathe. Heat fills my cheeks, and the way my thoughts swirl, it seems like if I don't calm down soon, I might throw up.

I pace around the room, using every mental exercise I can conjure up to soothe myself, but I'm trapped in this spell. The best thing to do in moments like these is to surrender, so I lock my door and curl into a ball in the corner of the room. I need a few minutes. Need to remember that as much as it feels like these thoughts will destroy me, it'll pass like it always does.

Easier said than done.

I grip onto my leg—no, my prosthesis.

Sometimes I forget what it is. What I'm missing. What I can never get back.

***

I head out of the factory and see a few of the employees still lingering as they wait for rides, most from their spouses—some from their parents.

I'm still rattled from the experience with Jay, but at least the tension and the physical discomfort has settled. I noted the experience in an app on my phone, so I can bring it up with Laura, my therapist—one I pay for myself since the VA's resources are shit. Fortunately, the factory has an incredible insurance plan that allows me to see Laura, my psychiatrist, and my prosthetist.

Painful and frustrating as this can get, I'm one of the lucky ones. Despite how the terrors haunt me and how bad it can get, it's manageable enough that I can live some semblance of a normal life—enough that I can hide episodes from my employees. And I can function well enough with a job—something I knew I needed. Something I desperately fought for, not just because I need the money, but because I need my fucking sanity. At least when I'm busy, I can distract myself from the thoughts and sensations that bombard me on a regular basis.

On my way to my car, I see Jay standing before the open hood of his Honda Civic, which is scratched up and has a few dents in it. I figure it's an apt representation of where he's at in life.

I should breeze past him and head home. I'm too on edge. It's too easy for me to be triggered right now. But as he curses under his breath, I shift my direction toward him.

I know what's drawing me. His guardedness—his attitude—they remind me of my friend. And as much as I know that's liable to make what I'm experiencing even worse, I can't resist this impulse that pulls me to him.

He's so preoccupied he doesn't see me coming. His dark hair is a mess. Sweat and dust covers his face from the work in the warehouse. We all get a little film of crud on ourselves from being in there all day. He's wearing jeans and a t-shirt. When I reach the truck, he turns to me, his expression wide with confusion. Just like when he was looking at me in the warehouse after he pushed me down and exposed my leg for everyone to see.

Just thinking about that moment pains me. To be humiliated like that in front of my guys is a serious bruise to my ego. They know about the leg, though. They knew I was injured in the war. It's not something I've kept secret. Something like that's hard to hide because of my limp. But even though they know, I don't need them to be reminded of my faults. My weaknesses. My vulnerabilities. I'm their boss, not their friend.

"Oh, hey, Mr. Kline," he says, his brown eyes shifting between me and the inside of his hood.

"Car troubles?" I ask, inspecting the inside.

He bites his lip and avoids my gaze.

"You mind if I take a look?" I ask.

He steps away, wiping his hands on his already dirty jeans. "Sure," he says.

I inspect the inside before I try to start the engine.

"Looks like you've got a dead battery on your hands," I say as I step out of the driver's side and approach him.

"Fuck," he says, and I can see in his expression and in his rage that he has contempt for the whole universe. Like it has conspired against him like this.

He doesn't know shit about how horrible and cruel this world can be.

Some of the guys start laughing on the other side of the lot. "Motherfuckers," Jay says as he notices them. He starts their way, but I

10

snatch his arm, gripping onto his thick bicep in the leather jacket he's wearing.

I can't help but immediately imagine pulling him aside in my office and roughing him up a bit. Wiping that frustrated look off his face and replacing it with one of pure joy.

"Did you already forget what I fucking told you?" I ask, shaking the fantasy from my thoughts. Although it's not that easy to get rid of.

"They're just loving this," he says, his expression filled with confusion and rage.

"I don't need you starting another scene right now, okay? Just be glad I don't have any other appendages you can share with the world."

His rage shifts to worry and guilt in an instant. "Dude, I'm sorry about that. I really didn't—"

"I was just trying to make light of it. Don't get weird on me, okay?"

He nods. "Yes, sir."

"I get that you want to be polite and all, but like I keep telling you, you can just call me Reese."

I don't like hearing the sort of *yes sirs* that were so common when I was in the service. Even worse is being called by my last name since that's what people were always shouting at me when we were in the thick of it, scrambling for our lives, wondering if the guns being fired around us would be the ones that finally took us out.

"Yes, Reese," he says.

It's like training a goddamn robot.

I close the hood of his car. "Just act cool, and I'll drive you home." I start for my car, but then turn back around. He hasn't moved. He stands there, staring at me, as if he's surprised by something. "You fucking coming?" I ask him.

"You're serious?"

"What part of that sounded like a joke?"

"Sorry. I'm just…Never mind."

I lead him to my car. We hop in. He notices how I tuck the prosthesis on my right leg under my left leg to drive.

I'm not thrilled about him seeing me like this, but he already knows, so what the fuck do I have to hide? We head onto the main road. He says he's staying off Moreland in East Atlanta, which is on the way to my house in Grant Park, so I won't have an issue dropping him off.

We have a twenty-minute drive before we get to his place, so I keep my country music turned up—Travis Tritt—hoping I won't have to worry about making conversation with him.

"I hear you were in Iraq," Jay says.

"Just because you saw my leg doesn't mean you have to chat with me about it."

"I'm sorry. I just...If I'd known..."

"Wouldn't have changed how you lost it today."

He silences and waits a few minutes before saying, "Look, Tyler's just been kind of a dick, and that's why I—"

"You let me worry about Tyler. It's none of your business anymore. My only suggestion to you is to not make any more enemies."

"Easier said than done. Seems like that's all I ever make."

I'm not surprised. The guy clearly has a chip on his shoulder. "It'll serve you to remember that."

"What?"

"I'm just saying if you make enemies everywhere you go, it's probably not because there's a problem with everywhere you go."

"You saying Tyler was right?"

"Nope. Everyone has a way with dealing with shit like that, but most people don't resort to flipping the fuck out is all I'm saying."

Jay looks like he's about to start a fight with me over it, so I say, "That was some friendly advice from a boss to his employee, so I suggest you keep your lips sealed and act appreciative of it."

He's quiet again, though I suspect he's less than appreciative of my suggestion. I don't care. From what I can tell, he's trouble. And that's not what we need at the factory. If he doesn't straighten up, he's getting the fucking boot.

I won't stand for his fucking attitude. Although, his attitude, his uneasiness...those are the things that remind me of Caleb. Ever since he interviewed, he reminded me of my bunkmate—my best friend in the whole goddamn world. And despite how careful I'm trying to be, I know that's why I'm really helping him.

3

Jay

I don't know what Reese said to Tyler, but it's been a week since the incident, and Tyler hasn't teased me or been an asshole. But as friendly as Reese was the other day, he hasn't gone out of his way to be any nicer to me. Greets me like he would any of the other guys—with a nod and not so much as a friendly smirk. I can see why everyone falls into line under this guy. He's intimidating as hell. When I was in the car with him and he was basically saying I brought this kind of shit on myself, I wanted to argue with him, but I didn't want to stir his rage again. I saw what that looked like, and it freaked me the hell out. I'm one to get angry. I'll explode during a situation like the one with Tyler. What happened to Reese is so far beyond that. It wasn't just like he lost his mind. It was like he knew he had and wasn't sure he could control himself.

I sit by myself at a table in the break room, taking fifteen minutes to grab a drink from the vending machine. With my earbuds in, I listen to an old Louis C. K. special. I have a bunch of comedy specials downloaded on my phone that I like to listen to—Richard Pryor, George Carlin, Joan Rivers, Rita Rudner.

Reese walks in, looking particularly agitated as he fidgets about. He's rattled, as though something's just happened to him.

He's prepping for a major inventory audit next week. He's been sticking around after hours for the past few days pulling all-nighters, and it's weighing him down. His beard appears a little rougher than usual—more uneven, like he needs a trim.

He heads to the vending machine and pops a dollar in before pressing a button. There's a thud as a snack hits the bottom of the machine.

He doesn't look at me as he kneels down and retrieves a Snickers bar. Not the healthiest of choices, but considering I'm planning to heat a package of Bowl of Noodles in the microwave for lunch, who am I to judge?

Some guys pass outside the doorway. The last guy has a cart piled with long sheets of metal. They're the repairmen who came in to fix one of the annealing machines that broke down on the other side of the factory. I'm guessing they're pulling the sheets from storage to make repairs—another task that's been agitating Reese since corporate's having a fit about how we're behind on our orders.

The repairman pushing the cart keys something in on his phone, not paying much attention. One of the sheets looks like it's about to slide free. I consider warning the guy, but I don't want to call him out in front of the boss. No need to get him into any trouble over something stupid. Worst case scenario is he loses it and has to put it back on.

My prediction comes true after he passes the doorway, and a loud clang echoes through the hall—the metal against the concrete floor sounding like a fucking gun going off. It shocks me, but then Reese slips behind the vending machine, disappearing out of sight.

I can't help but chuckle. *Oh, wow. What a fucking scaredy-cat.* My laugh is soft, and I wait for him to step out and admit he was a fucking pansy about something pretty stupid.

But he doesn't come out.

What the fuck is he doing?

I rise from my chair and approach him, pulling my earbuds out and sliding them into my pocket.

He's huddled in a fetal position, shaking. Trembling.

It only takes me a moment before the obvious realization hits me. This is about a lot more than some dumb fucking noise.

Post-traumatic stress disorder. I've seen it in movies and shit. Even known a few guys who've had these kinds of reactions to loud sounds after they served in the army. I've seen guys agitated, but not like this.

A voice comes from outside: "Holy shit!"

It's Tyler. I hear a few guys chuckle in the hallway. Judging by the way their voices amplify, they're on their way to the break room. Makes sense since they're in the first round of guys to take lunch.

I'm hardly thinking my actions through as I close the door and turn the lock.

"Hey, what the fuck?" Tyler says as he rattles the door handle from the other side. *Fucking douchebag.*

I turn to Reese, who's still shaking. Not moving.

A loud knock comes from the other side, which I know sure as fuck can't be helping Reese.

"You can't come in here," I say.

"What the fuck do you mean?"

I scan my stupid brain for any excuse that might remotely make sense. "Reese told me not to let anyone in the room. I was a dumbass and broke some bottles in here when I was coming to grab a drink, okay? He doesn't want anyone to come in until he comes back with some shit to clean it up with."

"You're just accident-prone as shit, aren't you?" Tyler asks, amusement in his tone.

Normally, I would be upset that he's referring to when he was a dick and tripped me, but right now, my mind is only on the fact that he needs to go the fuck away so Reese won't have to deal with another embarrassing situation. Maybe this'll make up for that dumb-shit move I pulled last week.

Tyler and his buds groan and their voices trail off as they move farther and farther from the door.

I turn back to Reese. His head shifts slightly back and forth.

I approach him and kneel so I'm at his level. I'm cautious. I don't want him to snap, but he needs someone here for him. And I want him to know he can trust me with this. "Reese," I say.

"Fucking…leave," he says through gritted teeth, his gaze straight ahead of him. He looks like he's concentrating very hard on something. Struggling to concentrate, even.

It's a harsh reaction considering I just saved his ass from being seen by those assholes, but I get why he wants me out of here.

"I'm not leaving you like this."

He moves his lips like he's trying to say something, but nothing comes out.

"Dude, I'm staying here until this passes," I add. "If I leave, any of the other guys can come in here. Is that what you want?"

He closes his eyes, muttering to himself.

I feel like crap. Wish there was something I could do to help him. Not just because he's tortured by whatever the fuck memory he's experiencing from Iraq, but because I know what it's like to feel embarrassed—to be ashamed and want everyone in the world to leave me the fuck alone.

I try to think of something to say, but everything that comes to mind seems trite. Like it'll just annoy him more than anything else. The last thing he needs right now is a series of clichés to pull him out of his very real pain.

Tears rush from his eyes, down his cheeks. I turn away.

"I'm just gonna come over here and not look at you, okay? I'll just keep guard, and you can do whatever you need to do." I head to the table, facing the wall.

He breathes intensely. Like it's nearly impossible for him to get air in.

"Do I need to call an ambulance?" I ask.

I wait. If he can't respond, maybe that's what I need to do. I reach into my pocket and retrieve my phone.

"No," he says in a deep, guttural voice that keeps me from doubting his sincerity. Judging by his tone, if I call anyone, the moment he returns to his usual self, he'll kick my fucking ass, and I'll be out on the streets without the sort of consideration he gave me the other day.

I'll stop talking. Anything else is going to annoy him, I figure. I just hope no one else swings by and disturbs him.

The sounds he makes intensify from heavy breathing to what sounds like weeping and then whimpering. I shouldn't be here for this. Shouldn't be witnessing it. He deserves a moment to recover on his own.

Not five minutes pass before the sounds settle, and I hear him moving around. I spin back around. He climbs to his feet and rests against the vending machine, tucking his face close to it.

"You can get out now," he says, his voice deep as ever. Severe.

He doesn't sound appreciative. He sounds pissed. Like there was a way to handle this and I fucked it up royally.

"I was just trying to help," I say quickly, but he points to the door.

I hurry out. Better this way. I don't want to see him like this, and at least now I know he's fine. I feel like crap knowing that he can never look at me the same way again. First I exposed his leg. Now this. Reese obviously isn't the kind of guy who likes people to see him weak. Or in pain.

And having a fucking PTSD episode right in front of me sure covers that.

I head back to work, and some of the guys start giving me shit about how long I was gone, but I say that Reese had me cleaning up my mess.

I don't give a shit about saving my own ass, but I'm glad I could save Reese's.

4

Reese

I can't believe he saw me like that.

For the past two years, I've done so well. I was nervous as fuck about even taking this supervisor position because when I first started working here, the noises freaked me the fuck out, and a factory is such a goddamn noisy place. But I didn't have any work experience outside the military training. This and construction were really the only options I had available to me—my only shots at creating a life for myself. Thanks to the meds and my work with Laura, I've gotten good at getting by day to day. The noises still freak me out, but few have transported me like the one that came from the hall today, one that evoked memories of me alongside my crew, dressed in full combat gear, as we raced through the smoldering heat. The sounds of gunshots fired all around us as we watched a few guys collapse onto the ground and eat the dirt-covered earth, their bodies going limp.

I'm better at handling everyday tasks now, but that episode reminds me of what I already know—I'm always a moment away from being back where I started, struggling to control the raging thoughts that are far beyond my control, falling prey to the sensations that overtake my body and paralyze me.

I already know why this one affected me so much. I haven't had much sleep the past few days. I knew I needed more rest, but it's not easy for a guy who never wants to sleep—a guy who needs Ambien and Nyquil so his mind will shut down. I don't have the nightmares like I used to, but my lingering fear of them makes it easy for me to stay up. Once again, I'm reminded of why I need sleep. Getting on edge like I've been for this inventory audit puts me at a greater risk of an episode.

I think Jay is partially responsible for them, too. From his first interview, he reminded me of Caleb. How closed-off he was. How he couldn't look me in the eyes. A guy who doesn't trust anyone. The sort of guy I'd have to earn trust from. The memory he awakened is one of the reasons that even when the guy at his last job told me not to hire him, I went against my better judgment and gave him a shot. Because even though Caleb had a short temper, he was a hard worker. And a great man. I want to believe the same thing is true of Jay. That I'm not just desperately trying to keep Caleb's memory alive.

But part of the similarity triggers those things that I work to bury within me every day, and it's even worse now that he knows about my issues. The other guys have seen me act weird, but I've always been able to sneak away before losing it. Even with loud noises, I've been cognizant enough to get the fuck away from everyone to have my breakdowns—panic attacks, mainly. And the other guys are usually so unaware of what's going on or where I'm at that I don't have to worry about them bothering me in a moment of weakness.

I head out of the freight elevator and walk into the main part of the warehouse, where I see Jay securing some shipments with plastic wrap and tape. I stand tall even though I want to curl back up like I did earlier. Because seeing him takes me back to that moment in the breakroom.

As he spots me, he stops what he's doing and runs his hand through his dark hair. He looks worried about me, which just pisses me off even more. I don't need his pity. I'm a fucking grown man. I've been to fucking war, which is more than this whiny-ass, entitled kid can say. I've been getting help for eight years, so I sure as fuck know I can control it. No, not control it. Manage it.

Sympathetic as he acted, as he looks, I imagine him getting a kick out of letting the other guys know he was there for me when I burst into tears like a wuss. Even though everything about his expression suggests he wouldn't do that, I don't trust him. I try to remind myself that this paranoia I have about him exposing me is just part of the feelings that overtook me earlier. But it doesn't make me feel any better or any more trusting of him.

My rage toward him mixes with my awareness of how fucking hot he is, and I imagine taking all this frustration out on him in the sack. Taking his body and making him beg for me to come inside him. Dominating him so that he knows I'm not just the weak thing he saw me as earlier.

He returns his attention to his work, wrapping up the pallet of crated bottles.

I approach William, who sits on the forklift, riffling through a few sheets on his clipboard. I don't need to talk to him, but I want Jay to see I'm perfectly capable of handling my job. I can do this. Although I wonder if I'm proving it to him or to myself. I chat with William about some inventory

20

issues I'm trying to sort out. Some misplaced equipment and a couple of shipments we're rescheduling because of the damaged annealing machine.

I feel Jay's gaze on me, and I'm sure he notices how I can't keep my clipboard from shaking. He must know it's about my episode and not just from me being tired as fuck, which I am too.

I have to push through this like I learned in therapy. I run through a series of mantras, reminding myself I'm not in immediate danger, but it doesn't keep my palms from sweating.

Goddammit.

***

I've avoided Jay for the past few days, hoping we could both pretend my episode in the breakroom didn't happen.

But he keeps looking at me. I can tell he wants to talk about it, and that's the last thing I want. Not just with him, but with anyone. Laura says the more I discuss it, the less it'll feel like I'm carrying around this burden by myself. Helpful as working with her has been, though, there are some things I'm not ready to deal with. Some things I haven't even talked to her about because they leave me feeling so empty and horrible that they remind me that maybe it's not even worth it to push through.

I stock supplies in the main storage closet, where Jay grabs handfuls of nails from a box and puts them into a plastic bucket. He'll be working on packing the shipments that are going out tomorrow.

I figured this would be like a normal day where he grabbed his shit and moved on. Instead, he asks, "How's it going?"

He's itching to talk about it.

"Going good, Jay," I say, shoving a couple of boxes of screws onto the shelf as I act like I don't give a damn. "How about you?"

He doesn't move. Why can't he just forget about what happened and let us both move on with our lives? I haven't had a serious episode like that in almost a year. It isn't fair that he's caught me in two of the weakest moments I've had in a very long time.

He walks to the door, and I figure I'm in the clear until he turns back around and asks, "Are we just never discussing what happened the other day?"

21

Tension rises within me. Beads of sweat collect on my forehead. "There's nothing to talk about."

"I think I deserve to know what happened. And that you're actually getting help."

His words sound sincere, but there's this part of me that feels like he just wants to know so that he can get inside my head. Know my weaknesses and vulnerabilities…to what end, I'm not sure.

I can't let him in. Can't let him get to me. "I have help. Been working on this for a long time. That was a rare incident. I was just tired."

"Maybe you need to take some time off. You've been working nonstop for the past few days."

"Like I said, been handling this for a long time. I know when I need to take time off. Don't need some newbie who doesn't know anything about me or my life coming in and telling me how to run things."

"I'm not doing that. Just…well, if you need to talk to someone over some beers or whatever, I'm here." I don't think he could have found a more awkward way of saying that if he'd tried.

I didn't take him for the kind of guy who would have reached out to help me. Closed-off. Quiet. Aggressive as fuck to anyone who pisses him off.

Just like Caleb, who put up a strong front but was the most amazing guy I've ever known. The kind of guy who would've given a friend both his kidneys if they'd needed them. If Jay would show this side of himself to the other guys, they wouldn't give him nearly as much shit as they do. But the only reason he's bugging me about this is because he sees me as this feeble guy who needs assistance.

I don't need his help. I don't need anyone's help. I can do this by myself.

"I'm fine, but thanks." My words are curt. Almost mean, considering he was being generous with his offer, but he must understand that we have a working relationship and that's it.

Although I can't help but think that it'd be nice if I could have more than that. Not just with the guys at work, but anyone. It reminds me of a time when I could make friends. Hang with them after work. A time when I was carefree.

No one ever invites me to anything anymore. I just sit alone in my house, dreading the world. Dreading having to come here every day. Laura's always encouraging me to get out, but I never do.

He turns to the hall.

"Hey, Jay," I say. He spins around, and I look right at him for the first time since the other day. He appears shocked by it. "A drink would be nice. After work."

What the fuck am I doing?

5

Jay

I can't believe he took me up on my offer.

I'm glad he did, but also scared as fuck. He's been so quiet the past few days. I figured he'd never look me in the eyes again.

I tried to forget about the incident and ignore him the way he was ignoring me, but I couldn't. Something about seeing a full grown man fall apart like that…knowing he was in pain, struggling, made me feel for the guy. First thing I did after I got home the day it happened was google the crap out of post-traumatic stress disorder. I knew about it in the way most people do—heard about it, seen it depicted on TV and in movies. I've known other guys who've had episodes, but I've never seen one that dramatic before. Now that I know about his issue, I feel a little protective of him. When I hear the guys talking shit about the boss-man, it puts me more on edge than it usually would. Makes me feel like getting in their faces and defending him. They don't know his life or what he's been through, but then again, neither do I. I wonder if I'm defending his weakness or my own. Whatever it is, I just kept finding myself itching to talk to him. I know what it's like to feel all alone in the world. To be afraid of shit. To want to break down and cry sometimes.

Granted, that time in the breakroom is the only time I've felt anything close to a connection with Reese, but now that I know it's there, I'm drawn to him. Want to know more about him. I feel like we carry his secret about that day together. Like we're bonded in some strange way because of it. Maybe I'm wrong and having a drink with him will help me realize that. Maybe I can get him and what happened out of my head once we talk about it.

I sit in the bar, waiting for him to arrive.

We agreed to meet at this place in East Atlanta. He had to finish up some shit at work first, so I figured I'd get a few rounds in me in the meantime. I'm on my third when he walks in, that same stoic expression on his face—the one he's always made in the brief time I've known him. But since his episode in the breakroom, it's gotten even more intense. Seems like he's keeping his defenses up even more now.

He approaches, offers a polite *hey*, and sits in the stool beside me— keeping his eye on me in his periphery. He angles himself toward the door and checks over his shoulder at a couple of guys who sit in a booth in the corner of the bar.

The bartender swings by and takes his order. After he gets his Bud Lite, he takes a sip and sets it on the bar.

Now I'm left wondering what the fuck we're going to talk about. This isn't exactly the way to discuss PTSD, but I figure I'll let him direct the conversation.

"I really am fine," he says. Sincere as his words sound, I can't help but question them.

"Okay," I say.

"I was deployed for about twelve months back in 2003 when they needed guys for Iraq. I just wasn't the same when I got back. Six months went by, and it was really bad. Took me about five more years before I started to get treatment. At first, I didn't understand what was happening to me, but a lot of my buddies were going through the same thing, struggling even worse than I was. Fortunately, they knew more about it at that time than in previous wars, and I figured I'd get on top of it. Considering how this shit hits people, I guess you could say I'm one of the lucky ones." He snickers, as if calling himself *lucky* seems particularly amusing.

He takes a swig of his beer, and I take one of mine.

"I've been getting treatment for about eight years now," he continues, "so just get it through your head that I know what I'm doing. Yeah, I should have gotten more rest when the inventory was happening. I knew that. Sometimes I go too hard, but at the end of the day, I got it under control."

"By 'got it under control,' you mean like a shrink and stuff?"

"An arsenal of people to help me out. But I don't need this getting around work, okay? That's why I wanted to meet you out here because if I find out you're spreading this shit around the factory, making my guys worry about my ability to do my job, that's gonna piss me off. I gave you a break, and I'm just asking you to show me the same respect. They know I've been to war. They know I lost my fucking leg because of it. They know I act a little screwy every once in a while. I'd like to keep them from knowing any more than that." The way he says it, in a deep guttural voice, he sounds like he'll rip off my head if I start spreading rumors about him.

"I would never do anything like that. Speaking of the guys, though, this…meeting here…isn't like against policy or anything, right?"

"Do you think I'd be here if it was?" He takes another sip before asking, "So what's your story, kid?"

I'm irritated by him calling me kid. "I can't be that much younger than you."

"I'm thirty-three," Reese says.

"Twenty-seven."

"You're a kid. Get over it. Story?"

"Don't have much of a story."

"Oh, really? The guy who almost attacked one of my guys doesn't have much of a story?"

"He tripped me."

"I saw that look in your eyes. I've seen that look in people's eyes before, but it's when they're fighting for their life, not when they're dealing with some asshole."

Now I feel like the vulnerable one. I didn't come here to talk about me, but it's fair for him to call me out on my shit when I called him out on his. "I just got knocked around a lot as a kid. Don't see any reason to get knocked around as an adult, so I don't take a lot of shit anymore."

"Who knocked you around?"

His question is too personal. I want to ignore it, but again, I doubt he wanted me to know what I know about him, so I just blurt out, "My dad. Not just with me, but with my brother. I got out of there when I was sixteen. Stayed with my aunt and uncle for a bit until I could get out on my own. Been moving around ever since."

I recall the shouting matches and fists flying as my older brother protected me. Thinking about him reminds me of those dead, lifeless eyes as he lay on the floor. Not moving. Not breathing.

The day my brother…my best friend…was gone forever.

It breaks my fucking heart. Tears into my soul.

"In that interview, you said you came from New Orleans," Reese adds. "How long were you there?"

"About four weeks before I lost my job."

"Before you were *fired* from your job," he reminds me. "For being prone to lose your temper, as far as I was told."

"Some of the guys at work found out I was on Grindr. Don't know which of the closeted fags figured it out, but after they did, they started calling me faggot and giving me a hard time about taking it up the ass. Guess they figured they could gang up on me without me putting up a fight, but they found out they were wrong when I kicked their fucking dumbasses. They underestimated me. People always underestimate me."

He stares at me with cold eyes. Distant eyes. I wonder what he's thinking, but then he says, "Fair enough."

I drink a few more beers, but he continues to nurse his first.

It's unusually quiet between us until we start chatting about stupid shit. The sorts of ins and outs that we have to deal with on a regular basis. Nothing serious. As if we're trying to get as far away as possible from all the serious stuff we started talking about when we first got here. The bartender keeps swiping my empty bottles, so it's hard for me to keep track of where I'm at, but soon, I realize just how buzzed I am.

Feels good. Real good.

"Holy shit," I say. "And it's only Thursday."

He looks at me, an ease in his expression that I haven't seen since I started working at the factory. He smirks. "Yeah. It might be a difficult night for you."

I see something else in his eyes. A look that I'm familiar with. It's a look I've seen on a lot of guys before. One of interest—an "I wouldn't mind fucking you" look.

A big, hot machine like him must be a hell of a fuck in the bedroom. I imagine his beard pressed against my face as he takes me from behind— violently, aggressively.

It's been a couple of weeks since I've had a good lay. I nearly had a Grindr hookup last night, but the guy ended up flaking on me.

A more sober thought crosses my mind. What am I thinking? Fucking around with the boss? That's a horrible idea. Am I fucking looking for a reason to have to find a new job already?

"I guess I should head home," I say. I need to get out of here before I make a stupid as fuck mistake.

His expression shifts to one of disappointment. Maybe I'm right about him wanting to fuck me. Could he need this release as much as I do?

27

I run back through my memories of the guys in the warehouse talking about him, trying to remember if any of them ever mentioned him having a girlfriend. I can't remember anything like that.

Could he really be interested? The more I consider the possibility, the stronger my desire becomes. My dick shifts in my pants as it stiffens.

"I'm gonna head to the bathroom and then head out too, but I'll wait with you for an Uber," he says. "You're not in any position to drive right now." He rises, and I notice his own long, stiff cock in his jeans. I avoid looking at it, so he won't realize I've seen it.

Holy shit.

Like fuck. I don't know if I could even take something that big right now, but he's obviously as interested as I am.

6

Reese

I head into the single bathroom and lock the door.

Being in a bar reminds me of when I returned from Iraq, when my bud Mike and I would hit the bars together so he could pick up girls. Jay's really throwing them back, so I figure I'll give him another ride. But the stiff erection in my pants assures me of the kind of ride I really want to give him.

He's hot. I can't deny that, and now that the drinks have loosened him up a bit, he's easier to get along with.

We were just talking about stupid work crap, but as I started looking at his face—really looking at him, almost for the first time—his five o'clock shadow, his smooth baby flesh tainted by just a few tiny specks of freckles, his wide dark eyes glistening in the bar light, I found my dick getting harder and harder. He's got a good frame on him. I've seen him in a sleeveless shirt when he works in the warehouse, his chest thick with muscle, his abs so defined I could see the definition creating grooves in his shirt.

His physique combined with the look he gave me back at the bar—one that suggested he'd be game to mess around—are why I'm horny as shit right now.

I head to the sink, run the water, and splash some across my face.

Just need to cool down. Need to wait for this fucking erection to pass and then head back out there.

I didn't think my jeans were particularly tight until this moment. The Cialis I take to combat the libido issues I had when I first started taking my antidepressants makes it stone-fucking-hard when I get aroused. This is even worse than usual.

I open the door. Jay leans on the wall across from the bathroom, his arms folded. He has a smirk on his face as his gaze drifts down to my erection.

At this point, I don't feel the need to hide it. It's clear he isn't any straighter than me, and I'm not ashamed of being turned on by a hot guy. "Is that a problem?" I ask.

He glances down at his pants. I follow his gaze to his own lengthy bulge. Saliva fills my mouth.

He rushes forward and pushes me back into the bathroom, pressing his lips up against mine. He skillfully closes the door with his foot and reaches back and locks it.

I shouldn't want this…there are so many problems with doing this with an employee, but the kiss is so fucking intense that my body betrays my logic. I grab the back of his head instinctively and pull him close to me.

His kiss is fire. Feels so fucking good. Before I know it, the small of my back slams against the sink. I feel the sting, but it won't distract me from this amazing sensation Jay's stirred within me.

I don't let anything bother me. I forget that I'm fucked up. I forget that I'm his boss. I forget all those things I carry around with me on a daily basis and just keep on kissing him.

Relief. That's what it feels like. Something I haven't had in so fucking long.

Something I need so desperately today.

He slides his tongue between my lips, and I eagerly welcome it. He untucks my shirt and slides his hands up my belly, feeling his way across my abdomen.

It's nice feeling someone appreciating my body. And I want to appreciate his. I push him back against the adjacent wall and pull his shirt up over his head, breaking our kiss just long enough to throw it behind me.

I want to be inside him. I want to fill him so that he can't maintain that scowl he always wears at work.

I kiss my way down to his torso, carefully maneuvering until I'm on my knees, licking as I slide my hands down his sides. When my face is at his crotch, I run my nose along the length. He smells so good. Like a man.

He unfastens his jeans and slides them down along with the briefs he wears underneath. His cock springs forward. And now the pain in mine is even worse. I just need to rub one out.

I bury my face in his trimmed pubes, smelling and licking. Feeling his cock against the side of my face. I move my hands around, cupping his ass cheeks and squeezing.

I'm his fucking boss.

Finally a logical thought enters my mind along with a series of others that remind me just what a horrible idea this is.

"Fuck," I groan as I pry my hands from his ass cheeks and push them against the wall. I get back onto my feet and hurry out the door. I need to get the fuck out of here.

"Where you going?" he asks.

The exit's to the left just outside the bathroom. I push through the door and step onto the back porch of the bar. He follows me out as he tosses his shirt on, apparently having buttoned his jeans back up in the bathroom.

"I'm gonna go home," I say.

"I'll come with you. Like you said, I shouldn't be driving right now anyway."

"No. I can call you an Uber or something."

He freezes, a stunned expression on his face, as if he doesn't understand what just happened. "Where's the fun in that?" he asks.

"I'm sorry I led you on like that, but I'm your boss. You're my employee. That's all there is to it." I'm starting down the stairs when I feel him grab my arm.

I whirl around, my instincts reacting before I can even think it through. In a moment, I have my hand around his throat and I'm pinning him to a column at the top of the stairs.

"Shit, shit, shit! Sorry," he says.

Fuck. I release him quickly, staring at my hand in horror, as if it was responsible for my actions rather than me.

"I'm sorry," I say. "I just need to go."

How does he manage to activate every trigger—every defensive impulse—within me?

I grab my keys out of my pocket and start through the parking lot.

My thoughts race. I can't believe what I just did to him. He must think I'm a violent bastard. I crossed the fucking line. Serves me right for going out for a drink with a co-worker. I should have told him to fuck off when he asked if I wanted to talk. What if he wants to file a complaint for me fucking assaulting him? What if I lose my job over this?

"Reese, Reese," Jay says behind me. I don't turn to him. I can't look at him after what I just did. "It's okay. I'm fine. I didn't mean to surprise you."

As much as he tries to soothe me, he can't understand. It's not just about the fact that I hurt him. It's about being out of control. That I'm so fucking out of my mind that I couldn't even think before violently responding to him. That's not me anymore. I've worked so hard to keep myself stable. But I know why I'm on such high alert right now. I know what keeps nagging at me that I refuse to think about. That I never want to think about again. It's why I've thrown myself into work the way I have recently. Why I've been losing sleep. Why I was reckless enough to come out here today and let my guard down with a guy who reminds me so much of Caleb.

I'm a fucking mess.

"Reese, are you okay?" he asks.

I turn back to him. "I'm fine." Problem is, I know just how far from fine I really am. And I can tell by his skeptical expression that he doesn't buy the lie.

"I'm sorry," he says. "I didn't mean to make you uncomfortable. I was trying to do the opposite. I just… I assumed since you…" He glances at my crotch again. "I don't know what I assumed. I mean, you are gay, right?"

Even though there's no one else in the parking lot, it's weird that he's saying it out loud. Like someone's going to come around the corner and be freaked out by him broadcasting what we are.

"The only thing that matters to you is that I'm your boss," I say.

"Okay, I get it. But if you do want something else, I'm down."

My erection becomes even more painful. I do want something else. I want it so bad. Not just because he's hot as hell and because it felt fucking amazing in the bathroom, but because it would give me an escape from the thoughts that hound me every day.

I should say no and get him off my back.

I walk toward my car, and seemingly beyond my control, like when I assaulted him, I say, "Come on." He follows me to my car and hops in with me.

We don't talk to each other. I'm busy trying to convince myself what a horrible idea this is, but I've already surrendered to the primal desire within me. We've crossed the line. And now that we're less than a couple minutes from my house, I'm ashamed of how easily I caved to my horny-as-fuck impulses.

It's just been so long since I've felt any sort of ease, and after that kiss, I know he's what I need right now. He's the only thing that can shake me from my obsessive thoughts about Caleb for even a moment.

I've worked so hard to get where I am to fuck it up with this indiscretion, but reason can't save me from how much I want his body right now.

7

Jay

He blew my mind.

I was relieved when I saw that hard cock in his pants. Figured we could give each other some relief. I've wanted to give him that ever since I saw him in so much pain the other day. I've wanted to give him as much as he needed. I figured it'd be hot, but when I kissed him, something about our chemistry stirred a passion I'm not used to experiencing. I fuck plenty of guys. Not ashamed of it, which is why I know when it's beyond the mechanics. And Reese…Oh, God, I've got some serious chemistry with him.

He woke up every part of my body, every nerve in my flesh. I want the stroke of his strong hands running across my muscles and the taste of those lips on my tongue.

I thought I wasn't going to have any issue getting him to fuck around once he knew where we both stood, but when he fled the bathroom, I was totally thrown. What kind of guy doesn't want a piece of ass when it's offered up to him like I offered up mine?

Clearly he's attracted to me. I can't imagine that raging boner was for someone else in that piece-of-shit bar.

When we reach his place, a one-story house in a subdivision, we get out and he glances around at his neighbor's places, as if he's worried one of them will catch him bringing home his evening trick.

Considering how quiet he's been, I'm a little unsure about what's going to happen. He wants to fuck. Otherwise he wouldn't have brought me back, but he's uneasy about it. Ashamed. I'm not sure I want him like that. Normally, I wouldn't fuck a guy who appears as conflicted as he does, but the fire between us, I'm not going to turn that down for anything…even if that means he winds up punching me in my fucking face halfway through because he can't get this PTSD shit under wraps.

He leads me up the front porch and into the house.

It's a nice place. More than nice. It's OCD clean—something I'm a little shocked to see.

A living area with gray-upholstered sofas and chairs are placed in front of a wall-mounted large-screen TV. A few side tables have statues and some interesting, thought-out décor on them. Nothing like my place, which Reese would think was more like somewhere a frat guy might live.

On the other side of the room, a bar divides the kitchen from the rest of the place. A small stack of mail sits on the edge of the bar.

I wander inside behind Reese, glancing around, looking for pictures of his family or something. Some indication that he's actually a person. Nothing like that. Just some framed artwork. One of the pieces stands out more than the others. A gray framed painting hangs beside the TV. It looks like the profile of a man gazing down.

Strange.

As he reaches the bar, he turns back to me and rests his hands on his hips. His dick is still hard as a fucking rock. How can he maintain that raging boner?

I approach him slowly, cautiously. If he wants to do this, he needs to make the first move. He needs to show me he really wants to follow through. Otherwise, I need to get an Uber and go home.

He sizes me up. He's seen me plenty of times at work, so I can't imagine what the fuck he could be looking for now. When I realize he's not getting to this quickly, I try to make small talk. "That's a cool picture," I say, referring to the one of the man's profile.

He comes at me so swiftly I'm not sure if he's going to kiss me or deck me, but I'm relieved when his lips crush against mine. He pushes me to the side and shoves me against the wall like he did in the bathroom at the bar. He wraps his arm around me and presses his hand against my back, forcing my torso tight against his.

His hard dick is stiff against my crotch. And I'm pissed that we're still wearing clothes because I feel he should just be buried within my hole. Don't know why that's where my mind goes because I'm always the top, but Reese seems like the kind of man who needs to dominate someone. And I'd love to be the one whose ass he owned.

He pulls his hand from my back, grabs my arm, and spins me around. Pushing my chest up against the wall, he reaches around and unbuttons my pants before yanking them down.

"God, you have the sexiest fucking ass in the world," he says, feeling up and down my sides. He gropes at my flesh, his fingers tight against me as he probes.

"It's yours," I say because I don't give a fuck what he wants to do with it.

He squats, trailing his fingers down my obliques until his face is right at my ass. As he grips onto my cheeks, I pull my shirt over my head and throw it aside.

He pushes my cheeks apart and spits on my hole before shoving his face against it. He licks, exciting my nerves with a good rimjob.

"Well, you're obviously no virgin," I say.

"Tasted some good hole in my day." He takes a moment before returning to his work.

I spread my legs as much as I can with my pants around my ankles, and I arch my back so that my ass pushes even closer to his face, inviting him to take it as he pleases.

I glance back and catch him licking his forefinger and middle finger before inserting them inside me. "I'm really tight," I warn.

"Yeah, you are." He's excited about it. Like he's eager to get inside me.

I'm worried about taking that big cock. As much as I've fucked these past few months, I haven't bottomed once. And I'm also confused as fuck about how his fake leg is going to work during all this.

As he massages his way into me, I let those worries go and enjoy the sensations he stirs. "Jesus fucking Christ!" I say. He stops pushing in, but I don't want that. I think he mistook my eagerness for discomfort. "That felt good," I say. "Keep going. I need you to open me up."

He licks my ring as he pushes farther in, moving his fingers in a half circle before going back the other way. He adds another finger.

"Holy fuck!" It stimulates me just right. The guy might be quiet, but he's obviously no stranger to fucking.

"I just want you to be ready for my cock," he says. "I want you to be able to take all of it."

"I want to take it all."

He pulls back out, and I fear he might have changed his mind. Remembered what an absolutely shit idea this is considering our work situation.

I turn around as he starts to get up from the floor, but as he reaches halfway up my body, he wraps an arm around me, and before I know it, he hoists me into the air and carries me through the house, into a hallway beside the kitchen.

I wonder for a moment how he can be fucking carrying me like this with his leg, but I used to hit the gym with a guy who wore a prosthetic leg, and he could deadlift twice his fucking body weight. And it's obvious based on Reese's physique that he spends plenty of time at the gym.

Reese takes me down a hallway, into a bedroom, and sets me on a queen-sized bed so that I'm lying on my back. He pulls my shoes off and slides my pants and boxer briefs down my legs, tossing them onto the floor as he removes each one. He's still fully clothed, and here I am, completely exposed, totally vulnerable. Totally his to do whatever the fuck he wants with.

"You have the hottest little body," he says, as if he just now noticed.

"I don't hit the gym for nothing." I'm cocky about it, but I work hard, so I feel like I have a right to be, and his interest doesn't appear to let up, so I don't think he gives a damn how conceited I may be. He likes what he sees enough to disregard a lot just so he can be up in my hole.

He heads to a nightstand by the bed and retrieves condoms and lube. Wouldn't have mattered if he hadn't had condoms because I have one in my pocket along with a lube packet I left there when I almost tricked out with a guy on Grindr. Before the asshole flaked.

As he tosses the condoms and lube on the bed, I prop myself up on my elbows. "Why don't you show me that hot body of yours?" I ask. He smirks. It's clear by his expression that he's confident about what he's got.

He unbuttons his shirt slowly, as if he's revealing some great secret, which can't be all that secret considering I can tell he's got a great muscly bod under that shirt. Only so much he can do to hide that.

When he's finished unbuttoning, he slides it off, letting it fall behind him.

I was wrong. So fucking wrong. I knew it was good, but not this good. Four distinct lines cross through either side of his fucking eight-pack, creating sharp shadows beneath them. I'm jealous as shit at how defined he is. I work my butt off to look half as jacked up.

"Those are some fucking nice abs," I admit. "And that chest…and those fucking biceps…I bet that dick's just as good."

He removes his shoe on his left foot and his sock before sliding his pants and underwear down to the floor.

There's the prosthetic. A curved dip in the metal makes space for his knee, and what looks like some sort of gray liner extends over his leg, but I can't really tell how much of his leg he still has below the knee.

I wonder if he's leaving the limb on or taking it off. I want to ask, but I'm not going to. I'm just going to roll with whatever he's comfortable with, especially since I can tell by the sad expression on his face that his confidence has taken a hit.

He slowly steps out of the leg of his jeans. Then he looks up at me—I can tell to gauge my reaction. I look right into his eyes to let him know it doesn't bother me. I mean, it won't as long as he can still fuck me good with that fat cock of his.

He crawls onto the bed and positions his face at my legs. "You got a pretty good cock you're working with too," he says before he takes it into his mouth.

I toss my head back and run my fingers through his blond tufts as he goes down on me, proving that he's as good with his tongue in the front as he was in the back. He stimulates my cock with his lips and tongue before his hand joins in on the action. He grips onto the base of my shaft while he encircles the head with his tongue, moving his hand and mouth in sync with one another, creating a rhythm that leaves me gasping with pleasure. "You sure know how to suck a dick," I say.

He stops. "I sure know how to do a lot of things," he says before abandoning my dick. He grabs the condom from beside me and suits up.

My body tenses as he spreads my legs, and I know it's because he's so big. I'm fucking nervous as hell. But I want it.

I like the look in his eyes, full of desire and lust.

He lathers some lube on his fingers before sticking them back into me. It feels good, but not good enough. "Just give me what I want," I beg.

"What do you want?" I can tell by the way he says it he already knows. He wants me to say it.

"I want your fucking cock inside me. I want you to make me feel good. I want you opening me up like you do all your good bottoms."

He accepts the invitation, pulls his fingers out, and spreads some lube across his dick before pressing the head against my hole, pushing.

He studies me. "In case you're wondering, this *is* against company policy." Serious as he looks, I can tell by the way he says it, he's not discouraged.

Even after opening me up with his fingers, I'm still tight, my body unwilling to let him in easily.

"That fucking tight hole of yours just needs to be loosened up, doesn't it?"

I'm worried he'll push in too quickly. But he doesn't. He moves slowly, my body adjusting to his girth. As his cock pushes in just right, a shot of adrenaline races through my veins. I forgot how nice it can be to be filled, especially with one this thick.

He stares at me seriously as he keeps pushing in. A surge of excitement moves through my body, energizing my nerves with a thrill I haven't experienced in a long time. The intensity forces me to open my mouth and moan as I enjoy the sensations that overwhelm me.

Reese smiles again. He obviously likes the show I'm putting on, so I won't disappoint him. I keep calling out until he leans down and kisses me with those wet, passionate kisses like the ones we shared in the bathroom.

He picks up his pace, and with each push, I feel his cock jam against my prostate, making my cock stiff as a board. Sweat pours down my face as he thrusts within me, offering me the relief that I crave. I've never had a guy who could reach back into me like he can.

Pre-come drips from the head of my dick onto my abdomen. Reese leans back, leaving me desperately craving more of his kisses. He wraps one arm around my left leg and rubs the other down my body, feeling his way across my muscles, appreciating the work I put into it at the gym.

It's all his right now.

He speeds up his rhythm, and each movement hits that tender spot within me, leaving me wanting more and more. An ache that I need him to soothe. He experiments with lifting each of my legs up before he finds the position that makes me pre-come. My body's twisted slightly to the side as he fucks me with my right leg lying vertically across his body as he does his work.

His injury obviously doesn't hinder his ability to satisfy a man. "Fuck, Reese. God, that feels fucking incredible!"

He stops for a moment, breathing heavily, sweat rushing down his forehead. He pulls out. "On your knees," he orders.

I can hear the military training in his tone. I do as I'm told, and soon, he's ramming into me from behind. One hand on the headboard, I grip tight and release a guttural cry. I jerk off with my other hand as he weaves his fingers into my hair and tugs back. When he pulls a little more, I release the headboard and arch my body until my back is flush with his chest. This position feels even better than when he had me on my back with my leg in the air. The pleasure he activates soars through me, and I call out, moaning with delight until I feel his body jerk about in a frenzy…in a way that lets me know he's filling up the condom within me. His own cry hits the side of my face as he moves close for a few sloppy kisses.

I spray my load across his pillows…and it keeps shooting out, spilling across the bed. I always come a lot, but now I feel bad because I'm hosing down his sheets.

"Holy fuck, you're a messy shooter, aren't you?" But the way he says it, it doesn't sound like a bad thing.

"I've…never…come that much." It must be how his cock is still jammed up against my prostate.

We pant. Sweat. Fall from the high. He pulls out of me, grabs my shoulder, spins me around, and wraps his arms around me.

We kiss, embrace. I still can't get enough of him. I want to start all over again.

He slides his arm through the crook of my leg, the other across my back and hoists me in the air again, leaning all his weight on his left leg as he falls onto me.

We continue making out.

8

Reese

That was just what I needed.

I didn't think it could get better than the kiss at the bar, but this was fucking insane.

His body, his cries, his pleas for more. He was game for whatever I wanted to give him.

A fucking amazing bottom.

For a moment, the screaming voices in my head, the downward spiral of thoughts that so frequently plague me, dissolved as I focused only on our intense experience.

After using a washcloth to clean up the sheets he spooged all over, I lie beside him in the bed as we pant together. My body jerks a bit, a sort of phantom orgasm lingering. Finally a pleasant phantom sensation—one that doesn't remind me of the darkest months of my life.

I turn to him, see his massive chest rising and falling as he stares at the ceiling, his face glistening with sweat in the light that beams in through the window blinds.

"You sure know how to work that massive cock," he says.

I can't fight the smile his words force. I want to thank him for the experience he gave me, but that'd be weird. I'd come across as a creeper, and then he'd never want to do this with me again. "With an ass like that, this cock is at your service whenever."

That seemed like a safe way of saying it, but what am I fucking doing? He's my employee. The whole reason I didn't want to do anything with him was because this was one of the stupidest ideas I've had in a long-ass time. I'm putting my job on the line here. I could get in serious trouble for fraternizing with my employee. The company's fine with hanging out with people in my chain of command, but dating is a no-no. Although I've known a few guys who've dated people who report to them. They just fill out some paperwork with HR to avoid legal liabilities, and that's the end of it. But why put my job at risk like this?

I shouldn't have fucked him to begin with, let alone be planning to fuck him again.

But the look in his eyes, lit up with excitement, encourages me even more.

It's the only relief I've had since my stress about this time of year returned. I need it so much. I never let myself have anything, so in some ways, I feel like I deserve this. I know that's what this is really about. I'm a victim of these delicious sensations, thinking with them rather than the voice of reason that keeps telling me what a crap idea this is.

Jay rolls toward me, his tight muscles compressing together, stressing their impressive definition. His cock hangs down the side of his thigh.

I roll toward him so that we're both on our sides, facing one another. I offer a kiss, which he eagerly receives. It reminds me of this intense magnetism I feel toward him. Something I wouldn't have expected— something I never could have imagined before he planted that first hot kiss on me.

As he pulls away, he glances around my room. "You have a fucking nice house."

"Thank you." Although I don't feel all that proud of it since it's more about the OCD I developed alongside my PTSD. Laura tells me that's not uncommon. Sort of my way of controlling what I can.

"You'd die if you saw my place. I'm basically a rat that rents a room."

I chuckle. "I was a mess when I was younger, trust me. That's not a bad thing."

He looks like he's trying to figure something out about me. Like he's looking for something from my past. I shift my gaze because I don't want him to see back there. I don't want anyone to see the horrors I wish I could forget.

"That shit that happened in the break room...how often does it happen?"

Why did he have to take something that felt so amazing to such a goddamn awful place? I was finally enjoying myself, and he wants to dig up the worst part of my life. But he was there for me. As much as I wish he hadn't seen that, it was nice that he kept the other guys from seeing it. I'm appreciative of that, and I owe him an explanation.

"It's not usually like that. I can't ever get rid of it completely. But typically I can push through the hard parts, now that I'm on meds and shit.

I have my good days and bad days. Usually I'm better on the bad days than I was in the breakroom. If I'm on edge, I can kind of sense when things are coming. Like when you dropped that box of glass before you started the fight with Tyler. That was a loud-ass noise, and as I'm sure you saw, it got to me, but at least when I see the reason for the sound, it doesn't bother me as much as when it just comes out of nowhere. Fortunately, I'm used to checking around, being aware of my surroundings enough that that doesn't happen much. Used to be a lot worse. I was at a job before I came to the factory, and I wasn't there more than two months before I had an episode. They ended up firing me. Not over that, they claimed, but I know it was because that freaked them out. So I'm extra careful I don't get caught. Easier now that I'm a supervisor because I can at least sneak off and hide it from the other guys if things get really bad."

"What happens in your head when you hear a noise like that?" Jay asks.

"I don't just hear the noise. I hear the rumbling of noises from when we were running through the streets in Fallujah. Gunfire and the sound of bombs going off. Kids, women, men, screaming. They don't sound like echoes from the past as much as they sound like they're happening right now. As if I'm somehow slipping through a time warp that's taking me back to that moment."

"That's horrible."

"It's not as bad as it used to be," I say. Talking with him about it is hard. I'd rather just avoid the subject, but Laura and the group sessions have made that part easier. Only took eight fucking years for me to get to this point.

He glances down at my dick, which is still stiff as a board. "How are you that fucking hard right now?" he asks.

I blush. Not much can make me do that, but considering the reason, I can't help it. "I take a little something to help me out. Initially, my meds made it difficult to get hard, and I didn't want to miss out on one of my favorite parts of living, so my doc helped me out there."

"Viagra?"

"A very low dose of Cialis once a day."

"Well, with a hard-on like that, you must need someone on that cock all the time."

I smile, appreciating his playfulness about a subject that typically causes me some tension. Makes me feel somewhat emasculated.

"It's nice when I get the chance."

"You don't fuck like you have any trouble getting laid." Jay eyes me skeptically, as though he believes I'm some kind of man-whore.

"I think I have a very reasonable sex life."

"Like what? Five guys a week?" he asks with a whimsical smirk, one of his bushy eyebrows raised higher than the other.

He earns a smile. I like this playful side of him. If he showed this to the guys at work, I don't imagine he'd encounter so much resistance.

"I'm not that bad," I say. "Hell, considering the past few weeks with work, I haven't had much time for anything like that."

"Then I guess I'm just glad that you saved that load for me."

I smile and lean close to him, my lips right before his. "You know, I have plenty of loads to make up for it if that's what you want."

"If you need a cum-slut tonight, you can just have at it." He kisses me and that sweet feeling returns. I wrap my arm around him and push him down onto the bed.

I want it again. Need it again. I want all those thoughts he stirred about my past to dissolve and be replaced with the hot steamy passion between us.

The fuck is as good as the first time, and when we finish, he showers off and then throws on his clothes. I offer him a ride back to his car, but he insists on taking an Uber home and just getting another to take him to his car tomorrow.

I'm appreciative that he didn't want to stick around. I was worried I'd need to find a way to get rid of him. But he obviously understands what this is. And as long as that's the case, I wouldn't mind making this a regular thing. What the fuck am I thinking? Fucking one of my employees?

But as many arguments as there are against what I'm doing, as hard as I've worked to get where I am, something about Jay breaks down my defenses. Maybe because he's already seen mine. And because he reminds me of my friend. A good guy who pushed a lot of people away, but was one of the best men I ever knew. A guy who deserved better than the hand he was dealt. Maybe I'm just kidding myself that Jay's the same way, but considering the way he acted with me today, I don't think I am.

As long as no one at work finds out, it won't be a big deal.

I head into the backyard, into my garden. It's dark out, but I need to make sure I've tended to all my plants.

It's a small garden in a fifty-by-thirty-foot space. It's a reminder of what I've lost. A reminder of what I'm trying to hold on to.

And typically a relief when I start working the land.

I approach the security light I've rigged on the shed so that it illuminates the backyard at night. Then I check on my tomatoes, fixing a few of the plants where they've grown off the trellises. They're looking really healthy. I'll probably be able to pick a few by this weekend.

While I'm on my knees, tying a piece of yarn around a vine to bind it to the trellis, I glance around at the plants that are growing some healthy fruits—peppers, cucumbers, squash, bush beans. I've done a good job this year. Much better than the previous ones. It doesn't feel like all that long ago when I couldn't make anything grow. I never had a green thumb. But my obsession with this project has improved my gardening skills. And there's some relief in it, especially as that dreaded anniversary nears—Caleb's anniversary—the day that is the real reason I can't sleep. The reason I'm so on edge right now. The reason I've thrown myself into the inventory more than ever before.

Because I don't want to remember. I don't want to hurt.

9

Jay

I'm listening to a Rita Rudner comedy special on my iPhone when I enter the kitchen and see my landlord and housemate Charlie. He sits at the table, a bowl of cereal before him as he reads the morning paper.

When I pull out my earbuds, I realize I'm fucking whistling. I stop, but it's too late. Charlie says, "Someone's in a chipper mood this morning…"

A retired man in his seventies with a few gray hairs left on his otherwise bare head, he's usually around the house because he doesn't get out too much. When I first interviewed for the place, he openly admitted my rent covers the mortgage, but he bought the place twenty years ago, so this is the cheapest option available to me, and I was appreciative to have the opportunity to stay somewhere that costs less than five hundred a month. He stays out of my way, and I stay out of his, but we've had a few sit-down chats in the kitchen since I got here. He doesn't press. Never asks too many questions. Just cracks jokes and tells some stories from his youth.

He's the ideal living situation. Never invades my privacy but also not so quiet that it becomes awkward.

"Just had a good week at work," I say. He chuckles, as though he knows better.

I open the pantry and retrieve a chocolate Pop Tart.

"Another healthy meal?" he asks.

I eye his Peanut Butter Cap'n Crunch. "Really, Charlie? You gonna judge me?"

"I'm old. I can do whatever I want to this body. You gotta take care of yours a little bit, at least."

I tear the Pop Tart wrapper open and flex my bicep so that it stretches the sleeve of my shirt. "That's how I take care of this body," I joke.

He laughs. "Ooh…now you're just trying to get me all worked up," he says with a wicked smile.

Charlie was quick to call me out on being gay when I came over here to see about renting. At first, I was defensive. Guys never notice, and I thought he was trying to say I was some kind of flitty thing, but Charlie relaxed me with his friendly smile and a laugh, telling me, "Don't get your masc ass in a bind. I just have the world's best gaydar. Only way I could get the boys when I was younger." He had spent his youth in San Diego and would go prowling for guys around the naval base—something I've heard some fun stories about since I started staying with him.

We chat a bit more before I toss out my trash and start to head out.

"Don't forget your comics," he says. He has the comics section of the paper sitting on the table beside his bowl. He apparently picked it out for me since I've asked for them pretty much every morning that I've seen him from the time I moved in.

I retrieve them from the table. "Thank you, Charlie," I say before heading off.

I feel alive. It wasn't just the sex with Reese. Hell, fucking is nothing to me. The sort I'm used to can't hold a candle to what Reese and I shared.

I could tell he wanted me to leave his place after we fucked again, and I was cool with that.

I didn't want to overstay my welcome. Didn't want to make him uncomfortable with what was going on, especially since he's my boss. Shit. *My boss*. I fucked my boss, and I want to fuck him again.

It's a bad idea waiting to happen. I know that.

But isn't that the story of my life?

I head to the factory and get to work, feeling more alive than usual.

Today's a big pickup day, so I'm extra-busy, moving boxes on the forklift to the loading dock before the trucks arrive. I slide the fork under a box when I catch myself whistling again.

Shit. I need to stop that.

"Having a good day?" William asks with a smile on his face as he wheels a cart of boxes toward me.

"Oh, no. I was just…"

I don't really have an excuse, but fortunately, he doesn't seem to care. He just says, "I've got to get these nails over to Amy and Terrence for pallets, but then I'll be over to help you in about ten. That work?"

"Sounds good."

"Hey, guys," Reese's voice comes from beside us, startling me.

He approaches William. Starts chatting him up. He looks as relaxed as I feel. I like knowing I can help alleviate some of the stress he's been under. I know he can't make a big deal out of what we did, but every time he comes back into the warehouse, he ignores me. Acts like I'm invisible. Even now when I'm right next to him.

It reminds me of those days after he had his breakdown.

The first few times he was like this today, I figured it was a fluke, but now that I know it's intentional, it's getting on my nerves. I'm fine with leaving it at what it was, but does that mean I can't exist outside of that? Really?

Rather than cause a stir, I ignore him the way he ignores me. I back the forklift up and drive off.

But I'm a little worried. What if the moment I left his place, he started to rethink what we did? It was so hot that I'd love to go again, but what if he doesn't? What if he doesn't think he should be fucking around with an employee?

No, he wouldn't do that. He needs it, too. There's no way the passion during that sex was one-sided.

But maybe it was.

I shouldn't obsess about this.

I'm never this way with guys. I can fuck the shit out of someone and then just walk away.

I want to believe it's just how hot it was, but I'm intrigued by him beyond that. He's an interesting guy. Most of the blockheads I'm used to are so uninteresting that I don't give a shit about whether I get to know them or not, but he's mysterious. There's this whole other life that he re-lives on a daily basis. This world that he struggles with while simultaneously trying to exist in the present. I want to know more about that past. Want to know more about these nightmares that plague him. Of course, I know that's the last thing in the world he wants to tell me about, considering he didn't seem all that eager about sharing that shit he told me yesterday. He sounded like he was straining just to tell me that much.

When I'm finished moving some of the boxes into the warehouse, William asks me to help Tyler out with another pallet accident. We've had a few of these recently because of some crap wood that was ordered for pallets. We've had to go back and secure some of them in hopes that we won't ruin another batch of bottles.

I head over and give Tyler a hand with the cleanup. He hasn't talked to me much since that day when we fought, but he hasn't given me any shit either. I pick up broken bottles and toss them into a box we're collecting the broken shards into.

"Look, man. I'm sorry I gave you a rough time when you first got here," he says as he sweeps up some of the debris.

"What?" I ask. He's really caught me off guard. Is this some kind of a trick?

"I wasn't actually trying to trip you. I just wanted to tell you that. I mean, I was an ass. I was giving you a hard time and doing everything I could to make your job harder, but when I bumped into you that day in the warehouse, *that* was actually an accident. Until you started being a dick about it, I was actually worried about your fall."

Well, that was fucking unexpected.

I think about what Reese said about me in the parking lot. *I'm just saying if you make enemies everywhere you go, it's probably not because everywhere you go has a problem.*

"Why were you ragging on me when I started up?" I ask.

"You came here, and you were all quiet. Had this cocky look on your face all the time like you were better than everyone else. Just kind of bothered me."

"Is that really what you thought?"

"Yeah. Reese was talking to me. Said you're just quiet, and I get that. Sorry if I gave you a hard time."

I'm a little irritated that Reese said anything to him, but also relieved. Suddenly I'm seeing Tyler in a different light. He can actually not be a dickhead? While we continue cleaning up, we get to chatting while we work, and soon he's talking to me about his wife and kids.

"I'm trying to plan out this birthday celebration for my wife," he says. "It's her thirty-fifth birthday. You know, we've been together ten years now."

"Ten years? That's fucking impressive." My record with guys is far less impressive.

He smiles as though he's shocked that I'm even interested in hearing about his life. He wipes the back of his arm across his forehead. "She deserves something special. We've been through a lot of hard times together. And I was just trying to think of something she might enjoy, you know? Not like the usual dinner-and-a-movie sort of deal. We do that pretty much every weekend."

"Have you thought about maybe a surprise party? Invite some of her friends."

"Yeah, but I don't know if that'll really surprise her."

"Is there anyone she's good friends with or maybe a close family member you can talk into flying in for it? That'd surprise the hell out of her."

His eyes light up. "She has this friend from college who lives in D. C. now. They talk on the phone all the time. Oh, shit. I guess I should have thought of that. Thanks. That's a really good idea."

It's nice lowering my defenses for a change. I haven't had a chat like that with someone I worked with in a long time.

All that tension from when we fought before has completely dissolved. Maybe Reese chatting with him wasn't such a bad thing after all. Maybe this new gig is gonna be good for me. Although I know better than to believe that. Everywhere seems great in the beginning…until shit starts getting complicated.

Tyler's not a bad guy. And Reese was right about me finding trouble everywhere I go. It happens enough that I know I have to be at least partly to blame.

Tyler starts talking to me about personal shit about his life. Makes me wish I had a buddy that I could talk to about Reese. Someone I could confide in. Of course, there are so many reasons I can't talk to Tyler about my life. A shame I can't shoot the breeze about what's going on with me the way he can about his wife.

When lunchtime arrives, I head up to the breakroom. A few of the other guys lounge around, eating their lunches. Reese heads in and approaches the vending machine, still ignoring me.

Of course he is. I'm just this trashy trick that he doesn't give a shit about.

50

"Morgan," he says with that same military tone in his voice as when he ordered me to get on my knees on his bed. My co-worker glances up from his ham-and-cheese sandwich.

"Yeah?" he asks.

"Can you swing by my office later to review some ordering information with me? I've been looking at a couple of other vendors that might be a little cheaper, but I want to go through it with you before I make my decision."

"You got it, boss."

A soda bottle hits the bottom of the vending machine. Reese pulls it out and leaves without so much as glancing my way.

My chest aches as I'm filled with disappointment.

Maybe yesterday was all I'm ever going to get from him. He doesn't seem like the sort of guy who opens up much. Reminds me of why I keep everyone at a distance. Can't get disappointed if you don't let people in.

After I finish my lunch, I head back toward the warehouse, passing his office. I consider going in, but I don't want to make a complete idiot out of myself. Don't want to seem like this desperate fucker who needs his cock inside me again. Even though that's kinda true.

As I pass one of our supply closets, I feel someone grab me from behind, and as I turn, there's Reese. He practically shoves me into the closet. Before I know it, he's pushed me so that my back hits and closes the door behind me. He kisses me hard, the hairs in his beard pricking at my face.

His firm muscles are tight against my body. I wrap my arms around him, clinging tightly as this experience offers assurance that my delusions from earlier were totally unreasonable. His tongue slides between my lips, and I greet it with my own. I rest a hand on the back of his head as he kisses down my face, to my neck. The sort of kisses he gave me yesterday. Wild. Careless. Passionate.

Considering how good it feels and how every muscle in my body relaxes, I would have thought I had gone months without feeling this sort of excitement. Not just a day.

"I've missed that hot piece of ass all day," he whispers so that his breath slams against my neck. More confirmation that my worries were for nothing.

It's not that I like him. It's that I've had enough sex to know the difference between when it's good and when it's a fucking stick of dynamite exploding, crashing through my trembling nerves.

"I thought you were ignoring me because you were ashamed about what we did."

"The only thing I'm ashamed of," he says, "is that I'm not inside you right now."

"I have a condom in my wallet." I still have it from when I was planning to meet up with that trick the other night.

He pulls away, looking at me with serious eyes. Is he considering this?

But as soon as he starts unzipping my jeans, I know it's on.

He locks the door with one hand as he pulls my pants and briefs down with his other.

I pull my shirt off, and he kneels down to kiss across my chest, licking as his hands grope at my sides. He forces himself away from my body, and we scramble out of our clothes, stripping down until we're both stark naked, our bodies pressed tightly together as he assaults me with even more kisses.

He pushes me against the door, my back hitting the knob. It smarts, but I just slide to the side and take the pain. I've taken hits before. I sure as fuck can take them now that they're followed with such intense waves of relief.

He kisses down to my torso. To my cock.

He gives me that good head like he did the day before, his tongue going wild around my girth. Making me hard as shit.

I gasp from the intense energy that pulses through my body. It feels like it's too much for me to handle. I writhe in pleasure before he pulls my dick out of his mouth and rises and kisses me again. He grabs the back of my neck and leans forward, pushing me farther into the closet, chest-first against one of the shelves. I grip onto a metal rod that supports the side of the shelf as Reese kisses his way down my back. To my ass.

On his knees, he kisses into my crack and licks my hole. Spreading my cheeks with his hands, he licks and kisses in a frenzy. I kick my head back, savoring the sensations that pool through me. Appreciating however he learned to please a man so well. I figure some of his military experience offered him opportunities to learn a few things from some of the guys who were more experienced than he was at the time.

He licks his fingers and slides two inside me, working me up before adding a third. "Open me up," I beg.

"I have to," he says. "You got me so hard right now. And we don't have any lube. Unless you brought that with you, too, you fucking whore."

I chuckle. "I actually did."

"Shut the fuck up."

"I'm always ready to play," I say. "That's what happens when you're used to tricking out with guys. Most of them are desperate enough to want to be fucked anywhere, but not bright enough to carry the tools, you know?"

He fetches my pants and hands them to me, and I retrieve the condom and lube. I glance at his prosthetic leg for a moment, and he notices, but I just hand him the lube and spin back around, facing the shelf.

He must think I'm judging his leg. I'm not. It just surprises me when I notice it, but I worry he's already fucking self-conscious enough about it as it is. And I don't want that to play on his mind.

He tears the packet of lube open and spreads some on his fingers before massaging his way in. I gasp as the sensations crawl through me, as he pleasures those areas within me that his cock was so good at pleasuring yesterday.

He kisses my ass cheek as he continues penetrating me with his fingers. Considering how much time he spent opening me up yesterday, I'm surprised at how tight I am right now.

"I wish I didn't want to fuck you this bad," he says.

"Grab the condom and get inside me."

He pulls his fingers out of me. I glance over my shoulder as he suits up, adding some necessary lubricant on top of the condom. He rises to his feet, using his left leg to push up before bracing himself on his prosthetic. He's good at working with that leg.

He tosses the condom wrapper aside. He's so fucking hard. It looks even bigger than the last time I saw it, which can't be possible. He works his way in slowly, letting me open up even more for him. Taking his time.

I have to get back to my shift. Everyone'll be wondering where I am, and I'm running through a million different excuses until a sharp rush of delight sweeps through my body, scattering my thoughts.

His hand covers my mouth, like he was anticipating my moan. "You like having that cock inside you, Jay?" he asks.

I nod as he kisses the back of my neck and slides in deeper.

"Damn, you're so tight," he says, pulling his hand away from my mouth. "But it feels so good."

He pulls his cock back out, squeezes some more lube on, and sticks it back inside. All those sensations he stirs make me arch my back as a rush of sensation shoots through me.

I grip onto the frame of the shelf as he works into his stride. He wraps his arm around my neck and clings on tightly as he thrusts hard within me, kissing behind my ear.

A wave of heat washes through me, up to my face, filling my cheeks. "It feels so good having you inside me like this," I say. "Feels so fucking hot."

"I wish I could breed you with my come right now," he says.

And I do, too. Even the thought of having him shoot his load inside me is enough to have pre-come dripping from my cock, onto the cement floor.

10

Reese

It's wrong. I've worked so hard to get where I am, so knowingly putting my job on the line is the dumbest thing I could do right now.

But Jay's a pill that can make me forget about how broken I am. About the pain that always seems to linger within me. When we fucked yesterday, he drowned out the noise in the back of my mind, and that's not something I get to enjoy often.

This isn't me. I'm responsible. I'm in control, meticulously so, of every aspect of my life.

Perhaps that's why I'm being so reckless about this. I've finally found something that gives me pleasure. Real, deep, profound pleasure, and I don't just want it. I need it—need the relief he gives me.

I've had such a hard time ignoring him, pretending not to be horny as hell for his body. Pretending not to want to experience those same delicious sensations that I got to enjoy yesterday. I'd been plotting a way to make this moment happen, and as soon as the opportunity arose, I took advantage.

My cock feels so good inside Jay's ass. My balls feel so heavy. Like they need release. I grip onto his abs, the flesh taut against thick muscles. His hole feels just as good as it did before, but this time, there's something so wrong about what we're doing since it's on the clock.

That just excites me more. Maybe because the thrill helps still the thoughts that race through my brain. I haven't felt this kind of excitement in a long time.

I've been dead for so long, and now I'm alive again.

"Own me," he whispers. "Own my fucking ass."

I pull out and turn him around. He looks at me, his eyes filled with confusion.

I lean down and wrap my arms around his thighs, hoisting him up. He wraps his arms around my neck, and I shove him up against the cement wall for support, feeling the pressure around the edges of my leg in the socket of my prosthesis. It's difficult for me to balance, but the struggle is more than worth it. I'm far more adventurous than I used to be in the bedroom, and I know it's because I feel like I have something to prove. That I have to show all my tricks that I'm more than the handicap they see.

"Surprised?" I ask.

"Impressed." He smiles. Keeping his leg in my arm, I maneuver my cock back inside him.

"Oh, yeah," he says, his wide brown eyes filled with eagerness. "Take me. Fucking own me."

I obey.

I ease myself in and then offer him the sort of fuck he needs. I thrust, and he curses quietly, twisting his head either way as he trembles, his expression revealing just how much he enjoys how my cock feels inside him. We curse together as I feel the pressure in my balls building and building.

And my shaft aches. The way I fuck his ass is like I have an itch and the only way I can relieve it is by ramming into him. Soon it's too much for me, and I'm spewing into the condom within him.

Our kisses are out of sync for a moment as I wince and groan with my orgasm. I think I'm going to have to get him off, but I must've hit the right spot within him because his cock spews like a geyser without him even touching it. His eyes widen even more like even he's shocked by the event.

The come spills across his abs like yesterday. Keeps going and going. I kiss him some more, amazed that this feels even better than the first time.

"God that was so fucking hot," I confess.

"You're a stallion."

We kiss some more before we break apart. I set him down, and we wipe off with a roll of paper towels from one of the boxes in the closet. Then we scramble into our clothes and get back out onto the warehouse floor. His excuse to Tyler will be that I needed him to help me move some boxes in the supply closet. That way he won't get chewed out for being late back from his break.

As I return to my office, guilt builds within me.

This is why I don't fuck around with employees. It's dangerous. We could get caught. We could both lose our jobs. For him, that might not mean much, especially for a guy who hops around as much as he does. But for me, I've worked too hard to get here. It's not his fault that I let myself get that reckless, though. It's just, there's something about how wrong it is that makes it all the more enticing. I've been playing by the rules for so long. This is the first time in a long time that the sex has been so hot that I can hardly control myself. And Jay never looks at me like he pities me, like some guys do when they see my leg. It catches him off guard occasionally, but then I see that desire in his eyes and know all he cares about is getting fucked.

But this is about more than him not giving a damn about my physical wounds. It's about the emotional ones that he eases. The chemistry between us is so powerful that when we fuck, I forget that I'm fucked up. I forget that there's something wrong with me. And for a moment, just a fucking moment, all those thoughts that never quiet down shut the fuck up and give me the peace of mind that I desperately long for. Just for a moment, I'm a normal guy like I was before I was deployed. And before I lost my best friend in the whole fucking world.

***

Shouting catches my attention. It's coming from the main warehouse.

And just when I was having such a great day.

I head inside and see Jay and William having at it. "Well, I don't see why you're getting on my fucking case," Jay shouts.

I'm pissed that it's him. Really? He can't make my job fucking easier.

"You were supposed to fill it up when you were finished," William shouts back.

"Hey, hey, hey, guys," I call as I head into the warehouse. "What's going on?" As I approach, I see Jay's face is bright red. He doesn't look at me.

"He didn't put gas in the forklift," William says. "I told him the gas gauge doesn't work anymore and that he has to refill it every time he uses it, so it died on me while I was trying to move some packages onto the loading dock."

"Is it going to kill him to do it now?" I ask.

William sighs like he doesn't understand why I'm being lax about this. Like I should be up in arms over such a trivial thing.

"I don't see why I forget to do one goddamn thing, and William is all up in my fucking face about it. Can't a guy make a fucking mistake?" Jay's tone is severe, his body tense, his face red. I don't know why he's so fucking defensive about this. Or why it has to be a fight. It's not something that can't be fixed.

"William, let me handle this," I say. I lead Jay back to my office.

"What's going on?" I ask him as I close the door behind me.

He sulks.

"Seriously?" I ask. "You were fine this morning."

"I'm doing my job, same as everyone else here."

"If you messed up with filling up the stupid gas in the forklift, you think I give a flying fuck?"

"William sure does."

He was there for me when I was having my breakdown. Now it's my turn to be here for him.

I saunter over to my desk and lean back on it, relaxing my palms on the edge. "Jay, talk to me. Seems like every time something normal happens— something that most people would just laugh off or chock up to nothing, you fly off the handle. What's wrong?"

He looks at his feet. "This is just how it always fucking is. No matter where I go. Everyone blaming me for shit. Acting like I'm the reason everything goes fucking wrong."

He doesn't sound angry anymore. He sounds sad. Like he's disappointed in himself.

"Talk to me, Jay. Please."

11

Jay

Reese has totally blown away all my defenses.

When I was shouting at William, I wasn't even thinking straight. I was just filled with rage and blindly arguing to get him off my back. But Reese is actually listening to me.

I'm not used to that.

I remember being a kid. Dad shouting at the top of his lungs. Always screaming at me for one reason or another. How I fucked up doing a chore around the house. How I fucked up in school. How I fucked up his life. No matter how far away I am from the little trailer in Texas that I grew up in, I'll never get far enough away to forget the tone in his voice when he berated me and my bro. Every moment that we needed something from him was a moment of inconvenience that was liable to set him off, sending him flying into his latest tantrum. And he proved with Miles just how much he never wanted kids. Just how much of a pain in the ass we were for him to have to deal with.

"I don't understand why I'm the one who always gets fussed at," I say. "Everyone fucks up, but they don't have to hear about it all the fucking time. They don't get screamed at over stupid shit. I'm always getting shouted at."

Even though we're discussing William, I'm talking about Dad. Feels like I carry him with me everywhere I go. Every co-worker who screams at me is just another chance for Dad to lash out at me through them.

Reese gazes at me in silence. I know what he's doing. Judging me. Blaming me.

"I wouldn't fucking do this to myself," I insist. "This isn't like Tyler. He was just being a dick. William is seriously getting on my case over something stupid."

"I don't think you do it to yourself. I just wonder if sometimes your attitude toward people is more what turns it into a big deal than the thing that starts these kinds of fights."

"So you're blaming me?" He's just like everyone else.

"I'm not saying William was right to get that fired up about putting the fucking fuel in the forklift or that Tyler was right when he was being an ass to you. I'm just saying that I'm sure your reaction to them doesn't help things any."

"No shit. Whatever. If you got a problem with how I am, I can walk today."

"Why do you have to take it there? I'm trying to help you, Jay."

"I don't need any help, *Reese*." I stress his name, emphasizing the way he said mine.

But as he gazes into my eyes, I can't help but think how much help I really need. How alone I feel. How alone I've always felt. But I'll be damned if I'm going to get lectured by some trick.

Not a trick—my boss. This is how fucking in the workplace complicates shit.

"Everyone needs help," he says. "Every one of us. I didn't get here today without help or by pushing people away when they try to offer me a hand. Not that I haven't done that in the past, but at some point, you have to accept the assistance."

Considering all he's been through, way fucking more than me, I'd be stupid not to at least hear him out.

"Maybe next time something happens, you could walk away for a bit. Maybe just tell whoever is getting on your nerves that you need a ten-minute break and then head off. If someone accuses you of something, you can just say *okay*, even if they're totally wrong. Just find your bearings and maybe confront them again when you've thought things through. I don't think these sorts of things would turn into a big fight if you took a minute to think them through, but you just start going off like that, and then no one's listening."

He has a point. Several points that sound like they're worth considering. Now I see why he's the boss-man. He's the first I've ever run into who seems to actually give a shit about his employees. Although maybe he just cares about me because we fucked around. I wonder if he'd have been as understanding about my tirade if I hadn't let him up my ass a few hours earlier. But he was nice to me even after I threw him to the ground, and he wasn't fucking me then. So maybe he's just a good guy.

"I could do that," I admit.

"I'd appreciate that. And if you need to come chat with me about it, yell at me about it, feel free. I've already given Martin and Carter permission to come and vent to me any time things are getting hard during the day. Sometimes you just need to get stuff off your chest, but without getting in everyone's faces."

So he does this for more people than just me? Suddenly I don't feel as special. But in a good way. Like he just sees me as any other employee, not like I need special care because of anything we've done. I'm also a little disappointed. I don't know why. We just fucked around a bit. He doesn't owe me anything because of it.

He's the kind of guy someone would be real lucky to have. A real catch. Hot as fuck. A good guy. Good listener. Someone who's been through enough shit in his life that he understands what's important.

I don't know why I'm letting my thoughts go there. Not like he'd want to do anything with me, some asshole he works with…someone he's hooked up with twice. I could never be the kind of guy someone like Reese would want to be with. He'd want someone on his level. Someone successful. Someone with money. Someone who doesn't have all these fucking petty attitude problems, which must seem like total bullshit to someone who's been through such serious shit. Who's been through war.

God, why am I fucking thinking like this? I don't even know this guy.

"Thanks," I say. "Can I go now?" I need to get back on the floor. Need to get away from him.

He seems surprised by my curt response.

"Oh, shit. No—I didn't mean that like I'm not listening," I say. "I really do appreciate it. I just think I should get back to help out with getting this stuff shipped out."

He blinks a few times before saying, "Sure. Go ahead."

I start for the door.

"One more thing," he says.

I stop and turn back around.

"You want to swing by my place later?"

Of course I fucking want to swing by his place. "This ass is yours whenever you need it," I say with a wink.

His lips curl at the edges, assuring me that whatever I do for him must at least be good enough for him to keep coming back for more, which is a fucking relief. Because it feels good every time, and I want it again…and again…and for however long it keeps feeling as good as it does.

I head back to my work, but William doesn't give me any more shit about the forklift, which he filled with fuel after I headed up to talk with Reese.

As I help move some boxes onto the trucks, I find I'm filled with an eagerness that I've never really felt while working before. I actually have something to look forward to other than just getting home and desperately trolling Grindr for a trick.

I shouldn't feel this giddy about it. It pisses me off a little.

I don't do relationships. They're complicated. They never end well. I've only had a few in my early twenties, but after learning that the only way they end is catching someone messaging another guy behind your back, I decided I couldn't do that to myself anymore. It wasn't worth the fights or the screaming matches. It wasn't worth putting my heart out there only for it to get beaten up.

When my shift ends, I head back to my place for a bit. Shower off. Pick out what I'm going to wear. I don't have anything nice. Just my work clothes. Closest thing is a polo with a lube stain on it. I debate for a few minutes before I decide it's not noticeable enough for me to stress about it. I throw it on and head to Reese's place.

He's also cleaned up when I arrive, smelling of a fragrance that catches my attention. A striking cologne that's almost as hypnotizing as he is.

He leads me inside. "Want a drink?"

"A drink? Oh, I don't have to fuck and go?" I ask, teasing but kinda serious too.

"No," he says, turning to me, a serious expression on his face. It comforts me.

What am I doing? If this all goes south, I'm gonna have to quit this job and move on…to where next? How many cities do I need to bounce around to before I realize that wherever I go, I'm still there? My problems are still there. The pain and the hurt is still there.

"A drink would be nice," I say.

12

Reese

I fix him a vodka Sprite at the kitchen bar. He sits in one of my stools, looking cute as fuck in a burgundy polo, his chest filling it out real nice. I can see his nipples through it. Makes me want to skip any pretense and strip him down, take him the way I've wanted to since we fucked in the supply closet. But I don't want him to think I'm an asshole who only wants him for his body. He's a good guy. He's just guarded, and that's something I more than understand.

He looks around uneasily. I know he's still in shock from how clean my place is. He had a similar expression on his face when he was here the first time. Makes me self-conscious.

"It's the service," I explain. I offer him his drink and start making my own. "That's why I keep everything so clean. You don't really have the luxury of keeping things tidy when you're shacking up with a bunch of other guys and you're spending your nights roughing it around the desert." I'm trying to downplay the far messier explanation. One I'm not ready to share with him.

"That makes a lot of sense," he says, appearing sympathetic rather than judgmental, which is more often than not the response I get from tricks that I bring home.

"What was that like?" he asks. Tension rises within me, and he must sense it because just as quickly as he asks, he says, "Sorry, that was a stupid question. I guess you don't want to talk about it, considering—"

"No. I'm getting better. Laura says it's good for me. She's my therapist. We've been working on this together for a long time. Believe me."

He must think I'm all kinds of fucked up with the way I talk about this shit. He can't understand what it was like. Can't understand everything we went through. Can't understand what it's like to murder a human being and have to find a way to make peace with that in your own head. To go around constantly trying to justify putting a gun to someone's head and blowing their brains out because you were scared as shit that they were about to kill you.

"At first," I say, "it wasn't much different from how I was raised. I was with the state when I was a kid. You know the ones that never get adopted?

That was me. So I just moved around from one orphanage to another. Shared dorm rooms with a bunch of other guys. I signed up for the armed services because I was told it was a good way to pay for my education. That it was the only way I'd be going to college. So I was in the Reserves. Studied business at UT. And then we went to war with Iraq, and I was deployed. It was about a year that I was gone. Most people were deployed for fourteen months. That was it. I don't think most of us realized what we were getting ourselves into. We were kids. And at first, boot camp was fun. It was this bonding experience where you got to hang with all these cool guys and goof around. But then shit got real when we were being shouted at by our superior officers and being told to scramble to get away from the machine guns. And the IEDs."

"IEDs?"

"Improvised explosive devices. That's what caused a hell of a lot of injuries during the war. It's how I…"

I can't say it. I try to get the words out, but I choke on them.

"Got it," he says as though he's trying to give me an excuse not to finish my sentence. I appreciate it.

"I think a lot of guys thought the war would be real black and white. But is the woman running down the street an ally or is that baby she's carrying really a bomb? You don't know. And you have to make split-second decisions, a lot of which you regret."

He stares at me wide-eyed. I got so lost in telling him about my experience that I almost forgot he was here.

"That sounds horrible," he says.

"It's not something a bunch of eighteen-year-olds should be expected to do. Die for their country. Suffer for their country. Too many guys I know came back from that messed up."

I imagine the distant look in Caleb's eyes. His agitation whenever we tried to go out with some of our old friends. The way he broke down when some of his anti-war buddies gave him a hard time about having participated. That all bothered me too, but not the way it bothered him. I loved Caleb so fucking much, and now he's fucking gone.

Forever.

Jay's eyes are still on me. I'm trying to figure out what he's thinking, but as he glances down, I realize I've stopped making my drink. I grab the Sprite bottle and pour some on top of the vodka in the glass. I stir it with the spoon I left out from making Jay's drink. Then I take a sip.

"Sorry. I needed a little something."

"I would, too. Jesus. Crazy to think it was that long ago…the war in Iraq."

"Yeah. Over a decade, and there are days when it feels like I'm still right there. Like I never came home to this life. Like everything that's happened between now and then is the dream and the war is the only reality."

"That's crazy," Jay says. "How that short amount of time can fuck a person up so much."

"Yeah. Real crazy."

"So the post-traumatic stress disorder…do you mind if I ask you about that?"

Yes. I mind a lot.

"Started having a lot of episodes after I got back," I say. "Intense. Unforgiving. Unbearable. Made it difficult for me to go to work. After I started a job at a distribution warehouse in Vinings, I had a serious episode. One of my co-workers had actually been through 'Nam and encouraged me to get help."

It's not a complete lie. The story about the episodes and my co-worker's well-meaning attempt to help me are true, but really, I quit that job shortly after and found another, hoping to avoid the issue. It wasn't until a year later that I sought treatment. But that's something I don't want him asking questions about. Something he surely doesn't even want to know about.

"Well, I think we've talked enough about my grim life," I say. "What about you? You seem like you're pretty well-traveled. Like you've been around the block a few times. What's your story?"

"I don't have much in the way of a story. Not like yours. I was raised by my aunt and uncle from the age of twelve…until I was old enough to get out on my own, and I never really liked school and didn't have the means to go anyway, so I had to start looking for work right after. Picked up odd jobs wherever I could. This and that. I don't like people ordering me around. Well, except in the bedroom that is."

He winks at me, and my cock twitches. A rush of adrenaline shoots through me. He's so fucking sexy that even something so simple gets me all worked up.

"So I obviously have trouble staying in one place."

"But why do you move around so much? Why not just find a new job in the same area?"

He takes a sip of his drink and shrugs. "I guess I just haven't found anywhere I really like. You know, it'd be nice to settle down somewhere. To find a place that I really like. But nowhere I've gone has really impressed me."

"And what do you think of Atlanta?"

"Nice enough. Got a lot of horny guys on Grindr, I've noticed." He has a sly look in his eyes and a fat grin across his face.

"Oh, yeah. We have plenty of those."

"The weather here could be better. Damn, it's a hot-ass summer. Humidity isn't very forgiving. Especially in the factory."

"No, it isn't. But you think you'll stick around?"

"Maybe. If things keep working out as well as they are. You know…with the guys."

Despite the playfulness of his tone, I feel like he's totally serious.

"So that's how you live your life?" I ask. "Some place doesn't work out, then you just move along?"

"Look, I don't need a lecture right now."

"I'm not trying to lecture you. I'm just asking a question. Not everything has to be a fight, Jay."

He takes a breath, once again reminding me of how Caleb would have to calm himself when he got short with me. "It's just easier that way."

"How many cities have you lived in?"

"Let's see…San Antonio, Dallas, Houston, Baton Rouge…Mobile for a while. Boston for a bit. New Orleans. And then here, I guess."

"You got a place to run to next?"

"I do, actually," he says, his grin suggesting he's always ready to be out the door as soon as things start heading south. "Was thinking that Chicago might be nice. I figured I might at least like the weather better."

"The cold?"

"It'd be a change from this humidity. At least for a bit. What? You haven't lived in a lot of different places?"

"I grew up in Tennessee, but I moved here shortly after I got back from Iraq."

"Why Georgia?"

I tense up. I don't like the conversation shifting back to me, but I've spent years learning the art of ambiguity, so I can handle it.

"To stay close to someone," I reply.

"Ooh. A lover?"

"A good friend."

"Must have been a really good friend if you were willing to move here with him."

"He was. The best of friends. A guy named Caleb." I choke a little on his name as I say it. "Met him when we first went to war. We hit it off real well." The tension rising in my chest is intense. I worry that if I'm not careful, I might have a panic attack.

13

Jay

I can tell this guy means a lot to Reese just by the way he struggled through his name, but he's become even more rattled than when he was talking about the war. It makes me wonder why this Caleb guy isn't in his life anymore. They must've been a couple. Surely this guy had to have been more than a friend, like Reese said he was. That would explain why he acts so weird when he says his name.

Reese drinks from his cocktail, but he takes his time as he gulps down what must be at least a shot's worth of vodka. I'm waiting for him to continue, but he just stares off.

"What happened to him?" I ask, figuring that's where the story was leading.

"He passed away," he says, his face turning red, his jaw tightening as he seems to be trying to keep himself together over it.

"Sorry," I say. "Didn't mean to hit on a sore subject."

He looks at me, but not really *at* me. Through me. Like he's still thinking about this friend.

"Not your fault," he says finally. "He was a Georgia native. We didn't get along very well when we first met. He was like you—a stubborn shit who got into trouble with his mouth. Didn't like to take orders. He had a beautiful body because every time he talked back to the sergeant, he would have to do push-ups. He'd tell everyone that boot camp was the best thing that ever happened to his six-pack." He chuckles. "One night, maybe a week after we'd been put in the same squad, we were all drinking, and he turned to me and said, 'I don't like the way you look at me.' He seemed really serious about it, too. He must've caught me looking at him in the showers, which I would do sometimes because he was hot as hell. Never had any intention of doing anything with him. He just…was gorgeous, so it was something that would catch my eye occasionally. I figured he was going to be an ass after that, but the next day, he wrapped his arm around me and started chatting me up about this other guy he didn't like in our squad. We were inseparable after that.

"He was a good guy. He got into the Reserves because, like me, he didn't have a lot of options outside of it. He grew up in a small town in a big family…a single mother who had a hard time keeping up with them all. She passed away when he was in high school. She didn't have much of anything to leave to the kids, so he had to make it on his own. He figured it was either the army with the possibility of getting a real education or winding up a mechanic in a shop. He studied engineering. When he got back, he wound up being a mechanic for a while anyway."

"What happened to him?" I ask.

"The PTSD got to be too much for him, and he just…"

He stops short, telling me everything I need to know. I can tell by the way he keeps moving his lips that he wants to go on, but I don't think he can right now.

"Sorry," he says. "Wasn't planning on talking about these kinds of things tonight."

"What were you planning, then?" I ask, raising my eyebrows suggestively, hoping to distract him from the pain the memory of his friend obviously stirred.

Reese forces a smile. I rise from the stool and head around the bar, eyeing him with a look that surely makes my intent clear. He appears to slip out of whatever trance he was in as I approach him.

I kiss him. Hard. I want to yank him from the darkness before it grabs him and leaves him shaking like I've seen it do before.

He sets his hand on my face, and my cheek pricks with excitement as I enjoy our kiss, tasting the vodka and Sprite on his tongue.

He turns and guides me, pushing me back against the bar, pressing tight against me. Even padded by our clothes, his muscles feel so good against me. I like the sensation. I like that he's such a fucking tower of a man. I want to be crushed beneath his weight as I'm filled with him.

"You're a damn good kisser," he says as he pulls away and gazes at me.

I'm enchanted by those blue eyes. They're right on me. Not somewhere else. It feels so good. Good enough to concern me. It reminds me that the moment things don't work out between us, I'll have to hop on a flight to Chicago and say goodbye to this city…and to him.

"You're a damn good top," I tell him. "I've never let anyone dominate me like that. Take complete control, do whatever he wanted."

"You usually top?"

I nod, and he smiles.

"Mmm..." He kisses me briefly. "No wonder you're so tight. I wondered if you were going to be able to take it that first time."

"Oh, that little thing?" I tease as I glance down at his crotch.

He beams, apparently amused because I'm sure plenty of his previous tricks have let him know just how big he is.

He cups his hands around my ass cheeks. "Well, I sure as fuck can take it now," I tell him.

"Why don't you show me?"

He leads me to the bedroom, and we do what we do best. Hot as ever. His hands grope my body as his cock fills me. He makes me scream out again and again. I don't hold back at all tonight. Sweat drips from our bodies onto the bed as his muscles glisten under the overhead light. I get a good view of every part of his room as we change positions, each time with him hitting my prostate in a more satisfying way than the last. And soon, we're lying spread out across the bed, gazing at one another.

He never checked out during our fuck. He was ever-present. With me. Totally wrapped up in the experience. I like knowing that our fucking can do that for him. At least, for a moment, help him escape from the demons that haunt him.

I sigh a long, drawn-out sigh. "I don't know what I'm gonna do about this," I say. "I don't usually do regular things like—"

"What?"

"Oh, shit." I'm embarrassed. I shouldn't have fucking said anything. He probably just wants to hit it and quit it. "Sorry. I was just thinking...I mean, it was hot for me. I didn't mean to assume that you'd want to keep this going."

"I'm having a very good time, too."

"So you'd want to like...keep this up?" I feel dumb saying it, but I'd be lying if I tried to act like this wasn't the hottest sex I've ever had, and I'm just not ready to quit it yet. "You know what, never mind. I want to die right now."

Reese leans toward me and wraps his arm around me. "Jay, I can't get my mind wrapped around you. For a guy who confronted me outside a bathroom for sex and who'll start a fight about anything, you sure seem like you're getting awfully flustered right now."

"I don't ever do this," I confess.

"What?"

"Hook up with the same guy. Like more than once or twice."

Reese's expression shifts to surprise. "Seriously? Like ever? Obviously you've had regular hookups in the past."

"Not outside of boyfriends, and that's been a real long fucking time for me. This is very new. But I want to keep fucking…if that's what you want."

"That's definitely what I want." He kisses me. He's the one trying to calm me down now.

He runs his hand across my face, his fingers sliding through the sweat that still covers my flesh. When he pulls away, his breath slams against my skin as he rubs his nose against mine.

I need to be careful about what's happening here. The ease he makes me feel. The heat between us. All this is dangerous. All this is the kind of stuff that leads to me getting hurt. Has in the past, at least. I've been good about guarding my heart. Keeping myself from getting wounded. But Reese is already sliding past my usual barriers.

Nice as he seems, I know how guys are. They always seem nice in the beginning. Always seem like the last thing in the world they would do is hurt you, but in the end, that seems to be all they ever do.

"This is going to get a little tricky," Reese says.

I knew it. Not even a moment after he said he was fine with hooking up with me, he's found an issue with us messing around.

"We won't be able to fuck around at the office like we did today. I mean, maybe occasionally, but we're gonna have to be more careful."

"I have plenty of condoms," I say it playfully, but it's not really a joke.

"That's not what I mean," he says, his brows lifting in amusement. "I just think it'd be a good idea for us to keep this as quiet as possible."

"Did you think I was going to tell someone? Who are all these friends you think I have?"

He laughs. "Whatever. You know what I'm saying."

"I'm fine with keeping it however quiet we need to. I didn't come out here to start a riot in the office."

"Well, you sure as fuck found a way," he says, planting another kiss.

My dick shifts. His hand slides up my leg and he gropes my shaft. God, he makes me so fucking hot.

"Looks like it's time to go again," he says before kissing me again.

I'm all his tonight. Ready for him to take me in whatever way he sees fit. I just want to be fucked again and again until I can't think straight. Until I forget all about the past.

And I hope he's eager to fuck me until he loses all concept of all the horrible things that have happened to him.

14

Reese

Jay stands behind the glass screen that divides the shower from the rest of the bathroom. He faces the wall. It's an unspoken agreement we've made for when I'm entering. We never had to discuss it. He just knows I don't want him to see me come in, and he doesn't watch as I hop into the bathroom on one foot, across the rubber mat that covers the tile floor. There's a mat in the shower as well to keep me from slipping. For many years, I sat in a chair to wash off, like my prosthetist suggested, but this is how I prefer to live because I can have a shower that resembles the sort I used to have with my fully-functional leg.

I open the door to the shower and hop in, gripping onto the metal rail I installed along the wall. This is one of the many showers Jay and I have shared in the past two weeks—ever since we made this a regular deal.

He's the only guy I've ever showered with since I've had my prosthesis. I've gotten used to taking it off around him, and I'm not as shy about my residual limb, which cuts off mid-shin. Not fucking thrilled about him seeing it, but he never makes me feel like he's judging me because of it. Just the occasional uneasy glances, but he doesn't push. Doesn't ask questions— something I'm appreciative of.

He turns to me, smiling as he continues massaging some shampoo into his hair. "I think I got some in my eye," he says, squinting.

I chuckle. I doubt he really did, but he'll make a joke whenever I have an awkward moment like this. I think he just wants to take my attention off my issues.

"You're so full of shit," I say as I approach him. I study his face up close and he sneak-attacks me with a kiss. He grips onto the back of my head and pulls me closer to him so that my head's under the running water. I'm lost in the sensations he awakens within me, as I always am. Enjoying his touch like when we were both screaming out in ecstasy just a few minutes ago.

He pulls away and opens his eyes wide. "Okay, so maybe I didn't have anything in my eye after all," he says, his lips curling into a wicked smirk. I chuckle.

Never would've suspected a guy wound up as tight as Jay would be so playful, but the more we're around each other, the more he acts like a kid. Silly. Teasing. Carefree. And it helps me take some things a little less seriously.

We mess around a little in the shower before we finish up. He leaves first, and I wait until he's out to hop into my hands-free crutch. It's like a mini crutch that I can strap my residual limb into so that I can get around a bit to put on my prosthesis. It's a pain in the ass to get it on, but I prefer to wear it when he's here—usually won't take it off until right before we go to sleep. I'm thankful that he gives me the privacy I need when I'm getting in and out of it. That he doesn't act like it's some great inconvenience.

Once I get my prosthesis on, I slide into a pair of boxers and head into the kitchen, where he stands in front of the pantry, a box of Pop Tarts in his hand. I approach and wrap my arms around him as he removes a chocolate tart from the foil wrapper. He takes a bite.

"Stop it," Jay says, his mouth full of his midnight snack.

"Stop what?" I ask as I kiss along his neck. He chuckles as he tilts his head, inviting me to keep tasting the treat that is his body. A drop of water slides from his hairline, down his neck. He smells of my coconut body wash.

With just a towel around his waist, his body is mine to enjoy as I grope and fondle his muscles—this gym-induced physique that I'm so fucking appreciative of. I want Jay to know I'm grateful for every bit of effort he puts into developing these muscles. But his sexual charisma extends far beyond his body. He's the kind of guy who could be twenty pounds overweight, and I'd still want to drive my hard cock into him.

He backs his ass up against my pelvis, keeping his shoulder blades pressed against my chest. I love when he surrenders his body to me like this.

He takes another bite of his Pop Tart, and I smile into his neck. "Jay, you must've really worked up an appetite." He spins around so I can feel the hard-on beneath the towel against my boxers, my naked torso rubbing against his.

He swallows his snack and sets the remainder of it on the counter beside him. I notice a few crumbs slip out of the wrapper. "Oh, shit," he says, apparently sensing that my OCD impulses have kicked in. "Fuck. Sorry." He breaks away and picks up the Pop Tart. He grabs a dish rag and wipes the mess into the sink.

74

I fold my arms together and watch as he freaks out even more than I would have about the mess. He folds the top of the tart wrapper and places it back in the box in the pantry before turning back to me. "There we go. All better."

I chuckle. "You are too fucking adorable."

"I'm not going to be the messy lay you end up complaining to everyone about," he says.

"Oh, you already are the messy lay. It's just usually messy because you're covered in your own come."

"I notice you never mind that mess." He winks as he approaches me and moves in for another kiss.

"Mmm," I say, "chocolate. Delicious."

His grin makes me hard again.

So fucking hard.

He reaches down and grabs my girth, stroking up and down like he wants to get me worked up again.

"Oh my God, you're good to go already?" Jay asks. "I have to say, you might need to give me one of these magic Cialis pills if this is what it does to you."

As much as I've never cared to talk about needing help to get it up, the way Jay's so impressed with my constant hard-on doesn't just make me feel like any other man, but a fucking Superman.

"I've been with guys who can keep going," he adds, "but this is just fucking ridiculous."

I cup his ass cheeks. "Can I take that as an invitation to enjoy this ass again?"

He pulls away. "Shut up. You've already had it three times. We gotta at least finish this one episode."

The other night, Jay stumbled upon this series on Netflix, *Sultry Scandals*. It's a crime re-enactment show. All the stories they feature have a sexy twist to them. They're typically centered around a bunch of people with too much money for their own good who start having exciting affairs with the maid, plumber, or pool boy. It all leads up to a murder, so we spend each episode trying to figure out who's going to be offed by whom and why.

Fun as the show is, it wouldn't be as much fun if I didn't have Jay here to joke about it with. And most of the fun is in checking out the hot models they hire to re-enact the crimes—models whose bodies they scan up and down and all around while a boring-ass voiceover gives the show some excuse for existing.

Between the sex, our daily chats, and our TV time, I like having Jay around. He's started spending the nights here. He brings his duffle bag with fresh clothes and a toothbrush so we can maximize the amount of playtime we get. We've only missed two nights together since last week, and both of those have been so that I could see my prosthetist and attend my group PTSD sessions. Most of my other appointments are during the day, though. I just take some time off for them.

I would rather skip my group sessions for more time with Jay, but I know better. I know how bad shit can get if I drop the ball, and it's not worth it. If anything, that would put me at risk for not being able to enjoy the time I get to spend with him, especially now when I'm more fragile than usual. When I can feel the uneasiness lingering within me, ready to strike.

I've been trying to ignore it and pretend that losing myself in my greed for Jay's body can protect me from the pain, but I know better. Still, our time together is so valuable to me. I haven't been with anyone who knew about my issues in a long time. I don't feel as alone as I usually do. He dulls the pain that I'm so used to experiencing.

We return to the bedroom, kissing, our hands pressing against each other's bodies as we grope and fondle one another.

He fights out of my grasp and grabs the remote from the nightstand. The remote was sitting on the comics section of the newspaper—something I've learned he likes to peruse before he goes to bed. It's cute watching him chuckle while he's reading them. He gets this whimsical expression on his face, and his eyes light up like they do when I'm hitting his prostate just right…when he's getting so fucking close to blowing his wad.

"Come on," Jay says. "We just have to find out who did it in this one episode and then we can get back to playtime."

He wears this big-ass smile that is so distant from the scowl he always wore when he first started working at the factory. I like seeing him smile. Being the reason he's smiling.

"Unlike you, some of us don't have a quick refractory period," he teases as he sits up and presses play. I wrap my arms around him and pull him back down onto the bed. "Fuck!" he calls out, reminding me of how many times he's cursed when we've fucked. He turns to me, and we kiss.

I peel the covers back, exposing his dick, stroking it so that he gets hard again. "Looks like I'm not the only one with a quick refractory period."

"You fucking jerk," he says as he grabs the edge of the towel and slings it over his steadily increasing erection. "No, we have to find out who did it. Now be quiet." He shifts his attention to the wall-mounted TV across from the bed. This'll be our third attempt at finishing the episode.

I slide under the covers and lie back on my pillows before resting my hand on his head, still a little damp from the shower. He lies down beside me, placing his hand on my abs.

The voiceover continues as the camera pans across the body of a hottie redhead with massive pecs and a serious package that we can see in the jeans he wears.

I just want to say screw the show and get to fucking again. I'm not always this sex-crazed, but despite how much I'm trying to act like I'm just horny tonight, I know the real reason why.

The day after tomorrow's the big day.

The day I've been dreading, which threatens to yank me out of everything wonderful I've shared with Jay and drag me into my dark place again.

I'm scared as shit about that. I was agitated a few weeks ago, but Jay's offered such a good distraction. Helped dull my awareness of the impending pain and given me something to look forward to instead.

"Oh, fuck," Jay says. He grabs his phone off the nightstand.

"What's up?"

"I meant to download this new Louis C.K. comedy special to listen to while I'm on my break tomorrow."

"Louis C.K.?"

"He's a stand-up comedian. I've already listened to all the specials I downloaded. I heard he was coming to Atlanta in a few months, and when I went to check it out, I saw he had a new special out."

"So that's what you're doing whenever I see you with your earbuds in? You're listening to a comedian?"

"Not just *a* comedian. I love stand-up comedy. Richard Pryor, Tim Allen, Joan Rivers, Rita Rudner."

"Who the fuck is Rita Rudner?"

"She's one of my favorites. She's from the 80s. Razor-sharp wit. Clever-ass jokes."

There's that excited expression again, and that look in his eyes like he's floating on fucking Cloud Nine.

He keys into his phone for a bit before saying, "There. Downloading. It'll be all set for my break tomorrow." He looks like he's so damn proud of himself before he repositions himself in the bed, placing his hand back on my abs.

"Come on. You don't get to act this adorable and then expect me not to defile the crap out of you," I say.

"I didn't say we couldn't mess around, but we should at least finish this one episode." He winks at me as he pets my torso. I like when he touches my body like it belongs to him. His attention returns to the TV.

"God, he's incredible," Jay says as we both enjoy the model on the screen, more fixated on his hot body than giving any shits about the narrative that's trying to explain the crime his character committed.

"You think he's hotter than this hot slab of meat you're in bed with?" I ask.

Jay turns to me, beaming. "He's okay." He slides his hand down my torso and lifts the covers to reveal my fully erect dick. "And big as he looks in those jeans, I doubt he can compete with that," he admits.

"You just remember that." I roll over on top of him.

I feel frisky. Like I did when I was in my fucking early twenties. Seeing him all excited about stand-up comedians got me all worked up.

We start making out again. "The episode," he insists between kisses, but he's not trying to push me away again. He surrenders to me. I've won, and I know it. Now for some victory ass.

"I'd feel bad using you like a blow-up doll if you weren't enjoying it so much," I say.

My phone vibrates on the nightstand. Again and again. I try not to look, but one glance over, and I see the familiar number. My face flushes.

"You got a little trick lined up?" Jay teases.

"Shut up. The only nights you haven't been here have been the nights I have group sessions, so you sure as fuck know that isn't the case."

He beams, like he's proud of how my schedule has revolved around him the past couple of weeks, and he should be. I love being able to sneak home together and spend the morning coordinating exactly how far apart we'll arrive to work to keep anyone from being suspicious.

But despite my attempts at losing myself in him, I'm distracted.

Why did she have to call right now?

Couldn't I have had one more night?

I've already been dreading the next few days. Knew I'd have to find an excuse to get out of fucking around with Jay, but I've been in such denial since we started messing around.

I'd rather just pretend it isn't real.

But as with so many things in my life, my thoughts keep going back to the darkness.

The sound of my phone vibrating on the nightstand doesn't just conjure up my memories with her, but memories of the crippling pain I suffered with for so long…the pain that still returns on occasion, sieging my body and capturing my mind.

In an instant, I'm transported back to the days when I wasn't strong enough to battle my emotions. When I was alone and helpless and afraid.

15

Jay

Something changed the moment he got that call. He went from being silly and laughing to being totally serious in an instant.

Who the fuck could it have been that made him do a complete one-eighty? And why is he starting to sweat?

My insecurity creeped in when I first heard the phone vibrating against the nightstand. I thought it might have been another guy. Even if it was, it's not like we're exclusive. Hell, we've only been doing this for two weeks. I don't have a right to pry into his extracurricular interests, but I don't think that's what this is. He's not acting shady. He's acting like something scared the shit out of him. Like it was Death itself trying to get ahold of him.

Between the sweat beading on his forehead and his ghostly pale flesh, it seems to have set off an episode. Was it the sound of the phone vibrating? Surely that wasn't enough to surprise him.

Whatever the reason for the shift in his attitude, I know what my job tonight is: to help him forget.

I lean up and kiss him again, but he doesn't kiss back. As I pull away, I see that distant look in his eyes. I reach down to feel his girth. He's still hard, but I remind myself that it's probably just the meds. "Reese?"

"Sorry," he says. "I don't know if I can do anything else tonight."

"What's wrong? Talk to me."

His Adam's apple shifts as he swallows. "Nothing," he says. "I just...I'm not feeling it right now."

He must know I can tell his behavior changed entirely because of that call, but in the grips of this mood that's captured him, he can't face whatever it's stirred. He rolls onto his back.

I feel empty. Like he's just robbed me of my joy, of my excitement, of my playfulness.

"Who was it?" I ask.

"What?"

"Who just called you?"

He shrugs.

"Come on, Reese. One minute you're crawling all over me and the next you look like you're about to have a panic attack."

"It's not like a guy or anything," he says quickly, as though that was my biggest concern.

"That wasn't what I was worried about," I say.

He's quiet again. I can tell there's a lot more to it, but I recall what the articles I've read about PTSD said about pressing. That I need to give him some space and not overwhelm him.

"It was just someone from my past. Someone who reminds me of a lot of shit I went through."

I'm relieved that he told me that much.

He's quiet for a minute before he says, "Look, I know we've been going at this pretty regularly, but do you mind if I have a few days to myself?"

I tense up at the suggestion. Is he trying to get rid of me? Does he not want to keep this up?

No. I push my insecurity to the back of my mind. He just started acting this way over that phone call. And if it's someone from his past, maybe a friend he served with, then it's likely forcing him to relive all those nightmares that are the reason he has episodes to begin with.

"Whatever, that's fine." Shit. I tried to say it like I really am fine, but I can't hide my disappointment. Can't hide that I just want to curl into a ball and cry.

"I just need a few days," he adds.

Why does he have to be so goddamn vague about it?

And a few days? That could be two days…a week…longer? I'm spoiled with all the nights we've spent together…all these amazing nights. To think I'll have to do without even a few with Reese is painful. There's an ache in me—a hunger. Like he just told me I'd have to go days without food or water.

I try to tell myself he'll be fine. That he'll snap out of whatever funk he's in soon enough and things will be back to normal, but I'm scared as hell that won't happen. That if I give him space he'll just walk away from this and never call me again.

I don't want to believe he could do that, but if it's that easy for him to walk away now, maybe he needs to since I can feel that these fuck sessions are moving towards something else. Something that maybe neither of us is ready for.

"Okay, Reese. Just…let me know, and I'll come running back into your arms again."

It's a joke. I'm hoping it'll lighten his mood, but it doesn't work. He rolls off me and relaxes on his pillow, staring forward as *Sultry Scandals* continues playing on the TV. He breathes quickly, his chest rising and falling rapidly.

He's gone.

Lost in the past again.

Lost in pain.

I wish I could pull him out of it, but I don't think that'll be happening tonight. All I can do is be here for him.

When the episode ends, I turn the TV and the lamp on the nightstand off. I tell him, "Night," but he doesn't respond. I'm not sure he even heard me.

I lie down in bed, facing him. The moonlight that breaks through the blinds shifts in his eyes as he stares at the ceiling.

It's just a few days, I tell myself.

And maybe he'll rethink even that once he finds his balance again.

I hope so.

My anxiety about his uneasiness keeps me up for another hour before I drift off to sleep. When I wake up, he's already in the bathroom. Hasn't put on his prosthetic yet. He grips the sink with one hand for support as he dries off with a towel. I hope he's already recovered, but when he enters the bedroom, he skips our usual session of fooling around, puts on his prosthetic, and changes into his work clothes. We don't talk except when he plans out the time I should leave so that I can arrive at work without anyone suspecting what we're up to. We don't ever kiss goodbye, but for some reason, when he leaves today, I wish we had. I needed the reassurance.

I remind myself that we're not like that.

It's just fucking, and I can set aside my own insecurities while he recovers from whatever he's going through.

Still, I can't shake the fear that he might think there's something wrong with us.

I remind myself that all this started when he got that phone call last night, but the insecurity within me has my thoughts spiraling off into so many different directions.

I wish he'd just let me in and tell me why it was so goddamn important for him to spend these next few days on his own.

16

Reese

I knew I'd get another call today. I just didn't know what time. When her number pops up on my phone, I tense up. Sweat collects on my forehead and palms.

I can't answer. Not today. I won't even listen to the message. I know what she'll say. That she's sorry for my loss. That she misses me. That she misses him. That she wishes we could be a part of each other's lives.

I wish I could do that. If ever there's someone who wants to be there for me, it's Melanie. She was a saint—an angel who would have battled her way through hell for me. Not just because I'm the one she wanted to spend her life with but because she's a good person.

Guilt rises inside me as I think of all the times she's tried to reach out, and all the times I've just ignored her.

I should be able to talk to a woman I was married to…a woman whose only mistake in our relationship was how she continued to love me to the point where it turned on her. I remember years earlier when she would ask me, "Where are you, Reese?" It was before I looked for help. She'd encouraged me to do it, but I wouldn't. I didn't want to talk to some shrink who didn't have a clue what it was like to be in a war, who couldn't possibly understand what I experienced. Neither could Melanie, even though she wanted to. I feel bad about us for so many reasons. Because she loves me. Because she did everything she could, and it was never enough. She wants to at least be friends, but I can't since she just reminds me of all the darkness in my past, and I'm terrified that bringing her back into my life will invite back all those awful memories and drag me back to that nightmarish place I was once in.

Even worse, I'm scared that I'll hurt, not just myself, but her too. And I've already hurt her enough.

I wish I could push her call out of my head so that I can get through the day.

I considered not even coming in—taking the day off like I've done in the past—but I know where that leads. I'd just lie in bed, my mind wandering through corridors and labyrinths of thoughts that will only bring me shaking to my knees in grief and horror. The past two years, Laura's encouraged me to work through the pain, and it's been more successful than trying to grapple with these things on my own. I have her number if I need anything, but she's on vacation with her kids in Florida, and I don't plan on bothering her.

I head into the warehouse, not looking at Jay. I've avoided looking at him since I left yesterday morning.

He knows something's up. He can tell I'm agitated, and if anyone deserves to know the truth, it's him. But I don't even want to face this myself, let alone talk to him about it. I'm just grateful that he's backed off. All I've gotten from him has been a text to ask if I'd be interested in meeting up after work today. I just can't do it, though.

Not tonight.

It'd be better for me to have him over than be alone, but I'd be useless to him. Wouldn't be in the mood for sex or being playful. I'd be in my own world…and he'd be sitting there, watching me suffer. Feeling uneasy. He didn't sign up for that.

"William, do you have the BOLs for yesterday?" I ask as I approach him. "Just got off the phone with corporate, and they're trying to find out where a couple of shipments went missing. I need to fax that over so they can stop riding up my ass about it."

"On it," William says.

Jay stacks some boxes on a pallet. He wipes the sweat off his brow, taking a long breath before grabbing the next box and stacking it on top of the last. I imagine his body against mine as he offers me the sort of comfort I sure as fuck need right now.

He glances at me, his eyes narrowed like he's trying to figure out what's wrong with me, assuring me that he's as suspicious as I figured he would be. I avoid looking at him and return to my office.

I keep busy scanning and filing invoices. Soon I hear a knock on the door.

My body tenses up. "It's open."

Jay shuffles in. "Hey, man. You get my text earlier?"

I can tell by his tone he's worried. I just hope he's not worried about us because that would piss me off, especially after the past couple of weeks—

the amazing nights we've shared where he's made me lose track of all the pain of my past.

"I got the text," I say curtly. *God, I'm such an asshole.*

"Oh, okay. I know you said a few days, so sorry, it wasn't meant to bother you. Take as much time as you need."

Although I can tell by the way he says it that he's begging, *Please don't take too much time.*

As Jay waits in front of the door, me being quiet as fuck, I'm reminded of how I treat Melanie. Of this part of me that can be so cold and distant.

"I'll just leave you to your thing then," he says.

He starts out, but I can't let him leave thinking that I don't want to spend time with him, especially when he's the only thing that makes any of this any easier. If there's anyone I want to spend tonight with, it's Jay. He's the only person who can make me feel normal when the fireworks of memories constantly shoot through my brain, scattering and growing into an epic display. He's the only thing that can pull my attention away from that show to another one that is just as explosive when we're together.

"I'm sorry," I say. I ball my hand into a fist as I fight my impulse that just wants to be a recluse and hide from the whole fucking world.

Jay turns around in the doorway, and it's the first time today I've allowed myself to appreciate that beautiful face. Even covered in a layer of dust and sweat, he's hot as sin. His lips curl upward. I can tell that he's pleased that I went out of my way to catch him before he walked out.

"I've just been so stressed these past two days," I continue. "I'm doing the best I can, but it's just a lot."

He approaches my desk. "Who was it, Reese?" he asks. "I know that call triggered something. You're not okay, and I'm worried as fuck about you. You're not acting like yourself."

It reminds me of something Melanie might have said. Words so similar. Maybe even the same words on some occasions.

"It's like you were there one minute and then suddenly you were transported back to another time."

If only he knew how right he was. I feel so vulnerable with him being close enough to notice. I don't like feeling weak, but I've been willing to risk it to receive all the other benefits that I get from being with him.

86

"Today's not an easy day for me," I say.

Just tell him why. Laura would be so impressed if you could just vocalize it. But as I start to say it, I realize my mouth won't open. *Fuck.*

He waits patiently, and when I can finally bring myself to say something, I say the only thing that I know will help, but goes against everything I'm feeling right now: "This might sound weird…and if it does, just bail. Can you spend tonight with me?"

"Of course. I've spent plenty of nights with you."

"No. Like I just need you to be there with me. I can't promise that I'm going to be normal or shit. Probably not going to even be able to have sex, but I think it would help me out. I'm sorry if I'm being evasive, but I just can't talk about it, okay?"

"Yeah, I'll be there, Reese."

"I can make like dinner or something. Not like a date. Just to eat." Cooking and cleaning always are good distractions for me anyway.

"That'd be great," he says.

His words soothe me, and even though I'm not sure how I'll act around another person, at least I won't have to deal with it all alone. And at least I'll be there with someone who gets that I'm fucked up…who's seen me when it gets bad.

"No, like I'd really like that," he continues. "A lot. It's a date then." He must see me tense up because he immediately says, "Whoa, that was a joke. Trying to get you to relax a bit. Sorry."

"I'm just on edge. It doesn't have anything to do with you. And I can't promise that I'll be acting normal tonight. In fact, it might end up being the least sexy night we'll ever share together."

I notice I'm already suggesting there will be more nights. He must think I'm fucking desperate. Or that things are moving too quickly. God, this was a stupid idea, and I might just scare him off, but maybe if he comes over and sees me have a breakdown, he'll leave. Maybe that's what needs to happen before we keep on going with this.

His smile broadens. "I appreciate you asking me over."

"Good. Okay. Then you should probably grab some clothes from your place and come on over."

He chuckles.

"What?"

"Nothing. Sorry. You're making it sound awfully serious. We've done this enough that I know the routine."

I run my fingers through my hair. "You're right."

"No, it's cute. I'll grab a few things and then come by."

"Any allergies that I need to know about? Things you don't like to eat?"

"Pretty good in the allergy department. I'm not a big fan of pasta."

"No linguini then, I guess," I tease.

He winks. "Meat's always good. Big fan of bread, too."

"Who isn't?" I ask, feeling my tension subsiding.

"I guess I'll see you tonight then." He heads for the door, and as he reaches it, swings back around. "Reese," he says. "I get that you just need someone there. I know it's not like a datey thing. So don't stress. I'm not going to get the wrong idea or anything."

He says that as though that was my biggest concern, which it's really not.

Losing my fucking mind is.

But I feel better knowing he'll be there. At least I can have one thing in my life that has helped make me feel like I'm not a mess. Someone who has made me feel like I'm hot and a good lay.

Like a man.

17

Jay

While I grab my things from Charlie's place, I dwell on Reese's serious expression as he walked around the factory, looking like someone close to him had just died. I've been on edge on his behalf the past two days at work, terrified that something—some sound, some stray thought—would catch him off guard and send him into one of his panic attacks. I didn't want him to be in a place where I wouldn't be able to protect him. Keep anyone else from discovering his secret.

The time we've spent together has been so incredible.

I'm sure having a fuck buddy doesn't mean much to him, but this is closer than I've let myself get to a guy in a long time. Since I was in my early twenties when I had screwed around with guys I'd catch on Grindr or Scruff, working up their same schemes on other dumb kids. Guys who'd take advantage. Guys who are the reason why I'm so fucking guarded now.

I like waking up beside Reese, and I was sad when I woke this morning and realized I was in my own bed. And even sadder knowing that Reese was somewhere struggling on his own.

Today gave me hope, though. I figured he was going to let me walk out of his office. Tell me that he needed some more space. But when he actually pushed through his discomfort to ask me over for dinner, that filled me with excitement. Not because it'll be like any other night. I can tell from what he said that it won't be. That I'll likely be there helping him through his pain. But considering how I feel about it, it seems like this is moving somewhere beyond fuck buddies.

God, why am I even letting myself think like that?

I wasn't joking when I called it a date. I was testing. I wanted to see where Reese stood with us. If he could even consider something more. But I could tell by the way he tensed up about it that this is too soon. We've been spending so much time together I guess it got screwy in my dumb brain. But even though we're not at that place in our relationship, I want to be there for him.

The way he's broken reminds me of how I'm broken. He wants to keep to himself. Shut out the world. That's a painful way to live, so I'm happy to be there if I can make it a little easier for him.

When I arrive at Reese's house, I'm excited. This night feels different. More intimate because I know he's letting me share something deeply personal with him.

I open the door and head through the living room.

He stands in the kitchen. I've seen him in there, making eggs or cereal for breakfast. Fixing me a cup of coffee. But he has a few grocery bags spread out across the bar as he busily works at the adjacent kitchen counter. He glances over, his expression as serious as it was at work today, reminding me that as nice as it is that we're sharing this moment, it's not all light and playful.

Reminding me of the dark reason he's invited me over.

As I near the bar, I see he's using a rolling pin to flatten out some dough on the counter. "Pizza?" I ask as round the bar and approach him.

"Yeah. You said meat, so I was going to go for meat lover's, if that's what you want."

"Well, you know me. I'm fine with sticking some meat in my mouth."

He beams, seeming to forget, at least for a moment, the stress of his day. He turns from his work and offers me a tender kiss.

It's different from the kisses we shared when we first started fucking around. Something more sensual than reckless passion. Something more meaningful. Something that promises more to come. There's an ease about it that makes me feel confident in what we're discovering together. It gives me hope. I'm so used to feeling on edge. Like I'm five seconds away from sprinting on to the next place. But when I kiss him like this, I don't want to run. I just want to stay right here with him.

But this whole setup, dinner and all, makes me uneasy. As datey as it looks, I need to remind myself that it's not a date.

As he pulls away, I glance around at his various stations. He has bowls filled with vegetables and some filled with raw chicken, sausage, ground beef, and bacon.

"Mmm," I say. "What do you need help with?"

"No, no. I got this."

"Come on. I want to help. Don't make me just sit around being useless." He appears surprised by my offer.

"What?" I ask. "You thought I was no good in the kitchen?"

"If you want to cook some of the meat, I can take care of cutting up the vegetables."

"All over it." I fish around the cabinets and stack a few pans on the stovetop. Then I grab some wooden spoons and spatulas from the drawers.

I catch Reese looking at me instead of tending to the dough. "What?" I ask.

"I like watching you make yourself at home. It's a good thing."

And I like hearing him say that.

I get to work. I glance at him occasionally, noticing that he slips back into the same state he was in at work very quickly. I wonder if I'm supposed to talk to him to keep him from going there or if I need to give him space. It reminds me of that day when I was there for his breakdown. When I wasn't sure how to react. What to do. If I was handling it totally the wrong way or if I was actually helping.

Don't push, I remind myself. He's been dealing with this shit for a long time without me. He's not helpless, and he wouldn't want me to treat him like he is with the PTSD any more than he would about his leg.

We work together. He covers the raw crust in sauce, cheese, and sliced vegetables. We pile on the meats I've been cooking before placing our creation into the oven.

"Smells fucking amazing already," he says, setting the digital timer on the stove for fifteen minutes.

"Nice teamwork." I offer him a kiss. He wraps his arms around me and pulls me close, but I can feel his distance as he kisses me. I've only felt this occasionally since we started fucking, but it's a coldness from him. He's not present in the moment. His mind is off somewhere else, and as he pulls away, he looks at me, his expression filled with uneasiness, as though he's afraid that I've noticed.

"I'm sorry," he says. "And I'm sorry for being all evasive about tonight. It's… I'm not ready."

"That's fine. At least you warned me, and I'm amazed you're even able to talk to me this much about it."

"I never would have been okay with doing this before, but you actually respect all these ridiculous boundaries I have up."

"They're not ridiculous, and I have my own too, so I get it."

91

As patient as I want to be, I wish I could get inside his head. I want to know everything about him. And I want him to share those burdens that weigh heavily on him.

"I'm here," I say. That's all he needs to know right now.

He glances around the kitchen. "For not being a date, this sure is the most datey thing we could have done. Sorry about that. I just felt like I should make you some dinner, at least. For being here for me."

"I want to be here. For this, and I mean, in case you get a little frisky later."

"Shit. I thought I was clear earlier…"

"That was a joke, Reese. I was trying to be playful. Take your mind off the stress."

Normally he would have realized I was kidding, but he's not himself tonight. I have to keep that in mind when I tease him.

"I'm all about you fucking the shit out of me and vice versa," I add, "but not if you're not feeling it. Seriously."

He shifts his gaze to the side, twisting his lip.

"What?" I ask.

"Sorry. My brain's everywhere tonight. I probably shouldn't have asked you to come over. I don't even know why I did."

"Yes, you do. You knew when you asked me. And I did, too. So I'm not going anywhere, and we're gonna get through this."

He takes a deep breath. Then another. "I'm counting backwards," he says. "Something Laura told me would help calm me down. I have a lot of little tricks I use. That's one of them. Did you ever think you'd meet someone as fucked up as me?"

"Well, I'm hardly the epitome of normal."

"I lost someone today," he says quickly, as though he had to blurt it out or he wouldn't say it.

"Caleb?" I ask. "I kind of assumed it was something along those lines."

He nods. "I can't believe I said that much," he admits. He heads to the counter and grabs a glass that I assume is his cocktail before downing some of it.

"This day's never easy," he says before taking another deep breath.

"I can imagine why."

But my thoughts are on my brother.

It hurts as I remember the times we played together. How he would laugh so hard. How we would wrestle around and tease each other. To think that Reese could be experiencing anything similar tears at my soul. I wish I could take that pain for him so that he didn't have to deal with it. Although I don't know that I'm strong enough because I'm hardly strong enough to handle Todd's death.

I don't ever talk about it, but I feel like it might help Reese to know he isn't alone. Because I know that when he told me about Caleb, I felt some ease just knowing there was someone else who could relate to what I was going through.

"I told you about my asshole father," I say. I don't know that I'll be able to make it through this story, but I figure I can fucking try. I can bail at any point. When it becomes too fucking hard. When it becomes too much for me to bear. Considering the state he's in, I doubt he'd push or pry. Maybe this is what we both need right now.

"I think he was bitter about having to take care of us. Not a lot of room in his two-bedroom trailer. Mom left us with him. She'd swing back around the house when she needed cash, but she spent most of her time with a guy named Phil. He was her dealer. And she'd go to his house and fuck him for some drugs. She'd still need money, because evidently banging the dealer wasn't enough for her to get her fix. Dad would fight her a bit for it, but he always caved. I don't know if he loved her or just felt sorry for her, but he'd hand over however much he could afford, and make sure to give her a few words about how she left him with *her* goddamn kids. That's all we were to him. Her kids. And she didn't even see us as that. Probably because she saw too much of him in us.

"He liked to shout, and he liked to hit. We would kind of take turns with it. If one of us was getting on his nerves, the other would start shit just to redirect his attention. I don't even think it was on purpose. Just survival. It was always over the stupidest shit. If I did a chore wrong. Or if I got a bad grade in school, or had to come home with a note for getting into a fight. A burden. That's what I was. That's what *we* were. One day, I'd gotten into a fight at school. The principal called him. They were threatening to suspend me. I think he was just mad that he'd have me around the house annoying

93

him all day for a bit. So when I got home, he just started laying into me. I guess it was worse than usual. I told Todd to leave. Screamed at him to go, because when Dad was done with me, he was liable to turn all that anger on Todd. But I think he was worried because Dad was real mad that day. Mom had come by the house asking for more money that he didn't have, and I guess Todd thought he might take things too far. And Dad was laying in some good blows. Todd started screaming, begging Dad to stop. He grabbed Dad's arm, and Dad just tossed him back.

"I know Dad was just trying to move him out of the way so he could keep throwing me around, but Todd tripped over the side of the couch and fell back. His head smacked into the side of the coffee table. I knew he was hurt, but Dad didn't notice. So when I was trying to get away—get over to help my brother—he just thought I was trying to get out of my punishment. For the first time in my life I was able to beat him off of me so that I could check on my brother."

Reese stands before me in silence. In suspense. Waiting to hear what happened to my poor bro.

I can't say it, though. It reminds me of how Reese couldn't say it when he was talking about Caleb.

"I just remember his eyes. Wide open, like he was about to spring back to his feet and start laughing and smiling. Oh, God, I've never seen anyone laugh and smile like he did. Never seen anyone filled with that much life. And for him to be taken from me, that…that was too much." Tears stream down my face.

As much as it hurt to share, there was something about it that freed me.

Reese hugs me. "I'm so sorry," he says.

"It's hard for me when that day comes around, so I understand."

I feel so naked. And it's nice to feel safe in his arms. To feel like he's willing to shield me in such a fragile moment.

I'm amazed that I was willing to open up about something I've kept within me for so long. But I'm also so fucking relieved, and I just hope that it helped him, even a little bit. That it let him know, however bad it is, he's not on his own tonight.

18

Reese

I'm horrified by Jay's story about that bastard father of his.

I hold him close, not just because I'm consoling him, but because his loss reminds me of my own. And yet, helping him in his moment of pain gives me a break from my own hurt since he needs someone to be there for him right now.

He clings to me. I'm not sure if I'm still shaking or if it's just less noticeable because he is too.

"I'm so sorry, Jay," I say.

As he relaxes, he takes a breath and pulls away. "I'm fine. Didn't mean to dump that on you. Just thought...I don't know, it might make you feel like you're not alone."

"It did, and thank you for that." It means a lot knowing he cared enough to share something so deeply personal. Something that shook me to my core. "What happened to your dad?" I ask.

"He went to jail. He's serving his time. He won't be getting out for a long time, but he'll be getting out. Something he doesn't deserve, the fucker. When he does, I sure as fuck won't be there to help him get back on his feet." He wipes the tears from his eyes, and I pull him close again, offering a kiss. He relaxes in my hold and kisses me back softly. He sets his palm against my face.

I want to take away his hurt. I wish I could hunt down his motherfucking father and beat the shit out of him to pay him back for his crime, not just against his brother, but against both of them. No one should have to endure that cruelty at the hands of a parent. Almost makes me relieved I never had that issue. As much as I used to fantasize about having parents, I forget they can be a real nightmare sometimes. Not everyone is lucky enough to get good ones.

After the pizza finishes baking, we prepare two plates and eat at the kitchen table. "It tastes so fucking good," Jay says, scarfing it down like he hasn't eaten in days.

"Couldn't have done it without you."

He smiles as he fans his mouth. "Oh, shit," he says.

"Guess you put a little too much hot meat in there," I joke as he drinks from his glass of water quickly.

When he recovers, he says, "Fuck that was hot." As painful as that probably was, it's clear it distracted him from the story he told me earlier. Brought him back to the present.

He blows out and sucks in a few times.

"I can give you something to suck on if that'd make it better," I say with a wink. He laughs, and I find myself laughing, too. Letting myself get lost in the moment with him, appreciative that I had the strength to invite him over this evening.

Once he's recovered and starts eating again, he says, "These vegetables from your garden are good. Where did you get this green thumb from?" He's seen me working in the garden, but he's never really asked questions about it. Just assumed it was a hobby.

Tonight's not the night for him to get curious. "I…uh…I didn't really start gardening until after Caleb's death."

"Oh, sorry. Shit."

"It's okay. His mom gardened a lot before she started getting treatment for breast cancer, which is what she ended up dying from. Caleb always said that he kept the garden up in hopes that she'd be able to get back to it when she finished up her chemo regimen. But life didn't work out like he planned, and she didn't make it. When he got back from Iraq, he started gardening again. He actually taught me how to compost, which I think is the reason why I'm able to keep any of this shit alive. He always said keeping the garden made him feel like his mom was still a part of his life. When I was getting treatment for my PTSD, Laura encouraged me to find a hobby. Any hobby. It was the first one I could think of because of him, and also, I liked the idea that maybe it would be my own way of keeping him around."

"But you guys never had a…relationship? I mean, nothing more than friends?" Jay asks, and I understand why he's asking.

"Sounds weird, me being so attached to some guy I was in the military with even though we weren't doing anything, doesn't it? Maybe it was. Not that he wasn't gay. I always kind of assumed the reason he got along with me was because he liked me more than he let on at first. His family was Southern Baptist, and I could tell by things he'd say that he was into guys.

96

And I think that's part of what made him gravitate to me…because we were similar in that way, but neither of us wanted to take it further. We never had a conversation about it, but I assumed we both knew we were batting for the same team. But he was more like a brother to me than anything else."

I don't want to talk about it more than that. He doesn't know how hard he's hitting on the subject I'd rather not think about tonight, but my shaking starts to return.

Fuckin' A. "Can we talk about something else?"

"Oh, yeah. Sorry. I thought that would actually be a safe subject when I brought the garden up." The way he starts looking around like he's trying to find a way out of the awkward situation makes me feel like shit that I even said anything. I doubt he feels great about being the one who's reminding me of such a terrible part of my past.

"Don't be sorry," I say. "*I'm* sorry."

"For what?"

"For making everything a fucking trigger."

"You warned me it wasn't going to be easy for you. I understand. It's not a big deal." He reaches across the table and sets his hand on mine, stroking his thumb gently across my skin. His touch soothes me.

I didn't think I'd be able to feel this way tonight, but being with Jay makes that possible.

"You about finished eating?" I ask.

"Yeah. Why?"

I rise from my chair, gripping on to his hand. "I want you."

His eyes widen. It's clear he's surprised to hear that after what a big deal I made about tonight not being about sex, but he doesn't fight. Just hops up from his chair. He smiles and kisses me.

I don't just want him tonight. I need him.

He grips my hand and guides me back to the bedroom. So funny being led into my own bedroom.

We brush our teeth and strip down, me to my boxers, him to his briefs. He lies across the bed, gazing at me as I step out of the bathroom, a cocky smile spread across his face. It's the sort of smile that makes me feel safe.

I approach him and sit on the side of the bed, removing my prosthesis. I can see his surprise. I usually wear it, but I don't want to tonight. I want to be as I am with him. We've already pushed through so many barriers together, and this is another I want to share with him.

He watches me, and tonight, more than any other night we've shared, I don't feel uneasy. He knows this about me. He doesn't have a problem with my issue.

I suddenly don't feel like there's anything unusual or wrong with me.

I'm not a broken man. Not when we're together.

I slide under the covers and cuddle up to him, kissing him gently at first and then letting the intensity build. He sets his hand back on my face and runs his thumb through my beard. He pushes toward me more aggressively than usual. He must know that's what I need right now.

For him to be strong. For him to guide me through this. I want to be submissive to him. He's given it to me like that a few times since we started this, and he's good. Real good. And that's what I'm craving tonight.

He rolls on top of me, his body pressed tightly against mine. His dick is sideways in his underwear, pushing perpendicular to mine as we thrust against each other.

As we break our kiss, he says, "Let me give you this, Reese. Let me take away the pain. Let me make you feel so fucking good."

"Please," I beg.

He kisses down my chin. Down my neck. Down my chest and torso. To my boxers. He slides them down and pulls them off before swooping down and licking up and down my shaft. He angles my cock toward him before sliding it into his mouth, offering swirls with his tongue across the head before sliding it deep in his throat. He puts in the work, burying his face against my pubes as he takes it in. I fist my hand in his hair, imagining him swallowing my thick load as he's done so many times.

I turn to the nightstand and notice that he's already laid out the condoms and lube. I retrieve them, and as he lets my dick fall from his mouth, he looks up at me and grins. "Well, aren't you an eager beaver?" He removes his briefs and suits up while I remove my boxers. Soon, he's working his way into me.

The pressure feels so good. So distracting. I have to focus on loosening up because, as much as he gives me props for being big, so is he. Big enough that it takes some time before he can break into his stride and ride me good.

He moves in just a little too quickly, and I press my hand against his hip. "Wait, wait."

He settles, gazing down at me, his eyes wide. He strokes a hand up and down my torso, petting my body like he wants to set me at ease. "Sorry," he says. "I just want it to feel good. I want you to feel so good."

His words relax me enough that I feel more comfortable. I grip onto his hip and tug for him to push deeper in. He does, being cautious, watching my expression to make sure he isn't moving too quickly.

A rush of energy sweeping through me lets me know he's hit my prostate. Goosebumps follow the sensation, pricking across my flesh as he offers another thrust that electrifies my body.

"Take me, Jay. Own my body. Make me yours."

He accepts the invitation and pushes. His face is serious as he works like he would at the factory…his attention fixed on the task at hand.

He leans down and kisses me, each kiss wetter than the last. His tongue greets mine and our kisses become more frenzied and passionate as I delight in the sensations he fills my body with.

I need him to keep me in this moment. I need to seize it so that it never leaves and that nothing in either of our pasts can catch up with us. We just have to fuck until we both can escape all the demons that hound us.

Being with him between these sheets, I feel so vulnerable and safe at the same time. I spend so much of my day grasping for sanity. Reaching for this impossible dream of lucid thought. But in this moment, I can breathe and feel without any of the distractions.

And it's all because of Jay.

He grabs hold of my hair and yanks, pulling my head back, breaking our kiss. He breathes against my face as he continues to take me.

"I love it," I say, feeling liberated by how he's claiming my body.

"I want to make you come so hard," he says. "I want you to forget everything as I make you spooge all over yourself."

"Make me," I plead.

19

Jay

Each thrust provides a sweet sensation as his hole massages my cock. I wrap my arms around his thighs and bury my dick inside him, offering him the sort of fuck he wants right now. The sort of fuck he needs tonight. He kicks his head back and moans.

He sets his hand on my shoulder. "Fuck me just like that, Jay."

I look down at his cock, which he's just grabbed hold of. He strokes it as a long stream of pre-come oozes out of the head. Knowing how turned on he is only makes me even harder.

"God, you're hard tonight, Jay," he says.

I lift his left leg, twisting his body to the side slightly as I pull his thigh flat against my body. "Oh, this ass is all mine," I say, squeezing his ass cheek, which is clenched tight.

I work up a sweat, building into my rhythm. His cock continues spewing, dripping down his belly, onto the sheets. His mouth hangs open as he cries out, and I can't fight the impulse to shove my fingers in there. I feel around while he licks eagerly.

He looks at me, and I can tell that he's not seeing through me like he has been these past few days. He's looking right at me. Right into me.

He's lost in this moment and so am I.

This is what we needed. This escape. This freedom.

And I'm just pleased that I can be here to give it to him, even if it's as brief as this fuck.

"Flip over," I say, guiding him onto his knee and lifting his right leg by his thigh, holding him up as I fuck him from behind. He grips onto the headboard with both hands as I take him.

I've never been this bold with his body before. I've never taken command because I didn't want him to feel self-conscious, but he doesn't resist, and I'm glad because this position feels even better, and I can tell by the way he starts calling out that it must feel pretty damn good to him too.

"You're gonna make me come like this, you fucking bastard," he says.

I push in harder and harder because I want him to spew his load and enjoy a sweet-as-fuck orgasm. I lean down and kiss behind his ear as I continue penetrating him. I work even harder, encouraged by the way he calls out. Sweat drips off my forehead and slides down his back, into the chiseled grooves between his muscles—the ones that make me wish I had his fucking build.

"This body, these fucking muscles…everything about how beautiful you are just turns me on so fucking much." I pound even harder.

"I'm seriously not even gonna have to touch it," he says.

"Don't then," I say, gripping onto his hip with my free hand as I lean back and take what's mine. Give him what's his.

His triceps and biceps flex as he tightens his hold on the headboard. With his back arched, all his muscles are contracted, displaying how beautiful he is. How well he's sculpted this incredible physique. And it's all for me to enjoy right now.

I'm such a lucky bastard.

The pressure in my balls is so intense I feel like I might shoot at any moment. "I want to look at you," I say. "I want to see your face when I come."

He shifts, and I slide out. He rolls onto his back. He's frantic like he's just as desperate for me to be fucking him missionary as I am. He gazes up at me, his quick breaths and red face assuring me that I'm not the only one getting a workout.

I slide back in.

"Fuck the come out of me, Jay!"

I grab his wrists and pull them back behind him, pinning them against the pillow as I continue pleasuring myself in his hole. Before I know it, he's calling out like some sort of animal. It's not a sound I've heard him make before. This is feral. I'm freaked out for a moment as I look at him and see his head twisted to the side as he moans through his teeth, then unleashes a full-fledged scream, his eyes revealing just how intense the experience is.

The pressure in my pelvis pulsates through me, and before I know it, I am jerking in a wild, violent succession. His eyes go wide, and I look down to see him spraying his load across his rock-hard abs, the white semen flowing like a geyser. My own come shoots through me like a bullet, into the condom. I delight in the sensations that race through my body, sending a hot flash to my face.

My balls tighten like they're trying to squeeze every last drop out, and despite having come already, my hips continue thrusting like I'm still trying to rub one out.

I collapse on top of him, releasing his wrists, not caring about the come that I'm getting all over my belly. Because it's his, and I want as much of it on me as I can get right now.

My cheek pressed against his, I can feel his breath slamming against my ear and his sticky sweat on my face. "Oh my God," he keeps saying, clearly caught up in the power of his own climax.

We kiss with that same wild energy we had when we first hooked up. I don't think I realized how much we needed that until I'd shot my load. But considering how stressed out he was from today and how much I was after talking about my brother, I think we were both desperate for the release that we could give each other. And now I crave being close to him in a way I've never craved before. I want to cling to him.

I'm terrified he's going to make me pull out because I know how sensitive my prostate gets after I come, but I'm relieved that he doesn't say anything. That he just keeps kissing me.

As the high settles, soon we're just holding onto each other. We haven't gotten up to shower yet. Just stayed wet with our spooge and sweat. I don't want it to end. I want to hold on to this for a little longer. Being covered in his semen. Being all his.

I lie on my back as he lies on his side, his torso pressed tightly against mine. His gaze travels down my body, and I don't try to cover up because I can tell that he's appreciating everything he's looking at. "Thanks for the great fuck," he says, a sly smile sweeping across his face.

"Thank *you*."

"And thanks for coming over here tonight. I needed this. More than you can know."

His expression, filled with appreciation and ease, is so wonderful. And again, I find myself imagining that we could be more than just fucking. We already are that. We might not have called this a date, but that's basically what it is.

And here I am in his bed—the only place I want to be right now.

"I'm sorry for being such a downer earlier," I say. "I didn't mean to make it sound like I've had some bleak, miserable experience. I've obviously had good times with my brother. Great times."

"I'd like to hear about those."

I smile.

"No, seriously," he says.

"Todd was a funny guy. When we'd wake up to go to school, he would run out and grab the local paper and bring it in so we could read the comics section together. We each had our favorites, so we'd skip around on the same page at different places. When one of us found something really funny, we'd make sure the other read it when they were finished with the one they were on. But Todd was even funnier than some of them. He'd take a pen and re-write some of the dialogue bubbles, especially on the ones he thought were boring as crap.

"That's the kind of guy he was. We didn't have much, but he knew how to make me laugh. Even if Dad had gotten mad or started hitting one of us. One time Dad beat him up so much that when I found him crying in his room, I asked him if he was okay, and he said, 'It just sucks that he never learned how to throw a punch. I'm sorry. I didn't want you to find out like this.' I know that sounds disturbing as fuck, but that's how we survived. Whenever Dad would go off on one of his tantrums, we'd make jokes about it. One time when I got it bad, I was curled up in bed, and Todd came running in. He was so freaked out and then he was like, 'What are we gonna do now that Dad found the secret passage to Narnia?' And I couldn't stop laughing after that. He could break through tension like it was made of paper. Just that power he had made all the hard stuff that much easier to deal with.

"One night, we stayed up late watching TV. Dad wasn't home. He had gone out to play cards with some of his friends. That's what he told us back then, but I think there was a girl because it was kind of regular for a while. We flipped on this old George Carlin special, and we laughed so hard. We laughed until we couldn't breathe. And then Todd got to making jokes off of Carlin's jokes, and I fell off the couch, onto the floor. I seriously thought I was gonna pass out because I couldn't get any air in my lungs. And I was crying. I begged him to stop, but he just kept on, and I was as happy as I ever can remember being. We spent the next few hours laughing and giggling until we passed out on the couch. That moment…when I think of Todd, what I loved about him, that's what I always go back to. Seeing how happy he was. Remembering how happy we both were. That for just a few hours, we could escape the shitty trailer we were in, forget about Dad and all the bullshit, and just let go and experience real joy."

Tears are in my eyes, but for a moment, it's because I'm so goddamn thankful that I got to experience that beautiful moment with him. That I was lucky enough to have had that time to appreciate Todd.

"That's beautiful," Reese says.

"He was."

He leans down and kisses me gently, offering relief from the sting of remembering that such an amazing creature is gone forever, leaving only the memories that I so desperately cling to.

20

Reese

The constant drumming of machine gun fire competes with the blasts of automatic rifles. We race through the narrow alleys between the concrete buildings of Fallujah, scrambling after the fucking ambush we just encountered.

Drake checks the next corner and urges us to continue ahead. With Caleb to my left and Drake falling back on my right, we hurry along, the other guys tailing behind us.

A sound blasts through the air.

It's the sort of sound we've come to fear and expect.

An IED. It's deafening for a moment, but we don't see the blast. Just watch as the nearby building collapses toward us.

"Fuck!" Drake shouts. Energy shoots through my body like a bullet as I hear one of my commanding officers shouting orders behind me, but I can't understand what he's saying. I don't even think he's giving us orders as much as he's screaming for his own sake. To keep himself from feeling like everything's gone to hell.

"Reese, Reese!" Caleb shouts from behind me. I glance over my shoulder. No sign of the other guys in our squad.

No wonder our commanding officer sounded so distant. Because he was.

Fuck. When the wall behind us collapsed, they must've gotten stuck on the other side of it.

"Over here," Drake says as he races to a nearby doorway.

"Wait, wait!" I call.

Drake's in a frenzy, and we've learned throughout the week that he's getting sloppy. He's too bold. The kind of guy who has a death wish. Who joined the service because he's thirsty to be in the heat of battle, but without using logic or reason to keep himself alive. He's the perfect scout, but a shitty strategist.

He kicks down the door and barges inside, searching around for insurgents—the ones who are likely responsible for the machine gun fire that got our squad running into what was clearly a trap.

Broken boards are scattered across the floor. Some larger pieces of furniture are capsized. It's evident the place has been cleaned out by the Sunnis—surely to transform these buildings and alleys into the perfect trap for the Americans they've fought against since Saddam Hussein's fall.

We make a triangle as we inspect the room, aiming our rifles. We'll shoot to kill, as we've been instructed. We search for hiding insurgents that might be lurking—might have led us down this path intentionally to kill us.

There's an open doorway to my right and a closed door to my left. "This way," Drake says as he makes a dash toward the door on the left, I assume planning on heading back in the direction of our squad.

I turn to keep an eye on the door we entered through. "Just wait a second," I call, but I hear him kick down the door.

Another deafening sound fills the air, and the place fills with concrete dust and wood chips.

I lose my footing and dive forward.

I can't hear.

Silence. Eerie silence. Like when we first got to Fallujah days ago for Operation Phantom Fury. The sort of quiet that had all my superior officers concerned about what we were getting into.

Everything's still.

It feels like forever before I turn and see Caleb lying unconscious in the far corner of the room, on the wall adjacent to the one the blast came from. As my senses return to me, a strong burning smell like rubber fills my nostrils. I search for Drake, who struggles to get up beside the opening where the door he was about to enter used to be. My gun's a few feet away from me.

Disoriented, I grip onto the concrete wall beside me, but as I attempt to climb it, I notice I can't. My legs aren't working right, and as I inspect my feet, I notice my shoe's gone and the bottom of my pants is drenched with blood.

"Fuck!" I rise on my good foot. The pain isn't crippling yet. My body's in shock. And I just hope the adrenaline that's keeping me going will last long enough to get me the fuck out of here.

A scuffling sound comes from the adjoining room.

An insurgent? One of ours?

I turn back to my gun. With my foot like this, it'll take me a minute to get to it.

I look back to the doorway and see the end of a rifle slide through it. A man steps in, his face covered in a red scarf.

It's on. Life or death. Kill or be killed.

I don't have a choice if I'm going to make it out of this alive.

I slide my combat knife out of my belt and lunge at him. He turns, bringing his gun around, but I'm on him before he has a chance. I slash wildly before me. I'm an animal trying to survive—nothing more. Just prey in the wilderness, tearing a predator apart.

But even in this moment, as my blade pierces through his clothes and flesh, I have a hard time figuring out who the real predator is.

If I don't kill him, I'm dead. Caleb's dead. Drake's dead. We're all fucking dead.

I keep fucking stabbing, trying to keep my eyes open because if I so much as blink, it's over.

But I can't help it. Some of the dust in the air stings my eyes and forces me to close them.

I open my eyes back up quickly.

Total darkness.

I've lost my eyesight. Must've been the dust. Whatever happened, I just need to finish this guy and take him out before he kills me and my guys. Just to give our squad time to rescue us.

"Reese! Reese!"

It's a familiar voice. A voice that jars me from the nightmare. But my fist is already going, and as it makes contact with a cheek, I know what I've done.

I freeze in place as a loud thud fills the room.

My arms shake as I try to calm the powerful rush of energy that soars through me—energy that I realize belongs to another time. Not to right now.

The light flashes on. Jay stands beside the door, one hand on the light switch, the other on his face. He turns to me, his expression filled with confusion and hurt.

What have I done? He told me about his abusive asshole father. About how he grew up taking punches. And now I've just done that to him.

I'm a monster.

"I—I—"

"No, it's fine," he says. He picks up his clothes, but keeps his eyes on me like he needs to stay on his guard. "I just need to go." He puts his jeans on and heads out the bedroom door. I hop on my left foot. I'm desperate.

I follow after him, still hopping as I head into the living room. "Jay," I say.

He doesn't respond.

This is really bad. This is why he shouldn't have come here tonight.

"Jay, please," I say, setting my hand on his shoulder.

He whirls around, his face tense, his eyes wide with rage. "Just don't, okay? Don't fucking touch me."

I see the pink spot on his cheek where I hit him. I want to help him, but I know in his mind he must be equating me with his dad. And that fucking tears me apart.

He turns back to the door.

"Jay, I had no idea. I was just…"

Please don't leave.

But before I know it, he's out the door, leaving me standing in the living room, stark-naked, hating myself, still reeling from the shock of my nightmare. I lean against the wall for the support. The only thing that'll be supporting me for the rest of the night.

20

Jay

I toss my shirt on and head to my car.

I had to get out of there since all I wanted to do was deck Reese. He didn't hurt me on purpose. I keep reminding myself that, but that doesn't change the fact that when he socked me, I was transported back to a night when I fought against Dad to get to Todd—to help my brother.

I shake so much it takes me a few tries to get the key into the car door. It reminds me of how Reese gets when he has one of those flashbacks to Iraq.

I can't believe he hit me. The thought replays over and over again in my head as I get in the car and curl up in the driver's seat, locking the door. I don't think Reese will do anything to me. I just feel like I need to be somewhere safe. Somewhere alone.

I sit in his driveway, confused as shit, my body racing through so many emotions—excitement, rage, confusion. I shouldn't blame Reese since I know what it was—another episode—but I can't help what I'm feeling toward him. Hurt. Anger. Those wounds are worse than any shiner I might have tomorrow.

I'm relieved that Reese isn't coming outside to make amends.

I consider driving off, but I can't leave him. Not tonight. Not when he asked me over to be here for him. But I keep slipping back to that night, feeling Dad's fists against me, and seeing what I would soon discover was my dead brother's body.

I'm trapped in that night all over again.

I try to stop the thoughts, but they race through my mind, unbidden, making me hate Reese even more for making me suffer through this. I cringe and my chest constricts.

Get yourself under control.

I ball my hands into fists, the pain in them and in my cheek the only relief I get from the thoughts that race through me.

Fuck you, Dad. Fuck you for making me so fucked up. Fuck you for sucking all the good out of this world...for tearing it from my life.

After several minutes, the thoughts settle. I can breathe with ease again as the tension in my chest relaxes.

I'm sweating. Panting. I didn't notice before. Was too consumed by the thoughts to pay much attention to what was going on around me.

When I regain my bearings, I step out of the car and head back to the house.

I wish I hadn't needed to leave like that. Reese needed me to be there for him. Needed me to console him. He obviously had some horrifying nightmare that resulted in him losing his fucking shit, and I bailed on him.

I open the door and head back inside, searching around for him.

Silence. Eerie silence.

The air conditioning chills the moisture from the sweat I built up outside.

I call out for Reese, but he doesn't respond. I search for him, but he's not in the bedroom or anywhere inside the house.

As I head into the kitchen, I notice through the sliding glass door on the back wall that a light is on, illuminating the back porch.

Strange to think that as much time as I've spent over here, I've never actually been in his backyard. I've seen him working in the garden through the window behind the sink, but never had any reason to go out there.

I walk to the door and peer through it. A few yards away, Reese sits in the fenced-in garden, illuminated by a security light attached to a nearby shed.

I walk to the garden, and as I come to the fence, I open it and step along a narrow board that acts as a divider between different rows of plants. Reese sits in just a pair of boxers, his hands-free crutch strapped to his residual limb as he leans back against a wooden beam that the chicken-wire fencing is stapled to. As I approach, he doesn't glance up. Just stares at a couple of bush beans at his side.

"I'm sorry for running out like that," I say.

He tilts his head back to see me. He looks horrified by what I've said. As if I just told him to fuck off.

"You're sorry?" he asks. "I fucking hit you in the face and *you're* sorry?"

"You didn't mean to hit me. I know that." I sit beside him, on a wooden board that acts as a frame around the garden.

"How can you say that? I saw the look in your eyes. I knew what you were thinking. You were looking at me like I'd just done what your father did to you. I saw the way it affected you. How it tore you up inside."

"Obviously it wasn't easy, but it's not like you decked me during a fucking fight. That would be one thing. That would be unforgiveable, but an accident that happened because of something you can't control? I'm not going to fault you for that."

He raises his hand to his face, like he's trying to conceal it from me. "Maybe you should. Maybe I'm not safe to be around."

"That's bullshit. It was one fucking night. How many nights have I stayed over and been fine? You've just had a lot on your mind, especially today."

He moves his hand and looks into my eyes like he's trying to detect any hate or resentment over what he did, and he might find some. While I understand what happened, a part of me just sees red as I think about that bastard who hurt me far beyond any of the physical injuries he gave me. It's a whisper in the back of my mind, trying to scare me. Trying to spark fear within me about this wonderful thing I've discovered. I won't let it win, though. Not today.

"I don't want to hurt you," he says. "I would never hurt you intentionally. Never lay a hand on you. But I can't promise that I'm not dangerous. Because these things happen, and I can't make them stop. I can't make myself better. I know that. I have to find a way to live with all this every day. I wanted to believe that I was strong enough for this, but—"

I know where he's going with this, and I refuse to let him. "Please don't give up on this already," I say. "I don't have a lot of things in my life that make me happy, but this does. Spending time with you is one of the few things I have to look forward to these days, and I know the risks. I know what you're going through."

"I'm just terrified that it could have been so much worse. You don't know how angry I was. How afraid I was of dying in that moment I woke up. It was like I was right back in the war. It was like I was fighting with an insurgent that I had to kill to stay alive that day. When I was in the dark, I didn't even know I'd woken up. I thought if I didn't fight, I'd die, I was a goner. And the thought of doing anything that could have put your life in danger scares the shit out of me."

111

It scares me, too. Hell, I almost peed on myself when I tried to wake him and he went apeshit like that, but I don't want to lose him over this.

"You shouldn't have to keep suffering over something that happened so long ago," I say.

"But I do. Every day. Every night. And I'll suffer a lot more if anything happens to you."

"Nothing's going to happen. I'll just be more careful if I try to wake you up next time."

The way he shifts his gaze, I can tell what he's thinking. That maybe there shouldn't be a next time.

It saddens me.

"You wanna talk about the nightmare?" I ask.

He takes a moment before he speaks. I wonder if he's going to tell me, but then he says, "My squad was ambushed in Fallujah. It was right after we arrived. It was eerily quiet when we first got there. Not a lot of action. But then as we got farther into the city, that's when the guns came out and made me and my team scatter. Me, Caleb, and another guy ended up going into one building that had an explosive device—the one that took my foot. Crazy thing was, when it happened, I didn't even realize I'd lost it. Just thought it'd been injured in the blast. An insurgent came in, and I wrestled him to keep us alive. Stabbed him with my combat knife. To death. Then our guys found us and rescued us. Took us to the medics. That's when they told me that it wasn't just an injury. My whole foot was gone and some of my leg was shredded and they knew it couldn't be saved. One of the other guys we were with lost an arm. We were sent back home. Caleb stayed and fought.

"He came back a few months later. I was living in Tennessee, but he convinced me to move down here with him, so I did. He had a fiancée he was coming back to. They were going to start a life together, but he was so rattled. She found him distant…too distant. And she ended up calling it off. Said he needed to get help. I agreed. We weren't the same. Not just us, but any of the guys we served with. We didn't know how to just pick up where we left off and act like none of that shit had ever happened, especially those of us who had wounds to show that we were there. Some people I ran into would call me a murderer for even being in that war. I don't know that they were wrong. I guess that's what I am now. Anyway, Caleb would just act funny everywhere he went. Agitated. Same as me. He had the nightmares, and he wouldn't see anyone about it. Neither of us would. Then one day, I got a call from his ex-fiancée. He was back with his family and a bunch of them were going fishing. They didn't want him to go since he seemed off. He stayed back at the house and put a rifle in his mouth. Pulled the trigger with his toe."

"Oh my God," I say.

"That's when I realized I couldn't pretend that everything was okay. That if I didn't do something, I'd end up like him."

"I'm so sorry."

"I can't pretend that none of that shit happened. The world wants me to go on as if I'm okay, but I'm not. And everyone can see that I'm not." He looks down at his shin, running his thumb across the scars. "I'm not even a whole person anymore."

"That's not true."

"Yes, it is. And every day is just another day I'm scared as hell that I'm about to lose my fucking mind. Which is why I'm scared as shit of hurting you. And it's why I wish it had bothered you more than it did."

"What?"

"Because as much as I know I shouldn't put you in danger like this, as much as it tears me up, I'm so fucking selfish, and I don't want this to end."

"Then don't let it end." I lean in and force a kiss. I know that once I reawaken that passion that's between us, he'll realize how stupid he's been for even considering stopping what we have going on. At least, I hope so.

As we kiss, what remains of my uneasiness from the attack subsides and is replaced with my total appreciation for getting to share this moment with him.

He cups his hand around my head and pulls me even closer, so that my nose is pressed up against his cheek. Then he pulls from our kiss and rubs his face alongside mine, breathing in deeply.

"What the fuck are we doing?" he asks. "I don't want you to be here because you pity me. I don't need anyone to be here for me. I've been on my own, and I can take care of myself."

"The only reason I'm here is because of how incredible it feels to be near you. Because I can't get enough. And because I'm terrified that one crazy moment, you're going to take yourself away from me. Please don't do that. Life's such shit, but this isn't."

He pulls me in close and holds me. It's the most comforting of embraces in the world. Makes me feel like he's protecting me from the entire world. Like it's just the two of this in this little garden.

21

Reese

I was so fucking wrong when I thought I had to give up Jay that night.

It's been a month since the anniversary of Caleb's death, and I haven't had an episode like that since. The usual day-to-day things still get to me. I can tell by the look on Jay's face that he's always uneasy whenever there's a loud sound, but something about him being here has made it easier for me to manage. Feels as though at least someone is on standby in case I need help. I'm used to having to deal with it on my own. Be strong. Tough it out through shit. Therapy has obviously helped, but it's not the same as having someone right here with me. Being around him quiets my mind. Not entirely—I know better than to expect that. The rumblings will always be there, and the episodes won't go away, but it's nice having an ally.

With our inventory audit completed, I don't have that stress on my plate anymore. And Jay's not only managed to keep his cool, but he's become friendly with his co-workers. I like to think he's chilled out because I'm as good for him as he is for me.

Jay spends most of his free time at my place. I haven't even seen the house he lives in because he says it's basically a frat boy's room. But he's started bringing clothes over. I made space for him in one of my drawers just two weeks ago—space I hope continues to grow as we spend more time together. We've made dinners together and watched a lot of movies. We both have a thing for over-the-top comedies like *Zoolander*, *Anchorman*, and *The Other Woman*. And he's shown me a few stand-up specials from some of his favorite comedians, so we spend a lot of nights laughing together. Laughing helps scatter those distracting thoughts that come so frequently.

I file a few invoices away in my office, playing catch-up on some things I neglected while we were prepping for the audit. Finally, pieces of my world are falling back into place and moving in a positive direction. Not just with work, but with my life.

Jay and I drove to work separately from my house, and we'll be driving right back once we're finished. Then we'll clean up and mess around. We've already agreed to make Chicken Parmesan tonight for dinner. And then the rest of the night will take us where it usually does, back into each other's arms—back into the bliss that I've come to realize can exist for me once again, even if it is hindered slightly by the echoes from my past.

My phone vibrates.

It's probably a naughty text from him, like ones we've exchanged a lot more these days. But it's a call.

Melanie.

Oh, Melanie.

A knot twists in my gut. Every time she calls, my guilt consumes me.

She hasn't tried to call since the day Caleb passed.

I don't feel bad just because she's trying to reach out to me. I feel bad because I know I shouldn't be like this. She deserves better than me ignoring her calls. But especially while things are going so well right now, the thought of letting her invite all those awful feelings back into my life horrifies me. It's what keeps me from responding.

I let her call go to voicemail, as I usually do.

She deserves better than this. I'm a fucking asshole, and I know it. There are a lot of things that I regret, but the way I treat her is the one I regret most. Still, I can't bring myself to deal with her any more than I can deal with any number of the things from my past.

She leaves another voicemail. I should listen to it. I can't keep deleting them.

I call to voicemail. "Hey, Reese." It's her soft voice. A voice I was so familiar with—one that used to fill me with eagerness and excitement. Now, that voice only conjures up grief and sadness. "I need to talk to you. If you could give me a call back, I would appreciate it." She sighs. It's the sigh of a woman who's tired. The sound she made when she tried to talk to me during those last months when I was with her, when she just couldn't reach me.

I tell myself I'll call her back, but it's a lie. Something will come up. I'll make up an excuse to avoid it like I always do. This is the sort of avoidance we talk about in group sessions and during my time with Laura, but it isn't something I'm ready to face. Not while things are going well in my life. Not when, for the first time in so long, I feel like I have a chance at happiness. A chance at moving on. I'll wait until things settle down and then call her. Although, how many times have I said that?

There's a knock at the door before it opens and Jay enters. I can't help the smile that stretches across my face.

He closes the door behind him, his expression serious. Oh, no. I was enjoying him not getting into trouble, and now here he is because something's gone wrong. I hop up from my chair and head around the desk. "What's the problem?" I ask, frustrated but eager to soothe him.

He approaches quickly and kisses me, his lips firmly against mine as he pushes me back against my bookshelf, which rattles against the drywall.

My concern about his reason for being here dissolves. I'm glad he's here. Not just in my office right now, but in my life.

He breaks our kiss. "Nothing's wrong *now*. You don't know how fucking crazy it's been driving me that you're just sitting up here, and I can't do a damn thing to you."

"You sure as fuck didn't let that stop you," I say.

He grins and kisses me again. His mouth still tastes like Listerine.

He fidgets with my belt, and before I know it, he's unfastened my slacks.

No. We can't do this. Not again.

But the thrill that I got from that first time when we fucked in the supply closet is too much for me to ignore, and I'd be lying if I said that I didn't want to fuck him right now.

He pulls down my pants and grips my hips, urging me to turn my body. I spin around, offering up my ass to him. I glance over my shoulder as he reaches into his back pocket and retrieves a condom and packet of lube.

I eye him suspiciously. "Were you planning this?" I ask.

"I didn't trust that I could really make it through the day without getting inside you."

He sets the lube and condom on my desk. I remove my shirt and set it on the floor beside me. He strips down and piles his clothes beside my shirt. I return to my position, my jeans at my ankles as I place my hands on the bookshelf. He pushes up against me, his stiff cock sliding vertically into my crack as he pushes it against me.

I arch my back and press my ass against his pelvis. He wraps his arms around me and caresses up and down my torso. He kneads my flesh as he kisses along the back of my neck.

117

"You feel so fucking good," he says. "I just want to be inside you. Filling you. Making you happy. Making you beg for more."

"Don't leave me hanging like this. Just do it. Own this ass. It's yours."

He doesn't waste his time. He leaves me for a moment as he prepares his cock with the condom and lube and then before I know it, I feel that sweet pressure pushing within me. I spread my legs farther apart to invite him in.

He's hard. Real fucking hard. I thought I would have been opened up already from all the times he's fucked me, but I must be a little tense today because it's a challenge as he makes his way steadily deeper, until his cock is pushed back inside me, filling me, tapping that spot that sends a ripple of ecstasy racing through me.

"Damn," I say. My nerves feel as though they're swimming in a sea of pleasure. He strokes his hand up and down my side as he starts his work, pulling out and pushing back in. He wraps an arm around my throat and pulls back slightly. He does this sometimes. Like he wants to show me just how much he owns me. I love it. Love the way he makes me feel like I'm all his when he fucks me.

"This ass, this body...they're mine," he says.

Not just those, but me too. I'm totally his in this moment.

He licks the side of my face like he wants to disrespect my body just for the sake of letting me know he's free to do as he wishes with it. He pushes me against the bookshelf so that my face presses up against one of the wooden shelves as he fills me with his girth. My cheeks spark with heat as he slams into my prostate. The intensity of the sensation forces me to curse through gritted teeth.

He starts to slide it out. "No, no, no," I say, pushing my ass even further back, trying to keep him in, but he pulls out anyway.

I've been abandoned, my body aching with dissatisfaction. Longing for his cock.

I turn around to him, and he leans down, wraps an arm around my legs and then the other around my back before scooping me up off the floor. He's gotten more adventurous about throwing me around now that he knows I'm not concerned about my prosthesis.

"You're a strong little fella," I say.

He smirks as he carries me to the desk and lays me across it. He lifts my legs, unlaces my shoes, and throws them aside before removing my socks and jeans and throwing them all aside.

Take me, Jay. Fuck me good.

22

Jay

I raise his legs and push into him. He throws his head back and curses. The veins in his neck tense as he restrains his moans so someone outside won't catch what we're doing.

But knowing that anyone could hear us just excites me even more.

After I find my rhythm, I lean down and kiss him. He accepts it like he's desperate for my mouth. His kiss is frenzied, his beard soft against my face.

I imagine a time with him when this condom won't be necessary. When I can breed him. Because I feel like that's where we're heading.

I hope it is, at least. The thought makes me even harder. I slide my hand up and down his torso.

A knock.

Fuck.

I stop. He glances around uneasily, his face bright red, as though the person fucking walked in on us.

"Hey, boss." It's Tyler.

"Uh, yeah?"

"We just got this box in that William was asking me about. Says he thinks it was sent back to us from the wrong warehouse. I don't know what I'm supposed to do with it."

"Just…I'm just finishing something up," Reese says. "I'll be right out."

The doorknob rattles. Seriously? He's not just going to go the fuck away? I like Tyler and all now, but don't cockblock.

"I just have a copy of the label," he says. "I was going to give it to you."

"Not until I finish giving you my cock," I whisper.

"Leave it on the floor!" Reese says through his teeth. "I need to get this one thing done right now." His serious tone makes him sound like he's about to chew Tyler's head off if he keeps this up.

"Um…okay. I'll leave it right here. Let me know when you're free so we can sort it out." I hear his footsteps as he heads away from the door, down the hall.

"Jesus fucking Christ," Reese says, hitting the back of his head against his desk.

I wonder if Tyler killed the mood, but Reese's dick sure didn't get any softer because of the interruption. And I'm still stiff within him, enjoying how tight his hole got when Tyler scared the shit out of him.

Still, I don't want to interfere with his job. I start to pull out. Reese grips my wrist and squeezes. He looks back up at me, his expression filled with desire.

"You don't need to take care of that?" I ask.

He smirks. "I told him I had something I had to finish. And I do."

The excitement that rushes through me makes me slide into him some more. He takes it, a smile stretching across his face. I can tell by the look in his eyes he wants it even more now than before.

I fuck him as hard as I can. He grips the edge of the desk.

I pant as sweat drips from my bangs and showers across his chest. I cling to his thighs as I feel myself steadily building to that delightful moment. We're lost in our experience again, and soon he's spewing a thick wad onto his belly, into his navel.

"I just need another moment," I beg.

"Take it," he says, his face wrinkled up as he recovers from his own orgasm.

I speed up, the pressure in my cock painful until the promise of relief is fulfilled and my body spams and trembles, the energy racing from my pelvis to my head. It's all-consuming.

And it's the sort of hot-ass fucking sex that makes me so appreciative that I'm lucky enough to get to fuck Reese.

***

"You need to come to dinner one night next week," Tyler says.

I'm surprised by the invitation. "What?" I ask. We're packing crates of bottles onto pallets in the main warehouse. We were just chatting about the news when he brought up dinner.

121

"I owe you after you did me a solid with that idea for Shelley's birthday party. She's still fucking blown away because I got her friend to come into town. I've been getting action for the past few weeks, and it's all because of you."

"You don't have to do all that. It was nothing."

"Dude, it's an invitation. Don't be an ass and refuse it."

I'm fucking grinning over it. I'm not used to people being friendly and fucking inviting me to shit. It's nice. "Yeah, I can do that."

It'd be rude for me to say *no*, but I wish I could bring Reese. This is just a reminder that we're not boyfriends and that this whole boss/employee thing complicates things even more. It reminds me of when I was younger and guys liked to skirt around the idea of being boyfriends. Seemed like they didn't have a problem being serious with other guys. Just not me. I don't think Reese is like that, but I don't fit into his life. He's a hot, successful guy who has so much to offer. I'm trailer park trash, without any money—a guy who's never held steady employment.

A fuckup.

I accept Tyler's invitation for dinner.

After I get off work, I head to the grocery store to pick up ingredients for the Chicken Parmesan. Reese has to stay at the factory until six, so I can grab what we need and have everything ready for us to make dinner together as soon as he gets home.

As I scan the chicken on a shelf, a young couple holds hands as they pass me, the guy carrying a basket filled with their groceries. They approach the fruits and vegetables and stop before a crate filled with cantaloupe. I keep my eye on them, trying to act like I'm just glancing around. They're in their early twenties, I assume. They remind me of what was running through my head when Tyler invited me to dinner.

"You're gonna have to pick it out this time," the guy says.

"Why?" the girl asks.

"Because you have that trick you do."

"Oh, that thing Mamaw taught me?"

She picks up a melon and hands it to him. He looks at her like she's lost her mind.

"Tap it," she instructs.

He obeys.

"Listen to it. Does it sound like it's hollow or like it's really solid?"

"Hollow."

"That one's not going to work, then." She takes it from him and places it back in the crate. Then she grabs another. "Try this one."

He does the same thing. "It's like thud…thud…thud."

"That one's good then. If it's hollow or too solid then it won't work. You're just supposed to hear that light thud."

"Well, aren't you just a little genius?" he says, lowering the melon from his ear and offering her a gentle kiss.

Jealousy wells within me.

I wish I could walk around with Reese without being worried people would judge us for being gay. But he might not even want to be in a public place with me, knowing that someone from work could discover us. I don't want to put Reese's job on the line, but we shouldn't have to hide how we feel.

I shouldn't be thinking like this, considering we haven't taken things further. We're fuck-buddies who like each other a hell of a lot. I haven't wanted to push. Just wanted to be in his life. But considering how things are when we're together, I don't see a reason to pretend that we both don't want to take things to another level. Unless he doesn't want that, in which case, I should fucking find out before I get hurt.

I chase that thought away. Of course he wants more, but there's a part of me that can't believe anyone would want more from me.

After I finish grabbing ingredients for dinner, I head back to the house and start preliminary preparations for our meal.

I can't get that couple out of my head.

Even though it's only been a month, Reese has to feel the way I do—that this is beyond fucking around. No, there's no question about how we feel. Unless he doesn't want people to see that he's with a guy. Or even worse, with some employee who's beneath him. Who doesn't have nice things or a house like he does. Or a good job.

That insecurity about me not being good enough for him keeps taking over my thoughts.

What if he just wants to keep me as his dirty little secret? What if he's ashamed of me? What if he sees me like all those other guys did—a fun lay, but nothing more? I know what that leads to. How much it hurts when everything falls apart.

I don't know if I can do that again, especially the stronger my feelings become for Reese.

When he enters the front door and gazes at me with appreciative eyes, my insecurities subside. I don't think he'd have a problem being out with me in public. Surely he'd be fine with others knowing what we have going on.

I relax as we prepare dinner together. We share tender kisses during each phase—kisses that remind me that we've come a long way from just fucking. What we have now means more, so it's not ridiculous for me to assume that we should be able to take things further.

We sit down to eat, enjoying our creation as we chat about work and what movie we want to watch tonight.

Movies. Homemade dinners. Wonderful as they are, they aren't what I'm reaching for.

While he talks about his day, I build up the courage to finally get this off my chest: "I was thinking maybe we could go out to see a movie." Tension rises within me. I'm more nervous about bringing this up than I thought I'd be.

"Like, out?" he asks, eyeing me, not like he's excited to share an experience, but like he's worried someone will catch us and make our work life harder.

"Um…just like, whatever. You know, the way normal people who are starting to see each other do."

I see the hesitation in his expression. He clearly isn't a fan of the idea.

I suddenly feel rejected. "I mean, you have to admit that what's going on here is more than fucking."

"Of course. It definitely is, Jay. I know that. I really like you."

"Then a date is the next logical step."

His gaze shifts about. "Isn't that what this is?" he asks.

"I want to like actually do things with you. You know, out in the real world…like everyone else does."

He's quiet.

"What?" I ask. "Am I just your office secret?"

"No. That's not it."

"Am I not the kind of guy you want to be seen with?"

"That's not it at all. Jay, it's just complicated because of work. You know that."

"Then I can get another job, so we don't violate some company policy or whatever."

"Oh, don't be ridiculous. It's not that serious. We have two supervisors who are now married to people in their chain of command. People they met while they were working with the company. We'd just have to fill out some paperwork with HR."

"Then why can't we do that?"

"Because it's not just about the company policy. People aren't going to respect me when—"

"When they realize you're a faggot? Is that what you're worried about?"

He sighs, picks his napkin up from his lap, and sets it on the table.

"That's what this is about," I continue. "You like that no one at work really asks about your love life. That you can keep a distance from them. And you think that if they think some fairy is running things, they'll start getting in your face and not respecting you. Admit it."

"It's not like you're running around telling people that you're gay."

"But I'm not scared of letting people know that I like you, either."

I stare right at him, but he avoids looking at me. He knows I'm right.

23

Reese

Why is he being like this?

Here we were, having such a lovely evening, and he had to turn it into this argument about making a spectacle of ourselves in public. He's right. I don't want the guys at work to know I'm gay. Or that I'm dating an employee. And I don't think I'm wrong thinking they're going to give me shit about it. That they'll respect me less or think that I'm showing favoritism towards Jay.

I don't know how to win this fight.

"Jay, you know how guys are. I've worked my ass off to get here, and I don't need for everyone to start drama over something that isn't a big deal."

"We aren't a big deal?"

"You know that's not what I meant."

"Then what did you mean?"

"I don't need everyone talking about me behind my back because of some guy that I've been with for a month."

That was harsh.

I knew it as the words escaped my lips, but he's pissing me off by challenging me like this. He's not just *some guy* to me. But it doesn't seem fair for him to ask me to out myself to the guys in the factory I've been working at for years when he's been there less than two months.

"That's what you think of us?" Jay asks. His face is bright red. Last time I remember seeing him this angry, he was getting into it with William.

"No, I'm sorry. I was just—"

"Fuck you," he says. He pushes to his feet and heads into the living room.

I follow after him. "Jay—"

"Don't fucking *Jay* me. If that's all you think of us, then I want out. I don't need to waste my time chasing some guy who can't admit to people how he feels."

This is about a hell of a lot more than the conversation we just had. I've triggered some defense mechanism within him.

"Jay, please…calm down."

"Calm down? Oh, now you want me to fucking calm down?" His eyes water. "Whatever. I don't need to calm down. I just need to get the fuck out of here."

He approaches the front door, and I'm terrified that, considering how mad he is, if I let him go, he's going to walk out of my life forever. This is who he is. This is what he does. He runs.

I run past him and throw myself between him and the door.

"Get out of my way," he says, his body tense as he approaches me.

"Just listen to me, Jay. Please."

"You've said everything I need to hear." He's not looking me in the eyes anymore.

"I'm sorry. I didn't mean to be an asshole about this. I was just defensive."

And you are too right now.

"You meant what you said," he says.

"I'm scared of what people will say. I wasn't making that up. And I was upset that you were challenging me like it was something I had to do to prove something to you. That's why I got a little snippy about it, but this is something we can talk through. You don't have to leave over a fight."

"I don't see a reason to stick around where I'm not wanted."

The Jay who stands before me isn't the Jay I've spent all this time with—the guy I've laughed with and shared so many wonderful meals with. This guy is rigid. Tense. Afraid. He refuses to look at me. It seems like if I get too close, he might lash out—do something crazy.

I approach him anyway. I need to get him to lower these defenses. I want my Jay back. The Jay who isn't stubborn and obstinate. The Jay who listens. Who understands.

"Please talk to me about this."

"I've already played out this script too many times. I'm never the guy people want to be in a relationship with. You know what happened with the first guy I ever fell for? We did this. For six months we fucked around. Six

127

fucking months seems like it would mean something, right? To a dumbass twenty-one-year-old who never had anyone it sure meant a fucking lot. We made the dinners. He said all the right words and kept me believing there was something there. And then I got a call from a guy…telling me to stop seeing *his* man. That they'd been together for two years. So I confronted the asshole who played me, and what did he say? 'What the fuck did you think this was? We weren't even dating.'"

I see the hurt in his expression. Hear the pain in his words.

"I get it. I've never been the guy anyone wants to date," he says. "I'm a fun fuck, but I guess I'm just such trash that no one could possibly imagine themselves being with me. Everyone wants a piece of the action, but no one gives a shit about how I feel."

"I care about how you feel. I want to be with you, Jay."

He studies my face like he's trying to see if I'm lying—leading him on like that asshole from his past.

"You didn't deserve to be treated like that," I continue. "By anyone. You're not trash. I don't see that when I look at you. I don't want you to feel like that. I just didn't think I could do it overnight. That's a big step for me to take at the office. I don't let people in at all, so to be out to them and for them to know I'm seeing my employee, that's a lot all at once. But if you need me to step out of my comfort zone for us, I will."

For the first time since he snapped, he seems to relax.

I do the only thing I can think of to ease his pain. I kiss him.

He tenses up even more as I push on him, shoving him against the wall beside us. He resists for a moment, but then he wraps his arms around me and kisses me in a frenzy. I feel tears rush from his eyes and sweep past my cheeks.

They confirm what I've been feeling all this time—that he cares so much about what we've shared. And I'm relieved because it means I haven't been alone in feeling this way.

He offers passionate kisses like he's just as glad that we're enjoying a ceasefire together.

He needs me right now. Needs my support. Needs to know how much I care about him. I now realize that's all this has really been about. The only reason he threatened to leave was because he wasn't sure that I was feeling enough for him to want more. But I do want more. Every day that we're together, I realize how much more I want with him.

I pull away and gaze into his eyes. He wipes violently at his face like he's ashamed that he cried in front of me.

"I wouldn't be ashamed to have you as a boyfriend," I say. "In fact, I'd love it. You're an amazing guy, Jay. And I haven't met anyone in a long time who I actually want to spend this much fucking time with. Someone I want to get to know. Experience things with. I haven't done this kind of relationship for years, though. A lot of fucking years, so it's just taking me a little bit more time to figure out how to make it work. But I do want to make it work."

I press my hand to his cheek and caress my thumb across his flesh.

"I'm sorry I hurt you tonight. Or made you feel like I don't care about you."

"I'm sorry, too," he says, and he sounds like he's returning to his usual self. "I know it can't be easy being in your position and having to worry about what the guys think. I'd be worried too if I had something to lose. But I've never had much to lose. Not for a long time. It just scares the shit out of me that even this might go away. I'd rather get out before it gets too hard. Before I get hurt too much. It would be more than I can stand."

I know that's what this fight has really been about. Because this is the only way he knows how to live.

It pains me that he would think I'd do something to hurt him. I'm worried about getting hurt, too, but not for the same reason.

"It would kill me if I knew that I hurt you in *any* way," I say. "Just like it hurt me seeing you like this tonight."

He kisses me again, his kiss soothing what little fear I still had about him leaving.

We needed this fight. Eventually, everyone will know what's going on between us. We won't be able to hide it, and I have to face that. I don't like facing a lot of things, but this is one I'm willing to confront if it'll help Jay. If it'll keep him here with me, which is where he belongs.

We take a moment from our kiss. "Don't do that to me again," I plead.

"What?" he asks.

"Scare me into thinking you're just going to walk out of my life forever. I was so lucky to have found you, and to lose you like that would destroy me. I won't always agree with you, but I want to know that if we have a fight, you won't just leave."

"That's all I know how to do," he says, his lips curling into a wry smile. "That's all I've ever done when things have gotten hard."

"It's taken me a long time to realize that running doesn't solve anything. In some ways I'll always be running. And I'd be lying if I said I wasn't scared as shit about what we're doing."

"I'm scared, too. I don't want to get close. I fall too hard. Every time. I rarely let anyone in, but when I do, I'm all the way. So when shit goes south, it's bad. Real bad. I don't want that."

"But I want *this*. Us. That's important to me, and we can do it together." We kiss again, and his fingers slide under my shirt. I break our kiss and tell him, "Let's not play around anymore then. Be my boyfriend. I want you, Jay. I don't want you to be confused or scared about that."

His grin—eager and playful like when he's reading the comics—offers me so much reassurance.

"I would really like that," he says. "More than like that." He chuckles. Seems like a nervous reaction as his eyes water.

"I'm going to go to HR tomorrow, just to get ahead of this. They're gonna need us both to sign something about our relationship to cover their asses legally, but they'll keep it confidential."

"Oh, wow. I thought you said you needed to step outside your comfort zone. Not wave a flag about it around the office."

"Don't worry. Like I said, it's confidential. Everyone won't know right away. But I want to do this. I think we're worth it."

He looks so much more relaxed than he did before. "You'd do all that for us?"

"I'm going to do it."

He kisses me again. Our passion takes us to the bedroom, as it always does, and we share another night.

24

Jay

It was a lot for me to ask Reese to be totally cool with being out to his employees after being together for such a short time, but last night, his words assured me that all this time together hasn't been for nothing. That he wants to move toward something more.

This morning, he went to HR, and they called me in to sign the paperwork that he was talking about. It was just to keep the company from being liable if anything goes south between us. Feels like a big step. Huge. Here we are just now using the term boyfriends, but we're already having to sign forms about it. But I wanted to do it. Better that than to do something that would get Reese into trouble.

That was a big step, and I don't need him to scream about our relationship to everyone in the office. I can be patient and give him some time to find a way to bring me into his life in a way that's comfortable for him. It wasn't that I wanted him to be in an awkward position at work. I just wanted to know I wasn't going to spend months...or years keeping us this secret that I could never share. I couldn't do that. But what am I even thinking? Years with him? How can I already be imagining spending that much time with someone I'm just getting to know?

After our fight, I realized I was telling myself that there was something wrong so that I'd try to get out of it. Because I'm not used to having something actually working out for me, especially with a guy. And it really does scare me. As I open up to him and build trust in him, I know he can hurt me. That he can break my heart into pieces and leave me even worse off than before I met him, and that terrifies me.

I step along a row of shipments, inspecting the pallets to see which ones need extra securing. We've had to be super-careful after all the damages we've been dealing with lately. Most of the other guys are on the other side of the warehouse, unpacking some of the raw materials that just came in.

Reese rounds a corner, coming around some of the packed boxes we're shipping out tomorrow. He has a clipboard in hand and a stern look on his face like he's been dealing with some pretty serious shit all morning long. The black button-up he wears fits snugly, and having seen all those muscles, memorized them, I resent that his clothes are covering up all my favorite parts of him.

"Mr. Hinson, could I talk to you for a second?" he asks, his expression lit up with amusement.

"Feeling playful today, Mr. Kline?"

He leans against a box beside me. "I was just going to see if you might be interested in doing something a little different tonight."

"Cosplay?" I tease.

He smirks. "Not exactly. I was thinking we would go out. Catch a movie. You know, like you mentioned last night."

"Really?"

His smile is warm as he says, "I just bought tickets for us for eight o'clock. Some new Ashley Judd movie with Kristen Stewart and Scarlett Johansson."

"I think the fact that you called it an Ashley Judd movie lets me know exactly how old you are."

He laughs. "Whatever."

"What's it about?"

"Ashley Judd blackmails Kristen Stewart into working for her football-player nephew as his bodyguard, but his ex, Scarlett Johansson, is trying to weasel her way back into his life."

"Really? Who's the football-player nephew?"

"Zac Efron?"

"That's who you lead with! If I thought I was going to be watching Kristen Stewart and Scarlett Johansson duking it out for two hours, I'd be like hell no, but just the possibility of seeing Zac Efron take his shirt off, and I'm fucking in."

He beams. "Good. I figure we can grab something to eat on the way."

"Look at you," I say. "You know you don't have anything to prove, right?"

"I'm not trying to prove anything." He glances around and steps away from the box. "I just think you deserve someone who wants to show you off, and I want to show you off."

He kisses me, a gentle kiss at first, but he wraps his arm around me and pulls me close. I enjoy the sensations that race through me. He sure does know how to make up with a guy.

After we get off work, we swing by McDonalds for some burgers, scarf them down, and head on to the theatre, AMC at Phipps Plaza. We recline in the red cushioned chairs, keeping a tub of popcorn between us. I keep waiting for others to arrive, but after the movie begins, we quickly realize we're the only ones here.

"Did this movie get the worst reviews ever or what?" I ask.

"Right?"

I pull up Rotten Tomatoes on my phone and see that it has a two-point-three rating. "Oh, fuck." I show him the page.

"Shit. I should have checked."

"You kidding?" I ask. "I'm kinda even more excited about seeing it now."

The movie's horrendous, but in the best possible way, keeping us laughing all the way through it. And that no one else is here makes the experience even better since we're able to make fun of it the way we would if we were lounging on his couch. As we leave the theatre, I'm in tears from laughing so hard at Reese's impression of Zac Efron in a scene where Kristen Stewart had to give him CPR after he tried to eat ten fire-hot buffalo wings that he thought were going to rupture his stomach.

"I can't believe that just happened," I say.

"I know. We'll have to go to the movies more often."

We exchange a look. I see the eagerness in his eyes, and I can tell that he really would enjoy getting to share another movie with me.

"Boss-man?"

I recognize the voice, and we both turn sharply. Tyler heads toward us, holding a bag of popcorn as he walks beside a woman I assume is his wife, Shelley. Two kids tail behind them.

Shit.

We were having such a good time, so of course, something had to come and fucking ruin it.

"Hey," Reese says uneasily.

As Tyler glances between us, I realize why I shouldn't have pushed for this. There's a knowing look in Tyler's eyes. It's clear he's not confused about what's going on between us, and I'm worried as ever. It's nice knowing Reese can't lose his job over it, but it sucks that Tyler could tell the other guys, and they could give him hell.

"Sorry," he says after an extended pause. "Reese, Jay, this is my wife Shelley." He makes an introduction and chats about the movie they're heading to see.

"Jay, I know I invited just you, but both of you guys can come to dinner next week, if you want," he says, and I'm stunned. Who would've thought that the guy I had the most issues with when I first started working at the warehouse would be the most understanding about who we are?

I keep checking Reese's expression as we talk, and gradually he starts to relax. And so do I.

When Tyler and his wife continue to their movie, I glance at Reese uneasily. I'm curious to see what he thinks about what just went down. "All good?" I ask.

"Wasn't as bad as I thought it would be," he admits. "But now we have to have our first dinner as a couple. Damn."

"I'm sorry it's going to be going around the office, though." I assume Tyler will tell some of the guys. So even though he's okay with it, the guys who aren't will find out and probably give Reese a hard time about it. Not only will they potentially think less of him for being gay, but they'll wonder if I'll receive unfair treatment because of our relationship.

All those things Reese was worried about.

I wait for him to acknowledge his concern on our way to the car, but he changes the subject back to the movie. Clearly he doesn't want to consider the consequences of what just happened, which I totally understand.

We head to his place, discussing the movie some more. Chuckling as we talk about some of the funniest parts. He parks at a frozen yogurt shop.

"What are we doing?" I ask.

"Treating my man the way he deserves to be treated."

I'm blushing. Oh my fucking God, I'm blushing.

He's seriously bringing me out to get frozen yogurt. How much more adorable can Reese be?

We head in and order. He gets strawberry with almonds and fudge while I get some peanut butter with fudge and cookies and cream.

"No toppings for you?" he asks as we sit at a small table in the shop.

"You're the only top I need."

He fights the smile, but I've clearly earned it. He takes a bite of his combo.

"That's an interesting mix you have there," I say.

"Strawberry and chocolate anything is fine by me…and you know, I like nuts." He winks.

"I bet you do. I'm sorry about Tyler."

"I needed this to happen. To show me that it's not the end of the world. Even if he says something to the guys at work, I'll live. Plus, there's no reason to keep it from anyone. I already keep enough shit from people as it is."

"So are these the kinds of dates you usually take guys on?" I ask, trying to change the subject.

"It's been a long time since I've been with anyone…even flirted with the idea like this."

"Oh, come on. There had to be others."

"Not really. Considering the PTSD, I never felt comfortable letting things go far. I've tricked out plenty, but you know, this hasn't been an easy thing to deal with. Still isn't, and I've never thought it was fair to drag someone else into my life."

I reach out and grab his arm. "You know you're not burdening me, right?"

But I can tell by the apprehension in his expression that he does. "Jay, I don't need you pretending that this isn't stressful for you. You didn't sign up for this."

"I did. In fact, I knew before I even started liking you that this was part of the package, so I eagerly signed up for it."

My words don't seem to bring him any relief. "Since you brought it up, I think it's only fair that I should mention that you haven't seen the worst of it yet. And it's coming. It's always coming. One day, I'm going to wake up, and it's not going to be easy to manage. And it's going to hurt you when that happens. I love having you here with me. It makes me feel amazing, and in some ways, I think it helps, but I'm not naïve. And I know that nothing can make this go away. And it's not your job to make it go away."

"I've done enough research to know that this isn't going to magically disappear, Reese. You gotta give me some credit."

"I just don't want to wake up one day and find out that I'm the reason you're unhappy."

The despair in his tone is like a knife in my heart.

"God, I sure know how to ruin a fucking date, don't I?" he says.

"Reese, I'm not some fragile guy who needs you tiptoeing around him. I can handle this, and we can push through it together."

"It just scares me because I really don't think you can understand until it happens. Until one day I'm caught up in it, and you don't even recognize me."

For me, they've just been moments—moments when it feels like Reese isn't really there. Where I'm wondering where he's gone.

"I don't think you realize how lonely it can feel," he adds.

"I'm sure it feels awful."

"Not for me. For anyone near me."

Now I understand what he's getting at.

"It's like I'm drowning and then someone's come out to save me, but I just pull them under with me so that we're both suffering. So that neither of us can breathe. I don't want to hurt you like that."

"Who did you hurt like this?" Because I know that's what this is really about.

"Someone I loved. Someone who loved me. Someone who it was too much for."

"Well, it's not going to be too much for me," I insist, though I can tell he doesn't believe me. That he's still scared. "You gotta give us a chance, Reese. I've got my reasons for being scared it won't work and so do you, but I care about this and so do you."

"I know. I am trying, but as we both get more invested in this, that's what keeps playing on my mind."

"Well then maybe you need to fill your mind with sexier things," I tease, and he chuckles.

"All those comedy shows really come in handy, don't they?"

"Sometimes. And when they don't, I can just put on something sexy and distract you that way."

His gaze sharpens. Something about what I said stirred a thought.

"What?" I ask. "Do you have something you'd want me to wear? A jockstrap, maybe?"

He rolls his eyes. "Nothing. No."

But I can tell by the way he says it that he isn't being honest. Now I'm curious, but I let it slide.

We finish our frozen yogurt before heading back to the house, some Louis C.K. diffusing the tension from the conversation we had about his PTSD. When we get back to his place, we wind up on the bed, making out. We lie on our sides, groping each other's bodies.

"Tell me…what you…want, Reese," I say between kisses. I'm thinking about that look he had when I mentioned me wearing something sexy.

"You," he replies.

"Good answer, but no. Tell me your fantasy. I saw that look when I talked about wearing something sexy. What is it? What can I do to serve you?"

I feel so close to him right now. All I want is to fulfill his desires. To make him happy the way he's made me happy.

He pulls away and glances me up and down like he's itching to say something to me. I'm intrigued.

"I just want to make my boyfriend happy," I say. "The sex we have is great, but I mean, we all have little kinks. Things we don't typically disclose right away. I want to know what yours are. I want to get to know you…in every possible way."

I see something in his gaze that suggests he's got a good kink he's eager to explore.

"What?" I ask.

He shakes his head. "Nothing."

"That obviously wasn't a nothing. What do you want?"

He hesitates before saying, "There is one thing I'd be curious to try out."

"What is it? Water sports? Roman showers?"

He cringes. "Oh, God no. Nothing like that."

"Just show me, then," I say slowly, hoping he can tell just how game I am to explore his fantasy with him. "And I'll show you how good I can be to my boyfriend."

25

Reese

We shower up together and brush our teeth. I told him I'd show him after we cleaned off, but I can't believe I'm even considering this. He won't fucking understand. Who the hell would? God, this is what I get for watching so much porn. I knew when I stumbled across my little fetish that it was wrong, but I can't deny that it'd be hot as hell if Jay was game. But I think he's just going to call me a freak and wig out about it.

I shouldn't show him this, but I want to explore it with Jay. I want to take him in the way I crave. In the way I hunger for.

We had such a good night, and I actually confronted my fear of the guys at work discovering what we're up to, so in a way, I feel more vulnerable than ever. Ready to take on yet another challenge. Ready to embrace this desire within me.

Once we're cleaned up, we kiss and nip at each other, rub each other's dicks a bit. I strap into my hands-free crutch, and we head into the bedroom.

I put on my liner followed by my regular prosthesis, not being shy about it with Jay. Nowadays, I don't even feel shy about asking him where I left it if I happen to lose track of it.

When I've secured it to my residual limb, I say, "Just sit on the bed while I get it out."

He jumps on top of the comforter and runs his hand through his hair, which is still a little wet from the shower.

I head to the closet and push my way through the luggage on the shelf before retrieving an unlabeled white box from the back.

I'm already blushing just thinking about sharing this with Jay.

As I turn back around, revealing the box, Jay eyes it with interest.

I hand it to him. I want him to see for himself. Decide if this is really a path he wants to go down with me.

He pulls the lid off and looks inside, wincing.

"It's stupid. I shouldn't have said anything." I grab the box, but he grips onto it.

"Just wait a second," he says, snatching it back.

What was I fucking thinking?

He reaches in and pulls out the fuchsia-colored women's thong with vine lace print across it.

He grabs the strap on either side and holds it before him, studying it as though he's not sure what he's supposed to do with it. Of course, it seems pretty fucking obvious.

His gaze shifts to me. "You want me to put this on?" he asks.

"I'm mean, you don't have to. It's just something I've always wanted to experiment with."

"Have other guys worn this?" He looks disgusted.

"Oh, God no. I ordered that online. I watch a lot of porn where guys wear panties and I just thought…I don't know. I kind of wanted to get it."

"Have you worn it?"

"No. I'm more turned on by another guy wearing it."

"Oh, so you thought you'd just meet some little trick who'd be eager to prance around in this for you?"

I cover my face with my hand. Why did I fucking bring this out?

"I guess I was hoping that one day I'd meet someone who would be interested in wearing it. But never have. Or at least, I've never had the balls to bring it up until tonight."

He studies it some more, and I reach for it again. "This was a stupid idea. Just forget it."

He pulls it out of my grasp. "I mean, it's weird," he says. "Like, you know that, right?"

"You're not making this less awkward."

His lips twist down, and he tilts his head. "Won't kill me to give it a try."

My dick shifts as I imagine his balls trapped behind the lace. After he notices my expanding girth, he stands up and steps into the thong.

He has this apprehensive expression on his face, and for some reason, that's almost as hot as him wearing it. He pulls it up over his junk. It's a snug but perfect fit.

"God, you're hot as fucking hell," I say out loud, even though I meant to just think it.

His body's stacked with muscles, his abs stressed by the shadows created by the overhead light fixture. His cock runs horizontally behind the lace of the thong.

I bite my lip, stifling the impulse to throw him down on the bed. I want to appreciate this moment. Take in the beauty of his body.

Now he's the one blushing, looking everywhere but at me.

I know why this is turning me on so much. I love seeing him out of his element.

"Does it look dumb?" he asks.

"I wasn't bullshitting when I said you're hot as fucking hell. You don't have a goddamn thing to be blushing about."

"Whatever. I didn't think it would feel this weird, but it does."

He hooks his fingers into either side like he's considering taking them off. I approach him and run my hand up and down the sides of his legs, my fingers trailing across the side straps of the thong before gripping on.

I pull him close, so that our torsos touch. He looks me in the eyes.

It feels just as good as I thought it would. We're both so exposed right now. Him for wearing these, and me for him knowing that I'm into this.

We're on an even playing field.

I slide my hand between us and run my finger across his torso, up his chest. As I reach his chin, I squeeze it between my thumb and forefinger.

I'm in control of him right now. He wants to play this game, and he wants to play it my way.

I lean forward and kiss him. Cupping my hand behind his head, I pull him in closer, strengthening our kiss. Soon, I'm sliding my tongue between his lips, his tongue meeting mine.

I feel around his back and down to his butt, pushing my fingers beneath the thong, enjoying his firm cheeks.

He breaks our kiss for a moment. As he exhales, the warmth of his breath rushes across my face, the scent of mint hitting my nostrils.

It stirs desire within me. Something powerful. Something I can't fight anymore. I scoop him up off the floor and toss him onto the bed.

His eyes are lit up with surprise, but I can tell that it's excited him. "You like that?" I ask.

141

"Do you like it?"

I nod as I grin.

I want to ravage his body. I want to take him even more than I have in the past because he looks so delicious in those panties. I crawl onto the bed, and he lies down, stretching out across it like he's offering up his body to me. Letting me have him in whatever way I choose.

I wrap my arms under his thighs and bury my face in the thong so my nose is right next to his cock as I inhale deeply, nipping at the panties. He groans. I slide my tongue along the top edge of the underwear. He throws his head back as his dick shifts, sliding up in a clockwise motion until the tip slides out of the top of the undergarment.

"I want to fill my mouth with your cock," I say. "Make you shoot your load on my tongue."

"Do it."

"Not yet."

Because I don't want to waste the moment that I have him like this. Totally trapped in my fantasy, surrendering to me.

I run my nose back and forth along his balls, offering licks, which I can tell by the way he arches his back that he enjoys.

"You're driving me fucking crazy," Jay says.

I stop licking his balls and crawl up him, my knees resting on either side of his right leg as I offer licks and nips up his body, appreciating his torso, those rigid muscles that he's earned from his workouts.

I slide my hand down beneath the thong and grip onto his rock-hard erection, squeezing it.

"This is mine right now," I say. "Mine to decide when you get off. Mine to decide just how I want you to get off. You got that?"

I like to dominate, but this is a whole other level. Something about having him in this simple little thong makes me feel so powerful. And like I just want him to bend to my will.

"That's how I want it," he says.

I kiss up his body in a frenzy, offering open-mouthed kisses with licks and the occasional nip before I reach his mouth.

He wraps his arm around me and pulls me close. That ease that I always get when I'm with him sweeps through me.

He cringes. "God," he says, breaking our kisses, "I'm so fucking hard it hurts."

"So am I," I say.

I straddle his face, titling my dick down. He opens his mouth wide, and I shove inside him and lean forward on the bed, setting my palms on one of the pillows in front of the headboard to maintain the balance I struggle with because of my right leg.

I push in until I hear him gag. But he grips onto my ass-cheeks and pulls like he wants me to dive in even deeper, which just makes me even harder. He's normally eager to suck my cock, but not like this.

He sucks and licks, and I offer thrusts. He slides one of his hands around to my hole and massages his finger against it. The sensitivity of his tongue across the head of my dick assures me that I'm leaking. I like knowing that he's tasting me.

I pull back out and plant myself down beside him. "Get up and suck me off. On your knees." My own words remind me of being bossed around by one of my senior officers.

Jay follows my instruction, getting on his knees and shoving my dick back in his mouth, working it up. I grip his hair and force him to follow my lead, pleasing me the way I want to be pleased. Moving at the pace I want him to go.

He fights my hold and pulls back. I release him, and he slides my cock out of his mouth and gazes up at me, his eyes pleading as he says, "I need you inside me."

I turn around and lean over to the nightstand. Retrieve the condoms and lube.

He rolls over and slides the thong down his legs. "No!" I say before biting down on the edge of the condom wrapper. I tear it open and spit the loose edge onto the sheets. "You keep that fucking on."

He slides it back up, his eyes filled with confusion.

"Spin around and face the bathroom door," I say.

He does, positioning himself on his knees.

I squeeze a liberal amount of lube from the bottle before setting it beside one of the pillows. I crawl to Jay, who faces away from me, his back arched, his ass eagerly waiting to receive me.

As I reach him, I grip onto the straps on either side of the thong and slide them down, pulling it to just beneath his ass-cheeks. Setting one hand on his hip, I press my cock against his hole and push in.

He's so fucking tight. Even tighter than normal, and I wonder if it's because he's self-conscious in the underwear. "Come on, you gotta open up."

"I will. I promise."

His words entice me. I push in.

He reaches back and rests his hand on the side of my thigh. "Oh, God, that feels amazing," he says. He turns to me, his eyes wide, his mouth hanging open. "Come on. Keep going. I just need you inside me right now."

"I don't want to hurt you."

"Oh, nothing's fucking hurting."

I push my pelvis forward, my cock driving deeper within him.

He gasps. "Goddammit. God-fucking-dammit."

I let him adjust to my girth as I push.

He takes deep breaths. "Shit, your super-cock feels so good," he says.

"Probably better that way since you obviously need a big fat cock opening you up."

"Yeah, I do."

As he breathes, I rock my pelvis back and forth. We build into a rhythm, and when I can tell he's adjusted, I reach down and grip onto his brown locks, tugging him back. He arches his back even more and leans so that his back is pressed against my chest. I wrap an arm around him and feel my fingers across his ab muscles, even more rigid than usual as he struggles to maintain this position.

I fuck him, and soon, he turns to me, sweat streaming down his face as his body twitches slightly. I wrap my other arm around him, feeling my thumb across his cheek. He leans into it and sucks on my thumb. He's wilder than usual, willing to explore with the addition of our new toy.

"I like having you like this," I say. "I wish I could breed you like you need to be bred."

He reaches behind him and sets his hand on the back of my head, stroking gently. He opens his mouth, releasing my thumb as he says, "That's all I want too."

And that makes it impossible for me not to thrust. Again and again and again.

His body jerks around so much that I'm worried about him falling forward and off the bed, so I wrap my arms under his and place my hands on the back of his head, forcing his arms up above him. Forcing him to be mine. Do as I wish. Serve me.

"Like I said," I add. "No coming until I say so."

He whimpers. I've never heard him make a sound like this before. Something about wearing the girly underwear is making him behave more feminine that usual. And that makes me feel more like a man. His man. The one responsible for pleasuring him. The one responsible for giving him the best fuck I can.

"My cock," he says. "I need to come. Please."

As much as I want to withhold it from him, I can't. I want to please him so fucking much. I lower my arms and reach down, beneath the panties, gripping his dick. I lean so that my face is right against his ear, my breath slamming into it as I tell him, "Give me a big load, Jay. Give me the biggest fucking load you can."

"I will," he says, his body trembling with excitement as I fuck him. Judging by the way he moves, I'm hitting his prostate. He tilts his head back, gritting his teeth. I can tell he's about to blow.

And seeing how much he's enjoying taking my cock, I'm going to as well.

He twists his body side to side before I feel the familiar spasm of his body. I glance over his shoulder, seeing his load shoot across the sheets, a little hitting the edge of the bed.

The pressure in my pelvis builds so quickly that it hurts, surely as much as his cock hurt when I was hitting his prostate just right. When he was begging for me to let him come.

As I explode into the condom, a wave of heat rushes to my face. It's a powerful feeling, a climax unlike anything I've experienced with Jay before. My body trembles against his as I wrap both arms around him and hug him tight, appreciating all that he just gave me. Hoping that he appreciates it, too.

26

Jay

Oh...my...God. Fuck.

When he first suggested this, I almost told him that if he wanted to fuck a girl, he needed to find himself one. But his interest in something so strange fascinated me. I wanted to see where it would lead. When I put the panties on, I felt flustered. Embarrassed. Aroused. Maybe because it was a side of Reese I hadn't seen before. Maybe because I liked the idea of him humiliating me, making me an object just for his pleasure. Whatever the reason, it was hot as fuck, and I'd do it again in a heartbeat.

I'm still shaking from the excitement. Who would have known that wearing a woman's thong would transform our already incredible sex into something even more profound?

I lie curled up against him, the panties hanging off the corner of the bed. Normally, I'm not in the mood to get cuddly, but after what we did, I sense a different sort of connection with Reese. We just shared something really special, and I can tell by the way he holds me that he feels the same way. At least, I hope I'm reading this right.

"I...uh..." he says after a stretch of silence. Not an awkward, uneasy silence. A meditative one. A chance for us both to recover from the experience.

I shift onto my side so I can look at him. "So you really never tried that with anyone else?" I ask.

He shakes his head. "I wouldn't even know how to bring it up."

"You didn't have much of an issue telling me."

"Well, you practically dragged it out of me." He wears a sharp smile.

But seeing this sexual side of him, this darker side with these needs I knew nothing about makes me a little uneasy, too.

"What is it?" he asks.

How can he fucking read me that well?

I don't want to say anything, but there's a question on my mind that we both need to address before we keep going. "This might sound like a dumb question, but do you want to open up the relationship?"

"Is that what you want?" I can tell by his expression that my question makes him uncomfortable.

"No, no. That's not why I'm asking. I wasn't asking for me. I just meant that I want to make sure all your sexual needs are met, and with that titanium dick of yours, I just…I wouldn't want to keep you from anything, that's all."

"I assumed that we meant we'd be exclusive when we agreed to be boyfriends." He sounds upset that I've even brought this up.

"You're totally thinking about this the wrong way. I'm getting everything I need from you, but if you need to run around and get some things from other guys, I get that. But I think that I should be able to as well."

"I don't like the idea of other guys fucking around with you," he says quickly. His face turns red and the veins in his neck push forward. It's like just the thought of me messing around with other people pisses him off.

"I'm not doing anything with anyone else. And I wasn't planning on it. I just didn't want to step on your toes, in case you did."

"I don't want that." His response is quick, definite.

I'm glad he said it, but it stirs apprehension within me as well.

"Then no, I don't want to do anything either," I say.

"You don't look like that's what you really want, though."

"It's not about what I want."

I'm not surprised by the look he gives me—confused.

"Reese, I've been in enough relationships to know how things work. To know that asking for you to not hook up with other guys is like asking for the sun not to rise. Why spoil what we have going on with rules and limitations?"

"Are you saying you have a hard time being faithful—"

"No, no. I've never cheated on anyone. I just…I've been the one who's been cheated on enough times to know that it's just…well, it's not a fluke. It's something in human nature. Something that I think is inevitable…eventually."

148

"Do you really believe that?"

"The most serious relationship I ever had was with this guy Kyle. It was in New Orleans. We'd been seeing each other for about three months. Had the same conversation. He didn't want to be in an open relationship. I thought things were actually moving somewhere. It was so odd to meet a guy that I didn't want to just have sex with. I mean, it started out that way, but then it turned into something so much more serious. We started talking. Enjoyed staying up together and chatting about pretty much nothing, and then so much. After we agreed to just see each other, he had to go to Baton Rouge on business. He was in accounting for a pretty big firm that had offices there, and he needed to go help them sort through some paperwork. I didn't talk to him much while he was there. He was always texting, telling me he was too busy to chat. I just felt that things were off, and I knew what was going on. I mean, I didn't want to know, but I did, and it hurt. I thought I'd actually found a good person in the world, and then…Well…After he got back, I did what any reasonable person does when they're faced with skepticism. Went through his phone. Didn't have any texts, which made me feel like a fucking idiot for looking. Then a Facebook notification popped up on the screen. New message. Clicked it, and there it was: a thread of messages with this guy he'd been hooking up with while he was gone."

"Oh, God."

"He's not the only guy I've met who's been like that. I told you about that other asshole. And between that and seeing how I've never met anyone who hasn't had some story like that, I just know that statistically, that's how it goes."

"It doesn't have to be like that, though."

"I don't need you playing like you're something that you're not. Clearly you have sexual desires that you weren't telling me about, and I would rather not make the agreement than wonder later on why the hell we did in the first place."

He's quiet, and it concerns me because I don't want him thinking that I want to run off and hook up with other guys. That's not what it's about at all.

"I'm sorry," he says, catching me off guard.

"What could you possibly have to be sorry for?"

149

"That you've been hurt so much. That so many guys have left you feeling like the world is a terrible place. It doesn't have to be like that, though, Jay. I believe that monogamy is possible. And I don't mind being the one to show you that."

His words dissolve my defensiveness about this. As I gaze into his eyes, I believe him. I feel so vulnerable. Like I did wearing those panties. But just like with those, I want to take a risk. I want to take a chance that normally I wouldn't be willing to take. I want to believe that Reese can prove me wrong, but I wonder if I'm stupid for believing it's possible.

He pulls me close to him, looking me in the eyes.

"Come here, Jay," he says playfully. "You don't have anything to worry about with me. What I want is right here in bed with me."

"Just don't hurt me, okay?" I ask. "I'm fine if you change your mind, but talk to me. Don't make a fool out of me. That's all I'm asking. Because that…that's too much for me. Feeling like an idiot."

"You're not an idiot." He kisses me, and I relax into his hold.

He pulls away slowly, rubbing his nose against mine, his scruff scratching softly against my face. He leans back until he's looking into my eyes once again.

"I won't betray you, Jay. I wouldn't do that. I know we're still figuring each other out. Learning who the other is. But that's not me. And one day I'll show you that, and you'll trust me the way you should have been able to trust those other assholes."

I blush. He has me totally losing my cool tonight. Letting him through every barrier I've worked so hard to create throughout my life. It's nice knowing that I've met someone who I feel comfortable letting it all down around because it's so hard acting tough all the time. Hard to act like I'm strong enough to handle anything when all I really want to do is break down and cry.

He kisses me, his warm lips and wet tongue destroying what little remains of those boundaries within me.

Just don't let me down, Reese. Please don't let me down.

***

"Hey, man," Tyler says as he enters the break room.

Considering he saw Reese and I together last night at the movies, I've been wondering how he'd react to us at work today.

He didn't say anything about it while we were on the floor together. Acted like he hadn't noticed anything was up. But now that he's entering the breakroom, acknowledging my existence, I'm a little concerned. I kinda wish we hadn't been scheduled for lunch at the same time.

He heads to the wall of mini-lockers opposite the table I sit at. He retrieves a brown paper bag like the ones he usually brings his lunch in. He sits in the chair adjacent to me at the main table.

"Hey, Tyler," I say for politeness's sake. I take a bite out of a ham and cheese sandwich I made this morning. Tyler opens his bag and unloads his lunch.

"So how long you guys been seeing each other?" he asks without hesitation.

I eye him uneasily.

"I'm not judging. My brother's gay. I'm totally down with it."

"Really?"

"Yeah. Our parents are dicks about it, but it's not a big deal, and one of my wife's best friends is gay. Hell, if I'd known about either of you guys, I would've fucking been trying to hook him up. He's on the prowl for a new man right now."

"You sure weren't like this when I first started working here."

"I was a little nervous. I don't think anyone told you, but you were replacing my old job because I couldn't work fast enough. I had back surgery a few months before you got here, and it hasn't been an easy recovery for me. Your position opened up because Reese realized he had to move me around so we could keep up with deliveries. He thought he might not be able to keep me on because he wouldn't have a place for me. I was just lucky that he ended up fighting to keep me with the owners."

Once again, I'm confronted with evidence that Reese isn't just a good boss. He's a good person.

Not only for making peace between us, but because he didn't just let them sack Tyler when he was struggling—most people wouldn't have given a shit.

Reminds me I'm real lucky to be with him.

27

Reese

The Uber car heads through a neighborhood in Buckhead.

"Definitely not living over here on the salary Tyler makes at the factory," I say.

"His wife's an attorney," Jay says. "She handles domestic disputes. I imagine she makes plenty of money."

"Apparently."

I'm surprised he knows that much about Tyler. But I have noticed them chatting in the warehouse recently. He's not just that way with Tyler, either. He's started to warm up to the rest of the guys, and I'm impressed as hell because he's come a long way from the guy who started here two months ago—who couldn't get along with anyone—who was always ready for a fight.

The Uber driver drops us off at a two-story home, and as we walk up the drive, I note the well-groomed front yard with lush grass and bushes.

Jay knocks on the door, and Tyler answers. In a short-sleeved button-up and jeans, he wipes his hands with a towel as he offers a warm smile. "Hey, guys," he says. "Welcome. Come on in."

He leads us into the kitchen. Shelley stands beside the counter, holding a lid as she looks into the crockpot and studies the roast Jay told me she'd be making for tonight. Her hair is up in a ponytail. She's wearing a blouse and jeans, looking slightly more dressed-up than when we saw her at the movies, but still casual.

"Shelley," Tyler says, catching her attention.

She turns and a bright grin expands across her face—one that reminds me of Melanie's smile.

"Oh, hi. Sorry." She places the lid over the crockpot and approaches us, shaking our hands. "Good seeing you guys again." She glances at a pot on the stove. "I think we have about twenty minutes for the potatoes. Come into the dining room and I'll fix you a drink. Did you drive?"

"We got an Uber so we could get a little wild tonight," Jay says.

"Good boy," Tyler says with a mischievous smile like he's eager to get tipsy. I'm willing to have a drink or two, but I definitely won't go further than that around an employee.

Tyler leads us into the adjoining dining room. A table that seats six, with an orchid as the centerpiece, takes up most of the space. Jay and I take the seats on the opposite side of the room.

Shelley approaches a liquor cabinet on the wall behind us. "Uh-uh," Tyler says. "You go finish the potatoes, and I'll take care of their drinks. You can't do all the work around here."

"Aww…that was almost sweet," she says, giving him a peck on the cheek before she heads back into the kitchen.

Déjà vu. It reminds me of something I would have done when I was with Melanie before the war—before the pain. Before the heartache.

We were much younger than Shelley or Tyler. Our life was so simple then. But after I got back from Iraq, when we tried to simulate the same sorts of get-togethers, it was different. One time, we had Caleb and his fiancé over. It was a quiet night—one that reminded us all of everything that had changed and that they could never be the same again.

The look on Melanie's face that evening still haunts me, as she forced a smile. But she couldn't hide her sad eyes from me—that discouraged look that seemed to ask, "Can we ever get back to what we had?"

"What do you guys want?" Tyler asks. "Vodka? Whiskey? Tequila?"

"Beer is fine with me," I say. "I don't want to be any trouble."

Tyler rolls his eyes. "I'm not giving you a goddamn beer, boss-man. Let me make you this martini that we had when we were in New York last year. You both game to try that?"

For the first time, Tyler is ordering me around, and I kind of like it. Makes me feel a little more at ease. I was worried that being his boss would make him uneasy around me, but he seems friendlier than he usually is at the office.

We agree to try the martini, and after Tyler fixes them, he and his wife sit across from us.

"Where are the kids?" Jay asks.

"They're with their granny tonight," Shelley says. "We thought we could have a little alone time for the weekend. We get some of that every once and a while, which is nice."

"Yeah. We don't have many opportunities to get out these days," Tyler adds. "And since we both work full-time, we take free nights whenever we can bug our relatives into giving it to us."

"Oh, as if Granny was so put-out by it," Shelley says with a chuckle, evoking memories of Melanie in similar moments. It was the sort of banter we fell into. It was a fun game, playing off each other, knowing what the other would say or eagerly awaiting a clever remark.

We chat some more before the potatoes are finished. Shelley and Tyler work together, fixing our plates, laughing together as they distribute the food.

I glance into the kitchen and catch them kissing again.

That's what Melanie and I went from—loving and playful like Shelley and Tyler to being haunted by the cruel shell of a life that my PTSD left us with. She tried so hard. Fought as much as she could. She wanted to save me. But she couldn't, and she left because it was too much for her. And just like when I'm transported back to the pain of war, in this moment, I'm transported back to seeing her sad face as she sat beside me on the couch, trying to coax me out of my pain. Trying to help me. But knowing that, just like so many other times, it wouldn't do any good.

"You okay?" Jay asks.

"I'm fine," I say, resting my hand on his leg and squeezing.

He sets his hand on mine, and it comforts me, but it also reminds me of what I have to be afraid of. Things are going well now, but like I told Jay, they won't always be this easy. One day, the darkness will return, a lot worse than this.

I don't ever want to hurt him the way I hurt Melanie. I can't watch his eyes dull as he gives up on his own happiness because of my pain. He thinks he knows what he's signing up for, but he doesn't. He *can't*. He's seen previews of the stretches that can get so bad and unbearable—and can feel like they might last forever. I've been lucky since I've known him, but my time is running out because no matter how much help I get or how many pills I take, when it gets bad, it gets so bad. And being here reminds me of how much I could hurt Jay. How much I could let him down.

154

I won't ruin his life the way I ruined hers.

"Hey," Jay says again, pulling me out of my self-destructive thoughts. Feels like I've been trapped in them for hours, but it's just been a few moments. Shelley and Tyler haven't even brought the food in yet.

He kisses me softly.

I chase the thoughts away. It isn't easy, but at least as long as I have my sanity...and this beautiful, amazing man, I deserve to enjoy it. I deserve to have happiness for as long as I can cling on to it.

28

Jay

I pull away from our kiss and see the ease in his eyes. Whatever thought had seized his attention—trapped him in the past—has eased up, but it's still there, playing on his mind. I tighten my grip on his hand to let him know I'm here for him.

Once we start eating, laughing, and chatting, his tension eases up. He even starts joking around, and I'm relieved.

"Orchids are a lot of work," Reese says to Shelley, pointing to the one in the middle of the table.

"I know, but they're so pretty. My mom used to be a big gardener, and we had so many of them, so it reminds me of home."

"Reese has a garden," I say, hoping the conversation will distract him from the other bullshit he's dealing with.

"Oh, really?"

"Yeah. Just vegetables."

"I would love to have a vegetable garden, but I have a hard enough time with the front yard."

"You do all that yourself?"

Tyler grins. "Yes, she does."

They start discussing gardening, and I enjoy seeing the light return to Reese's eyes. Shelley tells a story about a rabbit they had to deal with in her mother's garden when she was little, and the moment she's through, I see that Reese is back. It reminds me of when he recovered from that episode he had in the break room.

He just needs time. And help.

When we finish dinner, Tyler fixes us some plates of pecan pie and vanilla ice cream.

"Tyler made the pie," Shelley says.

"Don't tell them that," he insists. "They'll think less of me at work." He sets my plate down before me and winks.

"If this pie is half as good as that roast, then it's great," I say.

Shelley smiles at my compliment. "Thank you."

Tyler retrieves his and Shelley's desserts before setting them down on the table so that we can continue chatting. They tell us the story of how they met, switching up to tell different parts and give the other an opportunity to defend their actions. It's cute watching them in action, and I imagine Reese and me being like this in the future.

Is it really possible that I could be the lucky guy who gets to be with him? It's too soon to be thinking that far ahead, but I can't help it. He's the first guy I've entertained the idea of sharing something more with in so long. The first guy who's made me want to tear through the barriers I've spent years building up so that I can have a future with him.

"Do you guys like bingo?" Shelley asks. "Tyler and I play at a place in Midtown every Tuesday night with some friends. We'd love it if you guys would join us sometime."

"That'd be nice. This martini is amazing, by the way," Reese tells Tyler.

"Thank you," he says, his face pink as he blushes.

"And so was the meal...and this pie," Reese adds. "This dinner has been wonderful. Thank you for having us over."

"It's been our pleasure," Shelley says. "Just nice to finally get a glimpse into Tyler's life. He's never talked about work as much as he does now that Jay's started working there."

I've never been good at making friends, but I've made one in Tyler. And that feels pretty damn good. Things have changed since Reese came into my life. Changed for the better.

We exchange a few more stories before we notice the time and realize we should head out.

"Sorry. We didn't mean to keep you so long," Shelley says as she guides us to the door. She's clearly at ease with us now, and we feel the same way with her and Tyler.

"It wasn't an issue at all," Reese replies. "We had a great time."

"We need to do it again," I add.

"Oh, for sure," she says. "We'll keep in touch with you about bingo night. A bunch of us get together for it, and I think you'd really like them. There are a few other gay guys in the group that I think you'd get along really well with."

"That would be awesome," Reese says.

I check the Uber app. I ordered a car about ten minutes ago, and we have about five minutes before it arrives.

We say our goodbyes and then we head out. As we walk down the drive, Reese snatches my hand, holding it tightly. "That was great," he says.

I turn and see the light in his eyes again. "Yeah, it was."

"Thank you."

"What are you thanking me for?"

"For getting me out of my shell. I never would have done this kind of thing in the past—on my own—but being with you makes me want to open my life up more. I don't want to keep living in a box. I've known I shouldn't be like that for a while, but I keep using work as an excuse to not make any friends or keep my distance with people. You'd think between the group sessions and Laura I'd know better, but this has shown me that I need to start living again."

"It's done the same thing for me. Getting to spend time with you has changed me. I'm not that asshole you met. You've made me open up the same way. And not just in the bedroom."

A wicked smirk slips across his face. He must be reflecting on that hot evening last week when I wore those panties. My dick hardens just thinking about it.

"Maybe we need to get you back in those panties tonight," he says.

"Ooh. Doesn't sound like such a bad idea, Reese." I kiss him softly, but as I pull away, I see that uneasiness return. I can't imagine why.

He gulps.

"Everything okay?"

"As we were sitting there at first, when I was watching Shelley and Tyler interact, I was thinking about something from my past that I feel like I need to talk to you about."

I wait for him to go on, but he doesn't.

"What's wrong?"

"It's just…someone I hurt a lot. I want to talk to you about it, but I'm not sure I'm ready."

"Reese, you don't have to talk to me about anything you're uncomfortable with. You know that, right?"

"I know. I feel terrible because it's a part of my life that was so important to me, and it's like as I try to get away from it, I'm shitting all over it."

"I can't judge you for running from your past. That's how I've spent my life."

He starts to say something, but I can tell by the look in his eyes that he's not ready for this.

"Hey, Reese. You don't need to do this. We can just have a good night. There's no rush. I'm not going anywhere."

He smiles again and kisses me, much more passionately than before.

I'm so fucking lucky.

A car pulls alongside us. That must be our ride.

I pull away, but Reese puts his hand on the back of my head and holds me in place as he continues our kiss.

I surrender, savoring the moment.

29

Reese

I head through the factory, spot-checking some of the maintenance that's been performed on the annealing machines over the past few weeks. Gotta keep on top of the contractors or they'll skimp on the work and have to come back out in another few months for something that could have been easily prevented if they'd just done the job right the first time.

As I descend the stairs, heading down into the main warehouse, I spot Jay in a tight-fitting T-shirt, on his knees as he drives a nail into a pallet with a hammer.

"How goes it?" I ask as I approach him. He turns to me, his eyes wide like I surprised him. Sweat rushes down his face. He wipes his forearm across his forehead.

"Hey," he says. "I'm just reinforcing some of these pallets. Loads of fun, you know?"

"I bet."

"How about you?"

"Usual shit. The maintenance guys fucked up a few things here and there, but nothing they can't swing by and fix next week."

"Lazy motherfuckers." He rises and glances around.

I know what he wants. A bunch of the guys are in the break room, and William is on the forklift on the other side of the warehouse, so I'm not too concerned about us being caught.

We meet halfway and kiss. It's tender. Soft. There's something reassuring within it—the promise that when we need the relief of each other's touch, it will be freely offered.

A popping sound comes from behind me.

I grab Jay and force him to the ground.

It's an instinct that sweeps over me in an instant, and suddenly, I hear the sounds of my nightmares—my memories. The explosions. The gunfire. The tension in my chest swells. My adrenaline races. I can hardly figure out where the fuck that sound came from because I'm trapped in the sensations that overtake my body.

I lie flat, my limbs spread out, my hands pressed tight against the concrete floor.

As Jay gets on his knees beside me, he says something, but I can't hear it over the memory of my commanding officers shouting at us as we worked our way through the labyrinth of corridors in the streets of Fallujah.

The more I scold myself—try to bring myself back to the present—the harder it becomes.

Laura always tells me to relax into it. Fighting only makes it worse. Fighting only increases my anxiety and makes me feel like the thoughts are overtaking me.

I try to concentrate on my breathing, counting to myself. As I start to feel myself coming back, I turn and see Tyler and two other employees heading down the stairs into the warehouse.

Fuck me. Fuck me to hell.

I try to break the spell of the episode, but the stress of knowing the guys are in here, seeing me like this, is too much for me.

"Reese?" Tyler asks as he hurries down.

"Can you just give us a minute, please?" Jay asks.

"Sure, no problem," Tyler replies. "Come on, guys." He spreads his arms out in front of them and leads them back upstairs, checking over his shoulder. When they leave, I hear Jay say, "Come on, Reese. Come on."

He grabs my face and pulls so that I turn to him, looking him in the eyes.

"It's okay. Everything's okay. Just look at me."

It doesn't shake the physical sensations that lock all the muscles in my body, but the sounds that felt so real to me for an instant disappear into the background and are replaced with the sound of his voice.

"I'm right here, Reese. Right here. Just breathe. Deep breaths."

I follow his advice, though really, as he continues talking me down, it's the sound of his voice that guides me back, starts to relieve the tension that grips my body.

It takes some time before I finally take what feels like the first good breath of air that I've had since I heard the sound. Jay helps me to my feet, his arm around me. I start to take a step, but my prosthesis doesn't work right. "Fuck." My anxiety intensifies.

"What's wrong?"

"I fucked up the joint on the foot. God-fucking-dammit."

"I got you."

I pull away. "No. I can do this." I limp toward the door. "I have shit in my office. I just need to…"

But the stress my body's under combined with my leg throwing me off sends me back to the floor.

Fuck.

I haven't felt so weak…so helpless…so embarrassed in a long time.

I can feel Jay's gaze on me. "I can do this," I insist. I crawl to the wall and climb it. I'm about to take another step, but the intensity of my episode and the utter defeat of this moment—being reminded of what a mess I really am—seizes my attention. I burst into tears as I rest my face against the wall, leaning against it for support.

"Reese," Jay says. I keep my eyes closed. I can't face him right now.

"Go away," I say through gritted teeth. "Please."

"I'm not leaving you like this. Just tell me what you need me to do to help you."

"I don't need your help. I can do this. I've been doing this long enough by myself."

"Reese, please."

I force my eyes open, so he can see how serious I am, but it just releases the tears, which stream down my face.

God, I'm a mess.

"I…can…do this…on my own," I say, fighting to get the words out.

"But you don't have to anymore."

He approaches me and ducks. I don't realize what he's doing until he lifts me up and throws me over his shoulder, and I surrender, because it's never felt so good to have an ally. To not be totally alone in a moment where I feel so helpless.

"God, you're fucking heavy," he teases, and I laugh through the tears.

"I fucking hate you," I say, really meaning the opposite.

"You can let my ass know just how much you hate me later." But then he becomes serious again, saying, "I got you. I got you."

And I feel safe in his arms.

He carries me to my office and helps me into the chair behind my desk. He squats beside me before stroking his hand back and forth on my thigh.

"I'm good," I say as my sense of control over my body returns. He glances around uneasily, like he's not sure what he's supposed to do now. "Thank you," I say quickly to diffuse any uneasiness he's feeling.

"No problem."

I grab the back of his head, pull him to me, and kiss him. A little more of the tension within me dissolves as I'm absorbed in the ease that always accompanies his kiss.

I pull him close. I need him close. I wish we weren't at work. I wish this was just another night where we're lying in bed, clinging to one another after fucking. Holding each other close and gazing into each other's eyes. Those moments, beautiful as they are, never seem to last. They come and go like a sunset. Enchanting just long enough to leave you wanting more, but never totally satisfying your desire to see its beauty.

We continue kissing until he gently pulls back and asks, "You okay?"

"Much better now. Kind of a shitty way for the guys to see me."

He kisses me again, as though he's trying to distract me from my self-consciousness. And I'm just thankful that he's here. Not just in the building, but in my life.

I'm thankful that I was willing to give him a chance despite his attitude and tendency to run.

There's a knock on the door. "It's Tyler."

"You want me to tell him to go away?" Jay whispers.

"No," I reply. "Come on in!" I call out.

Tyler enters. "Everything okay?" he asks, wearing his concern on his face.

"Better. Just trying to figure out what the fuck that sound was."

"One of the machines shut down."

"Fuck. I knew those lazy-ass contractors would do something to mess up our goddamn machines."

"Are you good? Is everything okay?" Tyler asks.

"Yeah. It's…I have some episodes occasionally…from the war. I had my guard down and the sound surprised me."

It was the kiss. It left me feeling vulnerable, so when the sound came, my awareness of how unguarded I was roused all those defensive parts of me.

"Guess I need to fix this leg and take care of the machines," I say.

"You can sit this one out for a minute," Jay insists.

"I can check it out," Tyler follows. "And I can call the repair guys to get them to come back out if you need me to."

Jay was right. I don't have to do this on my own, but I can't shake the feeling that if I don't tend to this, I'll let my boss down.

I can't let anyone else in my life down.

"If you can, look at it. I just have to check out my leg and make sure I can fix it."

"Okay. I'll report back." Tyler heads out.

Even though I'm still rattled, I'm relieved.

My nightmare finally came true. I lost it in front of the guys, and the world didn't come to an end. Tyler and Jay didn't look down on me for being weak. They didn't judge me. They helped me. They were compassionate and understanding. They reminded me that it doesn't have to be me against the world anymore.

I open my desk drawer and pull out a case with some tools that I carry to make adjustments on my leg. I set it on my desk and say, "Now, let's see if I can fix this mess I made."

Jay rests his hand on my shoulder. "Are you okay?"

"I am now."

And I'm not talking about the episode, which lingers, and will for several hours, I'm sure. Just about having someone as amazing as him in my life. More amazing than I deserve. Amazing as he was today, it only makes me that much more afraid of hurting him. Of watching him take on this burden the way he did today.

30

Jay

I gaze out the window behind the kitchen sink.

Reese spreads compost over the plants in his garden with a rake. The orange glow of the sunset makes his beard and face appear the same color. He's so beautiful in this moment. He doesn't look like he belongs in the real world, but in a painting.

His serene expression as he tends to his work is so different from the look he had when he had that episode at the factory two days ago. It was devastating watching him fall apart, but I was just glad he let me help him. That he didn't keep pushing me away. I was worried he wouldn't accept the help. I would've acted the same way if that had happened to me. But we've come too far, and he needs to know that we're in this together. That I want to be here for him, and I want to let him be here for me.

I enjoy watching him outside for a few moments before I continue marinating the steak we're having for dinner.

Reese's place is starting to feel like home. Some days I forget I live fifteen minutes away. I still have to swing by to pick up clothes, but Charlie's teased me saying that I'm the best damn roommate in the world. "All cash, no hassle," he joked last time I was there.

When Reese comes inside, covered in sweat, he gives me a gentle kiss before heading to the bedroom to shower off. He returns while I'm setting the table. He's just in a towel, his body fierce as ever.

I'm jealous of how big his muscles are. I go to the gym too, but damn, I could never have his chest, which is so big it practically makes the top buttons of his shirts bust off. We sit down at the table and eat. He slides the comics section from the center of the table to beside his plate and asks me which ones he needs to read, and I eagerly offer recommendations. We chat about work and then what movie we want to watch tonight, but I can't keep from scanning his body, appreciating it, appreciating *him*.

"You don't have to treat me like a piece of meat," he teases with a smirk as he notices my continual glances.

"I'm fine with that as long as you're willing to treat me like one."

He gets up out of his chair and opens his towel, revealing his stiffening cock. He approaches me slowly, a determined look in his eyes as he closes his towel, hiding that part from me.

"Why don't you help me clean up this mess so we can make a new one?" he asks.

"I like the sound of that." We take care of the food and dishes before freshening up in the bathroom.

I'm already lying in the bed when he steps out of the bathroom, having brushed his teeth. He removes the towel, sliding beside me. He grabs the sheet and pulls it up to cover his prosthetic. He glances at me awkwardly.

"You don't have to hide anything from me," I say.

I haven't had the guts to say anything before. I never wanted him to feel embarrassed or uncomfortable about it. But I've noticed he still tries to hide it when he can.

His lips twist into his dimples. "You're not the one I'm hiding it from."

"I'm sorry. I shouldn't have said anything."

"No, no." He slides the sheet down to reveal it.

"It's just a habit I've gotten into. It's always made me feel like there's something wrong with me. Just reminds me, not just of how I'm broken-down there, but in my head, too. But I don't want to live my life trying to hide it from myself. I realized that when I had that episode and the guys came in. I can't keep living in fear. This is my life. This is who I am. And it's not so bad. Not anymore. Not now that you're in it."

"Whatever. You were fine long before I came along."

"I was fine, but you've changed a lot in my life in such a short time, and I appreciate that so fucking much."

"You've changed a lot with me, too. Who would've thought I would be getting invited to dinners with my co-workers considering how we started out?"

He smiles. "But it's because you're an amazing person. A defensive prick sometimes, but an amazing person."

His words heal something within me—mend the broken person that I've been all these years.

His eyes shift for a moment before he says, "I was going to wait to share this with you, but I think now's actually a really good time." He slides off the bed and hurries to the closet. I enjoy watching his ass cheeks shake about.

"Another thong?" I tease. Not that I'd have any problem with that.

He turns to me, beaming as he retrieves an envelope from the top shelf. He returns, handing it to me.

"What is it?" I ask.

He just smiles. While he gets back in the bed, I open it. It's two print-outs. Tickets to the Louis C.K. show.

"Are you serious?" My heartbeat quickens as excitement rushes through me. Not just because I want to see the guy live, but because that's one of the most thoughtful things anyone's ever done for me.

"You told me that it was coming soon. I figured it wasn't something you'd do for yourself, but I feel like you need to be there."

"Thank you, Reese."

"It was nothing," he says, rolling his eyes.

"No, it really wasn't nothing. It was…a lot. Too much. These tickets had to have cost you a fortune. I can't accept these. But I appreciate the thought. It's just way too much."

"You can and *will* accept them," he insists. He rests his hand on my cheek, his thumb caressing in that all-too-familiar way. "Because you do deserve this, and so much more." He kisses me.

"Thank you so much for this. Reese, you can't realize how much this means to me. I could never afford to do something like this for you."

He takes the envelope from me and sets it on the nightstand behind him. Rolling back over, he whispers, "I think I have an idea of how you can repay me." His words stir a heat within my body—a passion for him.

I don't just want him inside me. I want him all over me. Not just his kiss and caress. I want to be totally consumed by him in a way that isn't even physically possible, have every part of him stimulating every part of me, reveling in that erotic touch that my body now craves. He takes me, and I let go of my inhibitions and let him have my body in every angle and position he desires. I'm his sex slave tonight. I'm his to totally use in whatever way he chooses, and even when he throws his legs up for me to top, I'm his then too. Just a toy to satisfy his own greedy impulses, because that's what's so satisfying to me right now.

We fuck the way I needed to fuck, and when we settle after our post-orgasm highs, I delight in all the sensations that pool within me. He holds me close, offering many tender kisses, which I relax into.

He pulls away and studies my face.

"I'm finding this really easy to get used to," I say.

"Your ass is easy to get used to," he jokes, and I laugh.

After a few more minutes of holding each other and sweet kisses, I head to the bathroom to throw out the condoms we used when I notice my clothes on the bathroom floor. I check the drawer and realize I just have one shirt left.

"Shit," I say.

"What?"

"I need to swing by my place on the way back here tomorrow. I have like one shirt to wear. I knew I was running low, but I guess I wasn't paying attention."

"You should bring over all your clothes."

"Shut up," I say. Nice of a thought as it is, I know we're nowhere near ready for that.

I head to the bed and crawl back up to him.

"Well, I should at least get to see your place by now," he says.

Tension rises within me. Since the evening began, this is the first tension I've felt that hasn't been related to his massive intrusion. The first one that hasn't been coupled with a steamy, erotic intensity.

Just disappointment.

"What? No. It's a dump."

"It's your dump, so I want to see it."

"No, please don't."

I think about the stupid little room. It doesn't even look like anyone lives there. I don't have anything up. My clothes are the only thing that decorate the room—the floor, the bed, the closet. It's the room of a guy who doesn't plan on being in any place for very long. It represents the nomadic life I've always lived.

"It's part of your life," he says. "I think, considering we're boyfriends now, I should get to see it."

"You're gonna think I'm a slob."

"You're here all the time. I already know that."

But the way he's smiling, I don't feel like he's judging or critiquing me. That he likes the slob he's spending time with.

His expression shifts from amused to serious. "Come on, Jay. I want to get to know you. I feel like every time I try to break through a little bit, you pull away from me."

"What are you talking about? I've told you about my past. About my dad. My…Todd."

"I'm totally appreciative that you felt comfortable telling me about all that. I really am. But that's not the sort of stuff I'm talking about. I want to get to know as much about you as I possibly can. And that's a part of your life right now whether you like it or not."

"It's just not something I'm proud of. I really don't think you get it. You think of someone's place as being like yours. Being a good representation of who they are. Maybe that's true, but if you see mine, you'll see it's a wreck, and…"

"And what? You think I'm going to suddenly hate you because you have a messy place?"

It's strange hearing him say it because it's true. I'm worried he'll think I'm this irresponsible guy…the irresponsible guy I really am. Maybe he's right. Because the reason I'm scared of showing him isn't because I fear it'll be a poor representation of who I am, but a far-too-accurate one.

But at this point, we're both in too deep, and embarrassing as it is, I want to open up to him. I want him to be a part of my life. Even the parts I'm not all that proud of.

"If you want, you can come with me tomorrow," I say.

"You sound like I'm making you go to the dentist."

He rubs the back of his thumb under my chin. "We don't have to do anything you're not ready for. But considering we're boyfriends now, it's not a big deal. And I do think it's strange that I haven't seen your place yet. Don't you?"

169

"You're right. I'm just bad at this whole dating thing. I never really had a chance to get good at it."

"I'm happy to be the guy you practice on," he says, kissing me again.

As relaxing as the kiss is, I'm still nervous as fuck about what he's going to think when he sees how shitty my place looks.

31

Reese

As we drive to the house he's staying in, I can tell by how uneasy he looks that this is the last thing in the world he wants to do right now. I'm sure he would like to take time to make it presentable, but this isn't about what it looks like. It's not about seeing a stupid room. This is about the things we don't know about each other, those things that we haven't shared with each other. Things we need to share if we're going to make this work. Being together isn't about using a label. It's about taking steps toward sharing our lives…to see if we really can make this work.

And Jay's the only person I've wanted to make this work with in a very long time.

But I know this isn't really as much about what he hasn't shared with me as it is about what I haven't shared with him. What's itching at my conscience?

And the longer I don't mention her to him, the more I feel like I'm living a lie.

I know he said I could take my time, but I want to push through these barriers. The more I keep from him, the more I keep him at a distance. And I don't want any distance between us.

When we arrive at the house in Grant Park, he leads me up the driveway. It's a decent-looking place with a trimmed yard. He unlocks the door and opens it, glancing around. "Charlie?!" he calls out.

What sounds like a chair sliding across the floor comes from an adjoining room. "Oh, well, look who it is. Guess you gotta grab some clothes so you can play slumber party with your new boyfr—"

Charlie steps through the doorway, his eyes going wide as he spots me. A smile spreads across his face.

"Look at this!" he exclaims.

I can't help but laugh.

He approaches and Jay introduces us. We're shaking hands when Charlie says, "Aren't you a big hunk of man?"

"And you're awfully friendly," I say.

His grin gets even bigger—something I didn't even believe was possible.

"I'm just glad you're taking care of this one. Figure you'll be moving in together in no time, but I'm appreciating the cash and the peace and quiet."

The living room is clean with a few houseplants, some of which look fake. Jay catches up with Charlie a little before he heads back into the kitchen, saying that he needs to work on his crocheting.

Jay leads me through the living room into a side hall with a bathroom at the end. He unlocks a door on the left side of the hall and guides me inside.

"Here we are," he says, and I can hear the disappointment in his voice.

The walls are bare. An unmade twin bed is set against a wall with a window. Light pours through the blinds, casting sharp white shapes across the hardwood floors. A duffle bag is tucked beside a wooden desk on the wall opposite the bed. Some clothes spill out of it, across the floor.

It's not as messy as he always made it sound, but it's so empty. So nondescript. Doesn't tell me much of anything about his life because it lacks personality. He hasn't put himself into this because he's not used to staying anywhere long enough to feel comfortable making it his own.

I didn't think seeing his room would make me uncomfortable, but it does.

Not because of the mess, but because it reminds me that Jay is the kind of guy who's used to moving on. If something happened, something that bothered him, it would be effortless for him to pack up his things and move along to the next life he wanted to try. He's arranged his life, his belongings, and his work so that he doesn't have to stick around in any one place for very long if he doesn't want to. And the idea of losing him so quickly concerns me.

"I told you it was nothing," he says, avoiding eye contact.

I'm sure he's sensed my discomfort, but I don't want to make him feel bad because it doesn't have anything to do with him.

"It's fine, Jay. This is totally normal."

"You don't look like it's normal."

"I'm not gonna lie and act like it doesn't make me a little uncomfortable. The idea of you just leaving when you feel like you're done with Atlanta."

His expression doesn't offer me any comfort. He's admitted that's how he is. How he can be. How he's never been able to settle in any one place, so he must feel that it's almost fate that he'll have to leave.

"You think you'll be moving on anytime soon?" I ask.

"No," he says quickly, his brow furrowed. "I just…I'm not used to having anything keeping me somewhere. Not for very long, at least."

"But you've obviously had boyfriends in other cities."

"Yeah. And I'm not used to them lasting long enough to bog me down much."

"Is that what you think of a relationship? As something that bogs you down?"

"No, no. I'm such an idiot. That's not what I meant at all. I just meant that that they've always gone south pretty quickly, and when that happens, I tend to not want to stick around."

Does he think that's going to make me feel more at ease? The idea that one fight and he could be packing his bags and running out of my life forever? Moving on to the next place…the next partner.

I notice a stack of newspapers sitting on the desk. I approach them. "More comics," I say, sifting through them.

He steps beside me, interlocking his fingers as he shifts his body like he's uneasy. "I shouldn't have brought you here, should I?"

I wrap my arm around him and pull him close, kissing him. "That's not what this is about. It worries me because I am scared of something happening and you just running out. Relationships aren't easy, and considering what I deal with, the idea of it being too much and you just packing and leaving scares the shit out of me."

But maybe that's what needs to happen. Maybe he just needs to save himself from all this.

"I don't want to leave."

"Maybe you'll rethink that after I share what I need to with you."

I don't know how to tell him this. There's no easy way. Something like this isn't the kind of thing that there's ever a right time for. It's like breaking up with someone. You just have to do it.

He eyes me curiously, surely wondering what I could have weighing on me that I need to get off my chest.

"I…um…I used to be married."

He tenses up.

"I'm sorry I didn't say anything, but it's just…not the easiest thing to talk about."

"That's not a huge deal, I guess. How long were you with the guy?"

"It was a woman."

"A woman?"

"Yes, a woman."

He opens his mouth like he's about to say something, but then closes it just as quickly.

"We got married right before I went to Iraq, and we were together for about another year before she left."

"*She* left?"

"Yeah. I…I was pretty distant and cold with her when I got back. Things just weren't the same. Could never be the same."

"So it didn't have anything to do with the fact that you're gay?"

"Well, I mean, I did care about her. And I was attracted to her."

His eyes widen, and he pulls away. "Wait, what?"

"Is that strange?"

The expression on his face suggests he's not just surprised by the news, but distressed over it. I'm surprised. I didn't think that would be the big deal out of telling him that I used to be married.

"So you like going down on girls? That's hot to you?"

"I never had an issue with it."

He scans over me like he's looking at a stranger.

"Jay, I'm still me. That doesn't change who I am or how I feel about you."

"That shit with the panties," he says. "What the fuck was that really about then?"

"What?"

"Were you trying to dress me up like that because you're more attracted to women?"

"No. That's crazy. I just…it's something I've always thought was hot."

His startled expression doesn't change.

"Whoa, I didn't think that I was going to creep you out about that part. I wanted to tell you I was married because it's something I feel like I've almost been keeping from you, but it was a big part of my life."

"I'm gonna admit, that's weird. Really weird. Not something I've come across before. So like, I don't want to sound ignorant, but do you need that, too?"

"What?"

"Is that what the panties were about? You can't just be with one or the other? Like would you need to bring in a girl, too?"

"What? I'm bi, not polyamorous."

"But obviously you have a thing for women that you need to act out while being with a man. That's what the thong was about."

"You're thinking way too much about that. It's a little thing that was fun and that I really wanted to try out."

"And it obviously has something to do with your attraction to guys and girls. Like some weird hybrid thing."

"Maybe, but I don't really think so. It's just hot."

His face is scrunched up like he's disgusted with me. And now I feel self-conscious about something that I thought was just good, hot fun. "Stop overthinking that one thing."

"One thing? You have to admit the underwear fetish is kinda weird. And I thought it was strange already, but now that I know you're into girls too, what am I supposed to think about that?"

"Would it have changed anything if you'd known about it that night?"

"I don't think I'd have been as willing to go along with it if I'd thought you were thinking of me as a girl while I was in those."

"I wasn't thinking about you as a girl. I was sharing this with you because I thought you would want to know that I was married. I didn't think you'd care about me having been with women before."

"Well, I do. How am I supposed to satisfy that need? I don't have that. I will never have that, and if that's something you want."

"That doesn't even make any sense."

"How does it not make sense?"

"Have you never been with a bi guy before?"

"No."

"Well, it's not like I need both at the same time. It's not any different than if I was a gay guy. Just because I might be attracted to maybe fit and twinky guys, wouldn't mean I would need to be with both. I can be with just one person."

His shoulders relax, but he eyes me apprehensively. "You don't think the thong fetish might be connected in some strange way?" he presses.

"Even if it is, who gives a shit? You're my boyfriend."

"Okay, okay. I just have to process it. Give me a minute. That's a weird-ass thing to hear."

"That's fine. I get that, but you do realize that nothing's changed between us because of it."

"Yeah, yeah."

He runs his hands through his short brown hair, taking a breath like he's still struggling with it more than I feel like he should be. I figured he'd think it was weird that I'd been married, not that I enjoyed fucking girls. I wonder if this has something to do with his fear of guys cheating on him. Maybe he suddenly just realized that I could cheat on him with so many more people than before—and now on top of his worry about cheating, he has to worry that he won't be able to satisfy my desire to be with a woman. It's a wildly misguided assumption, considering if I was gay, I'd be just as likely to want to have sex with other guys as a bi guy who wants to have sex with guys and girls, but I figure once he calms down, he'll be more rational about this.

32

Jay

Now I realize why Reese thought it was so important to come over here today.

We've been playing house together, but there are things we still don't know about each other.

I thought, based on some of what we'd shared, we were open about so many things, but after the bomb he just dropped, I realize there's a whole lot I still don't know about Reese.

Married to a woman? I've known plenty of guys who were married before they came out, but most of them haven't identified as bi. They were just trying to fit in. Reese, on the other hand, could fuck guys or girls. How has that never come up before? I guess I didn't give a shit what gender he was attracted to…just that he was attracted to me. But what the fuck?

It's not particularly a bad thing, but I don't get it. It's never been the way that I felt, so it's hard for me to relate. And whether or not he wants to admit it, I don't think it's an accident that he happens to like fucking girls and wanted to fuck me while I was wearing the thong.

He enjoyed it so much. I would have put it on again just because of how hot it was, but now I'm so fucking confused because I feel like I'm with a stranger. At least, someone I don't know as well as I thought I did.

On the drive back to his place, I'm quiet. Questions keep amassing in my brain, crowding each other, fighting for me to decide which ones are most important and which ones need to be asked first.

"So you loved this woman?"

"Her name's Melanie," he says. "And I did love her."

"And *she* left *you*?"

He tenses his jaw. "Yes. That's what happened."

"So you're hung up on her?"

He winces. "It's been almost a decade since I saw her. I've moved on, Jay. I'm not the guy I was back then, and she's not the girl she was. I mean, plenty of people get dumped without being totally hung up on the person for the rest of their lives."

"And you enjoyed having sex with her?"

"Did we not cover that question?"

"Sorry. It's just…damn, I don't even know what to think about any of it. Like who *are* you? Are there other things you haven't told me?"

"As much as there are other things you haven't told me. I've lived enough that there's shit in my past. Do you want me to make a list of all the people, guys and girls, I've ever slept with? I don't think you want that any more than I want to know about all your sexual escapades."

But he did just feed me a pretty good question. "What about a percentage?" I ask.

"What?"

"Guys-to-girls?"

"Oh, God. I don't know."

Why do I think that'll make this better? I guess I'm hoping he'll say that he's leaning toward fucking guys. Then I don't have to feel so weird about it.

"Like twenty percent."

"Twenty percent girls?"

"Guys."

Fuck.

"Why is that a big deal?" he asks.

"It just confirms that you also need to get your rocks off with girls."

"That doesn't make any sense."

He sounds irritated by my line of questioning, and I admit that I'm not thinking all of this through, but what does he fucking expect when he surprises me with shit like that?

"It makes a little bit of sense, at least," I say. "I've just never had to think about if I like girls or guys. I've always known it was guys. What is that even like when you're growing up? How did you know what to do?"

"It was a little difficult when I was a kid. When I was in middle school, there was this guy I was really hot for. My friend, Ryan. When we changed together in the locker room, I'd always feel a little twitch, and I figured I might be gay, but then there was this girl in one of my classes, and I had the hots for her, too. At first, I wondered if I was just making it up. Trying to convince myself that I was straight. But I pretty much got the same feelings around her. I decided to go with whatever I felt and trust that whoever I was really attracted to would sort everything out. The next year, I started messing around with this guy at the housing facility where we stayed. I figured that was proof enough I was gay because it felt good and I really liked it, but then a couple of years later, I ended up messing around with a girl at school, and we started dating. After that, I pretty much only had relationships with girls and flings with guys."

"What does that make me then?" I ask.

"Oh, shit. Jay, you know I didn't mean it like that."

"Didn't you? Are you saying that this is some temporary shit?"

"No. I wasn't saying that. I was just explaining that it's kind of all over the place. I don't have some one thing set in stone that can simplify what I feel for people."

Tell me about it. That would make it too easy.

"I like having sex with *you*. I like the time that we spend together." He turns from the road and looks me directly in the eyes. "I like you, Jay."

His words offer me some comfort. I must be a real dick for interrogating him like this, but this was a lot to digest in one morning.

We stop by Home Depot. He picks up some soil for the garden and puts it in the back of the SUV. I stop asking questions because I realize they aren't getting me anywhere. Just confusing me—frustrating me—even more than I already am.

If he'd told me right away that he was bi, I doubt I would be this confused, but it's the fact that I feel like I've been blindsided by it. Not that he lied. We never actually discussed how he felt. I just assumed that he was gay. Any other guy would have just assumed he was gay. He fucks guys, therefore he's gay. This is the first time in my life that it hasn't been that simple.

When we get to Reese's, he heads out into the backyard to work on the garden. I tell him I'm gonna take a nap, but I can't fucking sleep. Not after what I just learned.

I guess it's a combination of never being with someone I knew was bi and someone with a panties fetish that is throwing me off. If he'd just been gay and wanted that, like I thought, it would have just been this quirky thing that he liked. And I would have been eager and excited about doing it again. But now that there's this whole other layer to why he wanted that, I feel a little dirty for having entertained his fantasy. And admittedly, I'm thinking, "Was he thinking about his ex-wife while he was fucking me?"

He loved her.

She broke up with him.

He obviously enjoyed fucking her, too.

I know that we needed this. That if there's any chance of us actually being something serious, I have to know the truth about who he is. But why does the truth have to be so fucking confusing?

I hop on my laptop and google everything I can about bi guys, heading to different message boards. Not much help. I try "bi guys" and "panties" and just come up with shit about crossdressing. Not helpful, either.

I wasn't expecting a google search to answer my question, but I was hoping to at least find some people who were dealing with shit like this.

Maybe I'll try later.

Why does this have to be such a big deal to me? It doesn't change that I like Reese. Doesn't change that I want to keep being with him. Maybe I'm making a big deal because I feel like something has to be wrong. Things have felt too good, been too easy between us that now there has to be something about him that's totally going to fuck up everything that we're doing. That's going to bulldoze the relationship we're reaching for.

I can get through it. Maybe not today, but I can figure out how to make this okay in my brain. I like Reese. A lot. And it meant a lot that he opened up about this to me. And now that I'm calming down, I realize how big of an asshole I was for the way I reacted to him opening his heart to me, being honest with me. His honesty shouldn't have been met with questions and accusations, but support.

I'm a bastard.

33

Reese

Disappointed. That's how I feel.

I thought sharing my history with Jay would bring us closer together, but that was a fucking mistake.

I carry a bag of soil through each row of plants, pouring liberally. When I'm finished I'll go back around and spread it with my hands.

Jay said he was going to take a nap, but I imagine he's just replaying our entire relationship, trying to make sense of it within the context of what he now knows.

The back door to the house opens and Jay comes out. The serious expression on his face isn't reassuring.

Is he coming out here to ask me some more questions? I don't know if I can deal with them right now.

"Hey, man," he says as he approaches.

"Hey." I don't look at him. I just keep spreading the soil.

"Can we talk?"

"Shoot."

"No. Like, can you set the bag down for a minute? I want to say a few things."

I stop pouring, squat, and set the bag down. As I stand back up, I look into his eyes. He doesn't look as guarded or defensive as he did earlier. I'm hoping that's a good sign.

"I'm sorry, okay?" he says. "That was a real dick move of me. You told me something important, because you were trying to be open with me, and I just shut you down."

"That's about right."

"I've never had anyone share something like that with me. And I wasn't lying when I said that it kind of weirded me out with the…panties thing. I don't know. Put yourself in my shoes. It wouldn't go through your head at all that maybe it was because you were thinking about me as a girl?"

I look over his body, his muscles tight against the T-shirt he's wearing. "Trust me, Jay, when I fuck you, I don't think about girls at all."

His lips curl at the sides, and it's the first time I've seen him ease up since our conversation back at his place.

"I'm sorry for being an asshole," he says.

"Thank you for the apology. And thank you for taking me to your place today. And listening to me. Even though you were a dick about all that, it meant a lot to me to tell you. And to learn some things about you. The only reason I did any of that was because I want to take things further, and we can only do that if we're open with each other about who we are. I have to admit that you keeping your place a secret from me made me feel like we were delaying moving forward. And in the same way, that's what I was doing with my ex-wife. By not sharing that with you, I was keeping us from being able to move on together. That's important in any relationship. Getting to know the other person. The real other person. Not just this idea that we come up with in our heads of who they are."

"I get what you mean there."

I smile.

"So all that stuff you said about Caleb?" he asks. "About moving down here because of him?"

"I asked Melanie first, and she was more than willing. She did everything she could to help me. I honestly don't know how I would have handled the amputation without her. She was the one who stayed on top of my appointments with my prosthetist. She helped make sure that I was comfortable with the prosthesis. When Caleb came back, she knew I was having a hard time mentally. She had been encouraging me to get help, but I wouldn't. I think she figured that moving near him would help us both because at least we would have each other. But it didn't do much good. Just two struggling guys trying to lean on each other for help, grasping for answers that neither of us had. And dying inside the whole time. It got even worse after he killed himself. Then Melanie and I both knew how much I needed help, and she tried to make me get it. I was stubborn, though. I didn't think I could be helped. One time she made the appointment for me to see someone at the VA's office, and I told her I was going. But I went to the grocery store instead and walked around for a few hours before going home and telling her I didn't think it would do me any good. It was a long process, even after she left, before I got help."

"I thought you said you got help after that episode you had at work...when you talked to that vet."

"He did tell me to get help, but it was a while even after that. It wasn't until a few months later when I ended up on the floor of my house for about a week after I left that job. I was having one of the worst episodes of my life. And I was thinking the sorts of thoughts that I know led Caleb to take his own life. That I wasn't right in the head. That I never would be. That I could end it all and never have to worry again. It scared the shit out of me because I realized that I didn't have a choice at that point. I was either going to do what Caleb did or see if I could find a reason to keep on going. It wasn't easy, but I made myself go to the VA office, which was about as useless as you could imagine, but I was fucking determined. I wasn't going to end up like Caleb. And if I was, I was at least going to die having fought my ass off to live."

"I'm so sorry you had to go through that."

"Not your fault. Just a crazy, shitty world that we live in. And I figured it out. Well, I'm figuring it out. This garden's helped a lot. It was one of the first things I ever did to get my mind working on something else. It was hard as fuck, too. Building it was like fucking lifting weights. A constant battle. Not physically, but against all these things in my head that cripple me...cripple me worse than..."

I don't even want to say it. I don't want to remind myself of it again. Don't I have to deal with it enough as it is?

He approaches me and kisses me softly before running his fingers through my hair.

"I hope you don't see yourself that way, Reese. As some crippled guy. Because when I look at you, when I hear about everything you've been through, I just see this incredibly strong, brave man. A man who I admire so much for working so hard to find a way to survive when everything inside him was trying to destroy him."

I smirk. "Look who's sure not being a prick anymore."

He laughs. "Shut up. I said I'm sorry."

"Whatever. Maybe I can jump in the shower and we can get back to what really matters. I think I need a pick-me-up right about now." I move toward him quickly and wrap my arms around him, keeping my glove-covered hands away from the back of his shirt, since I don't want to mess it up.

"You're all sweaty," he says, though he doesn't make it sound like a bad thing.

"You like it?" I ask.

He gazes up at me, his eyes wide with eagerness. In this hot moment, he's obviously abandoned all that concern he was dragging around with him earlier.

"I like it a lot."

I kiss him, and he doesn't hesitate to kiss me back. He rests his hand against my sweat-soaked face. He slides his hand behind my head and pulls me in closer.

When I break away, he gazes into my eyes. "Let's get things finished up out here and take a shower."

He helps me put away the soil, and I figure I'll come out tomorrow and spread it. Right now, I just want to be with Jay. Remind him that the only person I want to be fucking is him.

We head to the bedroom.

I remove my prosthesis and put it in the corner of the room, and when we get into the shower, I grab onto a rail.

I run the water, allowing it to slam against my back, blocking it from Jay, but I figure I need to get clean more than he does right now.

Jay turns to a shelf in the corner opposite the showerhead and presses down on the soap dispenser a few times, collecting a thick wad in his hand. He rubs his hands together and turns back to me. "I'll take care of this," he says, excitement in his eyes. He lathers the soap in his hands before sweeping them in semi-circles across my chest, gripping firmly like he's just trying to get a good feel.

In all the time that I wasn't having sex before he came along, it felt like I was just working out at the gym for me. Trying to be fit on the outside to show myself that, despite my weakness, I was still strong. Now, it's like all that time in the gym was finally for something…like all those amazing times we've shared in bed together, getting to see him enjoy them.

As his gaze meets mine, I don't see any concern about my handicap or my past, and it sets me at ease.

He lowers his hands, sliding them across my abdomen, feeling into the grooves between my abs. "You've got one hot eight-pack, Reese," he says.

I reach my hand that isn't on the rail to him and run my thumb between his pecs, down the vertical dip between his abs. "You've got some nice abs on you, too."

He doesn't look at me. Just continues taking in my body. Feeling his slippery fingers across it. I like how easily his hands slide across my skin.

He caresses my hips, and I'm surprised by how firm they are as he massages them with his hands. My cock steadily grows as the delightful sensation of his touch stimulates a powerful desire within me.

"You really are like a work of art," he says.

His words come with a bitter reminder of Melanie.

"What?" he asks.

"That sounds like something Melanie would have said. She was an artist. Used to paint a lot. She painted me for some time. Called me her muse. She had a difficult time painting after I got back. The only thing she did was that painting in the living room. That was actually one of the last ones she did before we divorced. But clearly we needed to because that was what she saw me as...or that's who I was. Just a sad, lonely shell of a person. I felt like shit because it wasn't just her husband who had abandoned her...so had her inspiration. The thing that gave her real joy."

"I'm sure she understood."

"Maybe too much for too long. Sorry."

"You don't have anything to be sorry about. That relationship was a big part of your life, and I like that you're comfortable sharing it with me, even when I was such a bastard to you about it." He pulls one hand back and runs the back of his fingers up and down my torso.

It's strange standing here, being on display like this before him. It makes me think of the night he wore the thong. How vulnerable he was. That's how I feel now, but more because of the things we've discussed—how much better he knows me—than being naked before him, my physical weakness revealed.

He steps closer to me, moving his hand aside as he presses his abs up against mine. My cock pushes back into my leg, but he grabs it and repositions it, pointing it up so that it rests against his stomach.

I lean down to kiss him, but he tilts his head back, pulling away. "No," he says. "Not yet."

He gazes into my eyes, giving me a moment to appreciate his brown irises—a deep mahogany color glistening in the bathroom's fluorescent light. His thick lips beg for my kiss like that's all they were made for. And they remind me of so many nights where I've just been able to take them when I chose to. To have them withheld from me even for a moment is a struggle.

I shift my weight on the rail and step aside so that he can step into the water with me.

He takes my invitation, sliding beside me so that the water runs through his hair, flattening it against his scalp. He turns to me, the water webbing across his face, dripping off his chin. His mouth hangs open as if he's about to say something or as if he's about to slide my cock into it.

He moves close to me again, pressing up against me. Now the water is streaming down both of our faces, and I can't hold back anymore. I move forward quickly and wrap my free arm around him, my cock running vertically up his torso and his sliding up the side of my leg as his torso slides slightly across the soap on mine.

We kiss in a frenzy, his hands caressing my body as I cling to him with my free arm, kissing across his face. The water slides between us as we enjoy this passion-filled moment. I get so lost in it that I lose my footing.

Shit.

I tumble forward, but he props me up. "I told you I've got you," he says before kissing me again.

It reminds me of how he carried me at the factory. His words mean so much more than just about this moment, and I'm relieved to have him here with me. Because until he entered my life, it was without meaning or purpose.

It wasn't a life. It was survival. It was struggling against my fucked-up brain constantly. Now, I have a reason for all this fighting. For the war I wage every day.

34

Jay

We hurry through our shower, and I help Reese into the bedroom. He pushes me onto the bed and hops on top of me.

His lips travel down my body, kissing with licks and nips that shoot jolts of excitement through me.

I run my hand down his back, enjoying the sensation of his smooth skin, tight against his firm muscles. When I reach his ass, I grip on. I imagine him sliding inside me as I hold onto his ass and direct his speed. Needing him faster and faster.

"I need you inside me," I say. "Please, Reese."

He grabs the condoms and lube from the nightstand while I reposition on the bed. I grab a pillow and put it behind my back before spreading my legs.

I feel so silly for all the trouble I gave him earlier. In moments like these, I realize that I don't care why Reese wants me, only that he does.

"Get on your knees," he says as he tosses the lube and condoms on the sheets. I obey his command and arch my back. He grabs my ass cheeks and pulls them apart, diving his face in first.

"Oh, God."

With his skilled tongue, he works around my rim, enjoying himself. I hear him growl, and I glance over my shoulder. He wipes some pre-come off the head of his dick before crawling up my body.

"Eat my come," he commands as he slides his fingers into my mouth. I lap it up, and it tastes just as good as it always does.

"You like it?"

"Yes."

"I'm gonna try you while I'm at it," he says, and he runs his fingers over my sensitive head and takes my pre-come. He pops his fingers into his own mouth and tastes it slowly. "Oh, fuck, Jay. That's real fucking good."

He licks his fingers some more and then runs them over my hole. He takes his time before inserting two fingers, massaging gently. Steadily, he presses them inside me.

"Reese, give me that cock. Please."

"Shh. I'll give it to you when I'm ready."

"Please…"

He moves his fingers deep within me so that I feel them hit my prostate. I curse.

He pulls his fingers out. He suits up and lubricates before entering me. "Nice and easy," he says, taking his time.

I take deep breaths as I adjust to him. We work together, him moving in as I become more at ease with each push.

He caresses his hand across my back. "Good work," he says.

I moan out as he pushes farther in. When I feel his pelvis against my ass-cheeks, I know he's in all the way.

He moves in and out, and as he finds his stride, he grips the back of my hair, pulling as tight as I like it. But tonight, I don't mind a little more.

"Don't make it easy on me," I say.

He pulls back harder so that I have to lean farther back and balance on my knees. He thrusts powerfully as my shoulder blades meet his thick chest. He wraps his arm around me and grips onto my torso.

Then he slides his foot to the side and pulls me back. We fall together until I'm stretched out on top of him as he continues fucking from beneath me.

"Damn, that's right on my prostate," I say. It feels so good. Not satisfying, but just on the edge, building and building to that inevitable sweet release.

But there's a sting to it. An unfulfilled hunger that leaves me wanting…craving…more.

He yanks back on my hair even harder so that his face is pressed against my cheek, his breath slamming against my flesh.

Goosebumps creep across my body. My balls feel like they're on fire because the pressure in them is so intense.

"I'm getting too close," I say.

"I am too."

I'm relieved to hear that because I was terrified I'd spew out and leave him hanging. And all I want is to please him right now. To give him the satisfaction he craves because that's what's fucking turning me on right now.

He fucks me even harder, and it's too late for me because I spew onto my stomach just as I feel him twist with that movement that lets me know he's coming too.

I shake my head back and forth as come continues rushing out of my dick. Heat fills my cheeks, and I lose myself in the intensity of the experience. We pant and sweat as we fall together from our climaxes.

After we clean up, rinse off, and dispose of the condom, we crawl back into bed. His arms around me and mine around him, we gaze into each other's eyes.

He beams.

A sweet sensation fills me, and I imagine many more nights like this with him.

It's a safe feeling. It assures me that it's safe for me to settle down. Like I don't have to spend the rest of my life running.

Could this really work? Could I get to enjoy being with Reese for so much longer? It's a thought I wouldn't normally allow myself to have, but one that excites me. I want to be with him. I want to have so many more nights like this. And for the first time in a very long time, a calm sensation sweeps through me. That look in his eyes seems to be appreciating me as much as I'm appreciating him.

I care so much for him. More than I've ever cared for another guy.

The word *love* keeps running through my mind, but it scares me, too. It's too soon for me to be feeling anything more than lust. What I'm feeling is just an illusion...like I've felt with other guys I thought there might be a future with. I've never had this before, so it's just more than I'm used to.

But could it become that? The more time we spend together, could I get to the place where I feel that way for him...I know if there's anyone I could feel that way about, it's Reese.

"Jay," he says softly.

And by the way he looks at me, it's as though he's about to say what I'm thinking. And I want him to. I want to know that I'm not alone in this.

He starts, but stops himself. His gaze travels over my face before he says, "That was hot as hell."

Disappointment rushes through me.

I shouldn't be disappointed. Not after what we just shared. Not after what I just felt.

But I can't help it. As much as Reese has given me, I want more. So much more. I'll settle for what we have right now, though. We have all the time in the world to get to know each other. For what we feel to strengthen.

35

Reese

Being with Jay has been a dream.

He's given me something I didn't think I'd ever feel again: peace of mind.

Being with him relaxes my thoughts and every part of my body. Eight years ago, I never would have thought I would reach this place. That I could feel like I did before the world showed me just how dark and cruel it could be. With Jay, I feel secure—like at least in the moments we share together, I can allow myself to enjoy pleasure. I don't have to live in worry and paranoia.

The other night, I wanted to tell him how much I care about him. As I gazed into his beautiful eyes, thinking he looked adorable as fuck with the way a stray lock of his hair curled down across his forehead, I wanted to tell him just how much he means to me. I caught myself before I did, though. Reminded myself that words like those don't have to come yet.

We have plenty of time.

Tonight we're heading to the Louis C.K. show, something I'm excited about sharing with him. I'm so pleased I was able to give him a present he really wants—one that can take us out of the mundane world we deal with on a daily basis.

We need an escape.

I head up the driveway after a long day at the factory. Jay's running by the store to pick up some condoms and lube since last night we discovered we're running low. I told him to make sure he bought a twenty-four pack because at the rate we're going, we need it.

I retrieve my keys from my pocket.

"Reese!"

The loud, boisterous voice jolts me so much I drop my keys.

I'm on edge in an instant, my body filled with tension. The blood in my face drains. The joy I was experiencing vanishes.

My thoughts crowd with flashes.

Running through streets, avoiding gunfire.

Bombs going off.

The insurgent coming into the room after the IED went off. I feel the need to protect Caleb, Drake, and myself.

I turn and see someone coming at me and jump forward.

The man backs away quickly, throwing his hands up before him.

It's Damon.

My fucking neighbor.

Shit. Calm the fuck down! Act cool.

Sweat beads across my forehead. My body quakes with an intensity that's concerning as a sharp pain pushes into my chest. Makes me feel like I'm about to have a heart attack.

It's a familiar sensation—one I know all too well.

I keep trying to calm myself, but I know there's no use.

"Hey, man," he says. He looks completely non-threatening in his light blue scrubs. He works as a physician assistant at the hospital downtown. "Everything okay? Jesus, I didn't think I would scare you like that, but you're white as a ghost."

"Sorry, Damon."

He doesn't normally come over like this. I'll typically only see him on weekends when I'm mowing the lawn or doing yard work.

I kneel down and pick up my keys, hoping the action will distract me and keep him from picking up on my strange behavior. As I stand back up, he holds out a letter.

"This was in my mail today," he says, passing it to me.

I take it quickly. He tenses up. I can tell he's surprised by how I snatched it away.

"Sorry about the way I'm acting," I say. "I'm just a little on edge. There was a lot going on at the factory."

"Not an issue, bud," he says, but it's obvious by the look he gives me that he doesn't think anything that happened at work can account for how I'm behaving.

"Thanks for bringing it over."

"Yeah. And you know, if you and your friend want to swing by for dinner one night, you know you're more than welcome."

I can tell by the look in his eyes that he knows what we are, and that's the sweetest thing he could have said. "Thanks, Damon."

He grins and says, "Catch you later." He starts like he's about to pat my shoulder, but stops himself. He must sense that that's too much for me.

I take deep breaths. I try to remember all the processes that Laura's taught me over the years, but my desperation to soothe myself in this moment only makes it even worse.

I can't be like this on such an important night.

I count my breaths, but it just makes me hyper-aware of how much I'm shaking right now.

I want to fall down, curl into a ball, and disappear.

When I get inside, I lock the door and drop to my knees.

My chest tightens even more. The pressure is frightening. I can feel my fucking heartbeat. It's fast. Like my heart's about to pop out of my fucking chest.

Jay will be home soon, I remind myself. I have to get back to normal for him.

I drop the letter Damon handed me on the floor.

I see who it's from: Melanie Carmichael.

Oh, Melanie. She hurt me so much, but I hurt her more. Every night I wasn't there for her. Every night I recoiled from her touch. Every night she tried to get me to go out or to pull me from the grip of my despair only to be met with the cold shell of a person that I'd become after I came back home.

The combination of Damon freaking me out and Melanie's letter collide, generating the perfect panic attack.

I lie on my stomach, resting my hands beside me.

It's pointless to fight. I have to go with it like Laura says, but I don't want Jay to come home and see me like this. I don't want him feeling like every time I fall, he has to catch me. But my awareness of how this will affect Jay only makes it hurt even more.

I beg my body to help me.

He was so excited when he saw the tickets, and I've been so eager to spend tonight with him. However, this episode reminds me of how long things like this can stretch out…and how they can interfere with my life. Reminds me of a time when I could hardly function because they were so intense. Of the stretches that still occur…that leave me walking through life like some sort of zombie.

I knew the relief I was experiencing with Jay wouldn't last. That one day I would have to confront this dark part of me again.

You can do this.

But I know willpower only works against me. I always use it as a tool to beat up on myself.

Relax. Relax.

But I can't.

Jay can't come home and find me in this state.

I need to at least make it to the couch so I can look like I'm tired or taking a nap. That'll give me time to recover. We have at least two hours before we have to leave here anyway.

Come on.

I need to be strong long enough to get there.

I hear the familiar sound of Jay's car engine outside.

The couch feels so fucking far away, even though it's just a few feet.

Mental flashes of the urgency of war return to me. It's like I'm racing through streets, on high alert, knowing there could be a sniper aiming for me. That I or any one of my friends could be shot dead in a moment.

I push to my knees. It feels like I'm struggling against a three-hundred-pound weight. I crawl across the floor.

The sound of the car door opening and closing.

I don't have much time.

He's not going to find me like this. I'm not fucking this up.

I press my hand against the back of the couch as I start rising to my feet.

I hear the rattling of the lock on the door. Jay must have just put his key in.

The pain in my chest is like someone's sticking a knife in it.

Do it, I command myself before getting up and throwing myself over the couch.

As the door opens, I settle on my back, closing my eyes and hoping to God I look like I'm taking a nap. That I haven't been caught. I doubt I'm giving a good performance of appearing comfortable because I can feel that every muscle in my body is flexed.

"Hey," Jay sings out, stressing the dissonance between our mental states.

He closes the door as I pretend to wake up. "Oh, hey," I fight to say.

He eyes me uneasily. He can tell something's wrong, and I'm pissed at how shitty I am at keeping this shit from him. "You okay?"

"Just got a headache. I took some ibuprofen."

It's shitty to lie to him, but I won't ruin tonight. This was supposed to be a fun-filled date where we would laugh together and forget about all this shitty stuff. But now here it is, right in my face, torturing me.

"Okay," he says as he approaches and leans over the couch, offering a kiss.

I reciprocate, but I can't offer him the sort of kiss I usually would. I'm too busy fighting this demon within me.

He notices and pulls away. "Sorry," he says. "You need me to get anything?"

I see the same look in his eyes that I used to see in Melanie's. Helplessness. Worry.

He wants me to open up, but he doesn't want to push.

I don't want to talk about it. I don't want to spoil everything. And that's all that my goddamn brain seems to do. Spoil shit.

"I'm good," I say even though I'm far from it.

He twists his lips into a wry smirk. "Okay. I'm just going to shower up and make some dinner then."

"Just make yourself some. I'm not going to be hungry. Thank you, though."

"Sure." He heads on to the bedroom.

At least while he's showering, I have a chance at recovering. Although I can tell by how powerful this is that I don't have a chance of getting better.

Not tonight. I have to find a way out of this. This isn't like my usual episode—the ones he's seen.

It's like the ones I had back when I was with Melanie. Because I'm not just reminded of what I did to her, but what I fear I'll end up doing to Jay.

He's had to help me out of my attacks on several occasions. He's good at it. He's amazing. And I know he would be understanding about tonight, but he shouldn't have to be. He shouldn't have to live like this. He has his own problems. He shouldn't have to take on my demons, too—these demons that can creep up at any time and take what should have been a fun moment and turn it into something dark.

I knew this moment would come.

I kept warning myself, but I was so greedy to enjoy him that I wouldn't let myself fully consider the consequences.

A horrifying realization hits me. One I've known all along, but which in my emotional state and dread regarding the letter from Melanie is only amplified:

I could ruin Jay's life. If he stays with me, I could jade him the way I jaded Melanie.

I want him so much, though. Want him with every part of my being. It's a selfish desire. I want him here because he makes me better. Because I want someone to soothe my pain. What do I really offer him? What can I offer him in the long-term other than the misery of having to nurse me back to health every time an episode like this hits me? When they become so severe that I can't enjoy something I want to share with him so much? When I have to be a witness to him slowly becoming more and more disheartened by our life together?

I remember how alive Melanie was before I went to Iraq. Her bright smile. Her zest. Her playfulness.

We had the same sort of frisky fun together that I now share with Jay.

But then there was the defeated look in her eyes before she left. Those dead eyes, nearly as dead as mine because of how I killed her soul more and more every day. When she'd given up on crying or pleading for me to get help. When I wasn't sure she even believed she could be happy ever again.

To think I could do that to Jay—that he could wind up as sad and miserable and that I could let him do that like I did with Melanie—tears me apart.

As much as I want to believe I'm better—that things have changed—this reminds me it's not true.

This will never go away. It can't. This is a part of who I am now, and I've known it all along.

Some romantic part of me wanted to believe that Jay could make this go away. Could heal all these internal wounds. But that was just a fantasy.

This is the reality. This is what had to happen.

We shared a brief moment of bliss—a moment where I was free of the true depths of my despair, but my moods aren't ever static. The happy moments don't last forever. It's one thing to go to work and push through the hard days there, but it's another to have to pretend to be okay within a relationship when I'm falling apart inside. A coworker doesn't care if I'm distant. A lover does.

I won't do that to another person. Not someone who I care about as much as Jay. It's wrong. Abusive, even. How could I live with myself if I had to come face-to-face with a version of Jay that was as emotionally depleted as Melanie was?

How could I be happy knowing that I did that to my Jay?

Her words echo in the back of my mind: *"I can't do this anymore."*

It breaks my heart.

Tears into my soul.

You know what you have to do.

I have to hurt him, but better for him to get hurt now and move on with his life than for me to fill his life with the darkness that consumes me. To let it destroy him, too.

I won't let that happen. Not to him.

36

Jay

"Feeling any better?" I ask.

It's an hour and a half until the show. It'll only take fifteen minutes to get to the Fox, but between finding parking and getting to our seats, we need to leave soon.

"Jay, why don't you just go without me? That headache's gotten a lot worse."

"You need some more ibuprofen?"

"No. I've taken plenty. I just…I don't think I'm going to be able to enjoy tonight."

When I came in and saw him lying on the couch, I could tell he was rattled. Considering he was fine at work today, I know something's triggered him. Something changed between the time we got off work and when I got home. I've seen how quickly a sound can set him off, but if that's all it is, why doesn't he just tell me? He knows he can talk to me about this kind of stuff. Hell, I've seen him have episodes before.

"Did something happen?" I ask.

"No."

A lie. "You can talk to me if something set you off. That's not something you should be ashamed of."

"I just don't want to talk about it." His tone is severe enough that I know better than to push. I can wait till he calms down and this episode passes.

"We'll just skip the show tonight," I say. Sad as I am that we're going to miss something I was so excited about, it's for the best. He can't handle the show tonight.

"Jay, you should go."

"I wanted to go *with you*. I'm not interested in going by myself."

"I'm sorry. I just—"

"No. It's fine. Don't feel bad about it. Shit like this happens."

I'm frustrated, but I won't abandon him.

Disheartening as it is that just as soon as we had a chance to do something fun, an episode had to come along and throw a wrench in things.

I understand that this is what Reese was talking about. The sorts of issues I signed up for.

"You really need to go," he says.

"I'm just going to turn in for the night, I think. I'm tired anyway." I head into the bedroom and close the door.

Emptiness rises within me.

I'm all alone.

A part of me expects Reese to come in here and console me. To shake out of this state he's in and go out to the show because he cares about me so much. Intellectually, I get that it doesn't work that way. Doesn't keep me from wishing that something would change, and he would hurry in and apologize for his curt behavior, hop into some nice clothes, and dash off to the theatre with me. That's a pipe dream, but it's a shame that tonight won't be a fun, frisky time with Reese. This is part of the package. I knew that getting into this. I've seen him struggle with this before. I want to be here for him, but he isn't letting me, and it's frustrating as fuck.

I decide to get ready for bed, hoping he'll come in and join me when he's feeling better. But I wait…and wait…and wait.

He stays in the living room. I don't hear him get up and move. Not even to go to the bathroom, and it concerns me too much to stay in here and act like nothing's going on. He knows what's happening, and if we just ignore this, that's not going to help him get any better.

I head back into the living room. He's right where I left him a few hours ago.

He stares at the ceiling until I move closer, and he looks at me for a moment. I don't see the usual look of appreciation in his eyes. I see that distant cold gaze.

It makes me sad.

"Feeling any better?" I ask.

"A little."

If anything, he looks even worse than when I told him I was going to bed. Like he's just been stewing in self-destructive thoughts. I imagine him replaying that time in Fallujah again and again in his head. Thinking about all that happened. All that could have happened. I imagine him thinking about what Caleb did and how helpless he felt in it all.

I kick at the base of the couch, hitting my toe lightly against it. As I gaze down at it, I see something out of the corner of my eye. It's an envelope on the floor, on the other end of the couch. It has crinkled marks in the middle, as though someone gripped it tight.

My curiosity gets the best of me.

Is this what set him off? Is this the thing that made him go from being totally cool today to being this shell of a person tonight?

I meander over to it, trying to act casual. Like I'm not up to no good, but given the state he's in, I wonder if he'll even notice.

I grip the letter between my toes and kick my leg behind me, grabbing it.

As he shifts his head, turning to the TV, I take a glance to see who the letter's from.

Melanie.

His ex-wife.

"Reese," I say.

He keeps staring ahead. He's gone, and regardless of why he's gone, it's like he's not even here. And it's the most painful and lonely feeling in the world. This must have been what he would do to her. Why she couldn't stay.

My face trembles and my eyes water. I'm not proud. I shouldn't be about to break down when I know what's causing this. But as impersonal as it is, it feels so deeply personal.

I walk around the couch so that I'm standing in front of him. So that he has to look at me.

"Reese, why didn't you tell me you got this?"

I display the letter. He looks at it for a moment before his gaze drifts. "What about it?"

"This is why you're acting like this, isn't it? Jesus, Reese, you should have just told me."

"It's about more than that."

"This is clearly part of it, though. Talk to me. I want to help you."

"You can't help me, Jay. No one can help me."

I've never heard him like this. He sounds so hopeless. So overwhelmed.

"The Reese I know is a fighter. Even when it gets hard. Things like this come up, but he knows how to get through them."

"It's more than that stupid letter," he says. "All that did was remind me of a mistake I was about to make."

"A mistake?"

"We can't do this."

"Reese, you've gotten through shit like this plenty of times. We're just gonna—"

"This isn't about this episode. It's about us. This isn't going to work."

He might as well have decked me. I open my mouth a few times, trying to think of how to react to this.

"I can't do that again," he says. "I'm not ready for a relationship. That letter just reminded me that it's too much."

"What kind of bullshit is that?" Is he being fucking serious right now? Is that why he's so upset? Here I thought he was having some sort of breakdown over the past, but really, he's just been dreading the idea of a future with me?

No. My mind races through all the beautiful moments we've shared. The moments when I could feel us getting so much closer. That wasn't a lie. But I've thought that before. I thought that with Kyle and the other assholes. Have I been fooling myself this whole time?

Have I been feeling so much more for him than he's been feeling for me?

I refuse to believe that.

"Are you telling me that this whole fucking time that we've been doing all this shit together, you haven't felt anything for me? It's just been this fun thing without any deeper feelings behind it? More than fucking. Because it sure was more than that for me. I...I..."

Don't say it.

But I can't help it. I have to know. Because if he really doesn't feel this way for me now, then I need to get the fuck out of here. It's only going to hurt worse the longer he lets it go on.

"...I'm falling in love you."

201

He looks at me, his eyes wide in horror. Like that's the worst fucking thing I could have said to him.

I feel like I did when I wore those panties for him. Naked. Exposed. But in the worst possible way.

He sits up. It's the most he's moved since I came home.

He rises to his feet. "Love? Are you out of your mind?"

He sounds pissed.

"We've been seeing each other for two months, and you're going to tell me you love me? You don't know me. You don't know who the fuck I am, and I don't know you."

I've never seen him like this before. Has he really been hiding this side of himself all along?

"Why are you being so mean?" I ask.

His gaze drifts. "You can't handle this."

"What?"

"This is going to be too much for you, and you might not leave me today or tomorrow, but one day, you will. Just like Melanie did."

"How can you say that? You haven't even given me a chance."

"I don't need to give you a chance. I know how you are. You've lived your life running from your problems, and this one is too much for you to handle. Melanie was a strong woman…a dedicated woman, and it was too much even for her. That's what getting that letter reminded me."

"I'm still here, aren't I? I do always run, but you've given me a reason to stay. I can prove to you that I'm strong enough for this. After all that we've shared, are you really willing to just walk away from this?"

He looks into my eyes, and without hesitation says, "Yes."

It's like when he punched me that night when I woke him up from his bad dream.

I'm stunned. In shock.

And so hurt.

It's like his response was designed to hurt me, and the shock of his words unleashes my own defenses: "You're a fucking asshole."

I hurry past him, tears welling in my eyes. I don't want him to see how he's affected me. I need to get out of here.

I head into the bedroom, throw the letter from Reese's ex-wife on the bed, and collect my clothes from the closet and the dresser before placing them on the mattress beside it.

It feels worse than when Kyle cheated on me. Maybe because I was stupid enough to let someone back in. Opened myself up to be hurt like that.

I keep waiting for him to come in and apologize. To say that he's sorry. But the man out there isn't the man I thought I was falling for.

How could he say that? How could he throw us away?

I want to believe it's just this breakdown he's having, but I can't.

Maybe he wasn't even dwelling on the war. Maybe he was just sitting in there, stewing over us and how he realized I'm not the man he wants to be with.

After I grab some of my belongings from the bathroom, I collect my clothes in one big scoop off the bed and head back into the living room.

Reese sits on the couch, facing away from me.

Doesn't even have the balls to face me after what a dick he just was.

I think about saying goodbye to him, but that's more than he deserves from me now.

I head out the door, but something stops me. "Goodbye, Reese," I say, not because I want to, but because I have to. Because I need the closure.

I leave, and the moment I close the door behind me, the tears flow freely.

I hurry to the car and throw my stuff inside.

None of this feels real. How could we have spent so much time together, gotten so far, for it to end like this?

How could we have gotten so far for it all to come crashing down in a day?

It doesn't matter. I just have to get out of here. I have to get far away. I have to leave all this behind and forget all about Reese.

Even though I know I never really will.

I burst into tears and collapse onto the steering wheel.

I fucking love him. How could he do this to me? Why doesn't he want to be with me?

37

Reese

What have I done?

The physical pain I'm experiencing is more acute than ever.

Why did he say he loves me?

I love him too, but it didn't make what I had to do any easier.

I kept fighting doing the right thing.

But when he came out of the bedroom, I knew I had to find a way to get rid of him.

I had to save him from the hurt.

I was awful to him. Terrible, but I had to be. I had to make him feel like I was a bastard for not believing in him to get him to leave because if I'd just said that I didn't want to hurt him, he would have stayed. He would have convinced me that we could get through it, and I know where that leads. I had that same discussion with Melanie so many times before the end. And even if he was willing to suffer, I'm not willing to watch him become an empty person because of who I've become.

He may think I'm a terrible person forever for how I just treated him, but I would have been a selfish monster to keep him here any longer when I know how the story ends. When I've already played it out once before.

Now he'll run. That's who he is, but I have to believe he would have done that anyway. Once it all fell apart. At least now he still has life in his body. At least I haven't totally destroyed him the way I could have.

Running is what he knows. Running is what he's good at. He's a survivor.

But that doesn't make me feel better about how far I let it get.

I knew this was on the horizon. That the darkness would return. But I entertained the fantasy that he could make me better. I wanted to believe we could push through, but after the despair of this latest encounter crippled me, I knew better. I believed the same thing with her. With my poor, beautiful Melanie who I sucked the life out of.

This isn't a battle I'll ever win. No one wins with PTSD. And as much as I tried to convince myself that we could fight together, if it was that easy, Melanie never would have gotten so hurt.

I never would have ruined her life.

I promised myself I would never hurt anyone the way I hurt her.

He'll never know, but I didn't do this because I don't care about him or because I didn't believe in him. I did it because I care about him so much and can't bear the thought of wrecking his life.

Why did you leave, Jay?

The thought lingers even though I know the answer.

No, Jay. You deserve better than this life. So much better.

I sit in silence, reeling in the physical pain from the horrible reminder that Melanie's letter awoke within me. Still struggling with the powerful anxiety that's crippled me—the anxiety I had to fight with my everything to find the energy—the will—to stand up and help Jay get out of my life forever.

This isn't his fight.

I lie back down on the couch, waiting for the pain to subside. But after what just happened, the intensity and excitement of it all, that's not likely. I might even have to call out of work tomorrow and just lie right here.

Fuck me. Fuck me to hell.

I can't have happiness. Not like other people. I'm not kidding myself anymore.

This is my life. This is all I can hope for. The silence. Utter loneliness and despair.

I'm so sorry, Jay. I'm so sorry, Melanie.

At least I had a moment with him—a beautiful moment where the pain was dull and the pleasure so powerful. At least in more lucid moments I'll be able to cling onto that the way I once clung onto Jay's body.

38

Jay

I push my bedroom door open. I have to start packing.

I'm outta here.

How could Reese say that to me?

The other night, I could have sworn as we looked into each other's eyes, we felt the same way for each other. That he was just on the brink of telling me how much more he felt for me.

Was I so wrong?

And then on top of that to tell me that I'm not strong enough. That I'm just going to leave him.

How can he think that little of me?

It doesn't matter. I need to erase him from my mind. Tomorrow, I'm getting the fuck out of town. I'm heading to Chicago. That was always the plan anyway. I knew I'd have to move on at some point.

God, how stupid could I have been for fucking with the boss? Now I don't have any choice but to leave.

I can't ever show my face back at the factory.

Right when I finally find a reason to change—a reason to settle down—everything goes to shit.

I don't want to run. I'm so tired of always running.

I pack my duffle bag with as much shit as I can, take it out to the car, and shove it in the back seat. I return to the house and keep grabbing things, making a pile in the middle of the room.

At least I don't have much. My nomadic lifestyle makes it so easy for me to move on again.

I grab a pile of clothes and carry it out to the car.

Gotta go. Always gotta go.

I throw it in the passenger's seat with the other crap I grabbed from Reese's house. I try to close the door, but it jams on some of the clothes that are starting to fall out. I open it back up and move some shit around when I notice an envelope in the clothes that I piled in here from Reese's place.

It's the letter from his ex-wife.

I must have snatched it by accident with the clothes after I set that stuff on the bed.

This is what Reese is running from. His past. He can never escape it. It's always there. Whether it's a memory creeping into his thoughts while he sleeps or a letter from a woman who loved him, no matter what he does, it's always there.

I'm no different.

No matter where I go. No matter how hard I try to escape the pain, it's always there. Following me. It chases me, not in the way that Reese's demons haunt him, but in its own twisted way.

What's going to happen if I change the city one more time? Change of faces. Change of names. Change of jobs. But there will still be pain. There's always pain. That's what Reese has learned too.

I gaze at my stuff, piled up in the passenger's seat. Not even in a box or suitcase.

It's a great symbol of what my life really is. Messy, jumbled, chaotic.

Do I really want to head up to Chicago only to find myself running into this same fate?

I could do it so easily, but I don't want to. I'm tired.

I glance back at the house.

Charlie stands in the doorway. He doesn't have that playful expression on his face—the one I'm accustomed to.

"Want to talk about it?" he asks as he walks down the porch steps and approaches me.

He glances into the car.

"Man troubles?"

"Not really troubles. It's over."

"I know you probably don't want an old man butting into your life, but that's what I'm about to do."

"Won't matter. He doesn't want me."

"I saw the way he was ogling you when you boys were here. And I know the difference between a man who's smitten and a man who…wants more than just to fuck around. Maybe I wasn't always good at sensing it with the guys I was with, but I can sense it with others. That man cares about you."

"Whatever," I say. But I want to believe him, and considering everything we've been through, it's hard for me not to.

"A fight is just a fight. It doesn't have to be the end," he says.

It reminds me of what Reese said about not running.

Maybe this is the demon I have to confront.

He sets his hand on my shoulder. "You okay?" he asks.

I shake my head as my chin quivers. "Not really."

"Let's have some tea," he suggests. "Just chat with an old man for a bit. You don't have to leave right now."

"Thank you, Charlie."

He leads me back inside, and I tell him about everything that's happened between us. I share how I feel about Reese and how I thought he felt about me. About Reese's past, and then about our confrontation tonight. When I'm finished, Charlie says, "Well, here's some more unsolicited advice. He's been through hell and back. And now he's got this guy who he's getting serious with, who's pulling him out of his comfort zone, and he's scared as fuck of fucking up your life with his PTSD. Think about if you were getting into a relationship with someone who had cancer. You think they'd be eager to let you sign on while they had to endure treatments and basically put you through hell while they were dealing with it? That's what we're talking about here."

"It's more than that. He doesn't believe I can handle it. He knows how I live my life, and he thinks I'm gonna run."

"He was having an episode. I'm sure it felt painful when you opened up to him and told him you love him, but you deserve to talk to him about this again. Not just what he said in the middle of the worst of it."

He's right. I know he is.

"You can run off now and never know the truth. Go ahead. Prove him right. I know you're scared he might really not feel the way you feel, but do you want to spend the rest of your life wondering what might have happened if you'd stuck around to fight for him? He expects you to run, but if you stay, you can show him that this is important to you. That he's important to you."

"I don't want to run again," I admit. "I don't know what good it'll really do me. It's always the same story everywhere I go. Until I met him, that is. I can't keep living like that."

"So you're willing to work for the man who broke your heart? Even if he decides that he doesn't want you?"

"Yeah. I can't live like that anymore. If Reese wants me gone, he's going to have to find a way to fire me."

"That's the spirit, kid," he says with a wink.

Although just thinking about facing him again makes the tears pour from my eyes. God, I just know I'm going to lose it in front of him.

Charlie heads to bed, and I unpack my car, putting everything back in my room. Then I take the letter from Melanie and set it on my desk.

I'll give this back to him tomorrow. Can't wait to see the fucking look on his face when he sees me and has to deal with this letter all over again. And when he realizes I'm not the kid he thought would just run at the first sign of trouble. That I'm bigger than that now. Although he's the reason for that. He's made me better in so many ways, and even if he doesn't want me, I have to give him credit for that.

I lie in bed. It's going to be a lonely night. The loneliest night I've had in a while.

I'm used to him holding me. Used to the occasional kisses on my forehead right before he drifts off.

Mad as I am, I keep replaying our time together over and over again in my head.

The laughs. The pleasure. The connection.

I wasn't imagining it. Mean as he was tonight, I can't believe that he really meant it.

When I got home, he was cold and distant. That letter set him off. Made him think about his marriage to Melanie.

I'm half-tempted to open it just to pry, but I'm not going to disrespect him like that.

He said she left him because of how distant he became, and she couldn't handle it anymore.

Is he afraid that if we really let this turn into something, I'll do the same thing?

He doesn't understand how I feel. I don't give a shit about the episodes. Even not seeing a fucking show tonight. Does he think I would just leave him when it got hard? Abandon him?

As I dwell on his motives, I'm pissed that I left. I should have fucking stayed and duked it out with him.

It was my fight-or-flight response. And damn, am I ever good at flying.

It was just so hard to face his rejection. God, I nearly shut down when he pushed me away.

I remind myself of how much pain he was in when I got home. There's more to this than he's letting on, and like Charlie said, I deserve an answer. A real answer.

39

Reese

I feel like shit as I stand in my office, the tension lingering from my panic attack yesterday. It wasn't so bad that I couldn't get out of bed today. I pushed myself to come in to work because I knew I needed the distraction. But it was nearly impossible to get out the door. I even had to fucking take an Uber just to get here. I didn't have the strength to drive. It's not as bad as I feared, but it's bad enough that I'm glad I did what I did. That I saved Jay.

The door to my office opens, and Jay storms in.

Fuck, he's here? What the hell?

I would've sworn after our fight that he would take off. It kept me up most of the night, as I considered calling him again and again, apologizing for what an asshole I'd been. Begging him to take me back. But what I did wasn't to make me feel better.

It's to make his life easier.

As I stand up from my desk, he approaches quickly, as though he's about to punch me. The veins in his neck push forward. His face is bright red. His hair curls naturally, revealing how little he did to it this morning, reminding me of all those mornings when he let it fall naturally rather than gelling it.

He throws a letter down on my desk.

Melanie's letter.

I didn't find it last night after he left, but I didn't care. I wasn't interested in reading it anyway.

"I want you to fucking tell me what's really going on," he says.

"We don't have anything else to talk about."

"I call bullshit on everything you said last night. Really? A letter comes from the ex-wife who left you, you freak out over a panic attack and then try to spin it around like the reason you want out is because you believe I'll run when things get hard. I've been replaying everything that's been going on between us over and over again in my head, and unless you were one hell of a fucking actor all this time, I'm not the only one falling in love here."

Shit. It's even worse than I thought.

"Jay—" I begin. I was hoping it wouldn't come to this. I had the strength to get rid of him once. I was hoping that's all I would need strength for.

"I'm not done talking. Now you be honest with me right now, and tell me what this is really about. Do you really think that I would leave you like your ex-wife? Do you think that I'm that kind of guy?"

He breathes intensely, as though he just used up an inordinate amount of strength saying that.

Goddammit.

Time for the truth.

"Jay, I didn't think you'd be like my ex-wife because you'd leave. I thought you'd be like her because you'd stay."

All his defensiveness. His anger. His tension—dissolves. I've thrown him. Totally dismantled the only argument that he'd prepared for.

"You don't know what it's like to watch someone you care about, someone who was so happy, filled with life, disappear. She used to bounce around at parties. She was the girl who would make everyone laugh. That's how I fell for her. I was at a friend's place. There were about twenty people there, and she came up to me and said, 'You're cute. Mind giving me a ride?' I told her I didn't bring a car. She was like, 'Who said anything about a car?'"

I can't help but laugh even now about how forward she was. How bold.

"Throughout college, we would go to every party, and she was known for this loud, powerful laugh. When people heard it, they would just be captivated. It enchanted them. Made them think, 'Who the fuck is this girl and how is she so fucking happy?' And we were happy together. I honestly didn't know that it was possible to be that happy with another human being, but when I was with her, everything was magic. She was a vision. And everything I wanted at the time. But when I got back from Iraq, all I could see was darkness. And no amount of magic could save me from what I'd become. Day in and day out, I watched as the woman I loved tried to reach me. She did everything she could. And after Caleb died...after he killed himself...I realized it was just getting worse.

"I remember one afternoon, I was just sitting on the couch, staring forward, because like last night, that's all I could do. I was crippled with anxiety and paranoia. I was paralyzed by this fear that had overtaken me.

212

And she sat on the recliner beside me, being there for me, and I just looked at her and saw the dead expression on her face. She told me, 'I can't do this anymore.' She meant keeping on like that without me getting any help. And the look in her eyes, the despair in her voice, reminded me of what I had to look at every morning in the mirror. And you don't know how horrible it is to ruin another person's life until you have to be witness to the pathetic person they've become—the miserable empty void of a person they've become because of you. So I set her free."

"You told me she left you," Jay says.

"She did. After I told her I didn't love her anymore."

Tears slide down my face, but I'm not ashamed of how I felt about Melanie. I'm not ashamed of how I protected her from the person I became.

"It was the only thing I knew would get rid of her. If she'd known it was just to protect her, she wouldn't have left. She would have tried to be noble. She would have wanted to be there for me. But I didn't want that. I didn't want anyone there. I wanted her to leave so that I could curl up into a ball and disappear forever.

"I'm not okay, Jay. What you've seen are moments. You don't understand how bad it gets, and how much it can take over my life. All this time we've shared has been incredible, but it's a lie. I've been able to slide by for a little while because I was lucky, but just ask my therapist. She knows just how bad it can get even in a good year. I'm lucky to be able to make it to work during the really bad periods, but it's a fight every day to look like I'm normal. I can do that with employees, but not with someone I care about…someone I care so fucking much about."

"You don't get to make that choice," he says. "That wasn't right of you to make it for her, and you sure as hell don't get to make it for me. How dare you think that you had a right to decide, after everything we've shared, that you knew what was best for me? I'm not a child, Reese. I may fucking act like it sometimes, but I have a choice in this."

"But I just don't want you to make a choice that you're going to spend the rest of your life regretting. I don't want you to look back at all your time with me and wish you had been somewhere else…with someone else. To feel like you're dead inside because I killed you. Because I couldn't be there for you."

He tilts his head, a sober expression shifting across his face.

213

"Oh my God," he says. "This isn't just about Melanie, is it? You feel responsible for Caleb's death, too. Because you couldn't help him. And then you felt like you were doing the same thing to Melanie. Watching her die, on the inside though, and knowing there was nothing you could do because of everything you were going through. That's it, isn't it?"

I turn from him because he's so fucking right, but I'm embarrassed that he can see through me like this.

He moves toward me, but I back away toward the wall. "Jay, please. I was strong enough last night, but I can't do it today."

"Reese, this isn't fair. I get to choose what I do with my life."

"Why are you even talking to me after the horrible shit I said to you last night?" I ask, looking back at him again.

"Because I wasn't willing to believe you meant it, and if you did, I needed you to show me that again to shut down what hope I had that what we shared was real. What I felt was real. But now I know it was, so you can sure as fuck bet I'm not going anywhere. Granted, I'm gonna fucking hate you for a while because you were an asshole, but I'm not leaving."

"What about me having a choice?" I ask. "Don't I have a right to decide who I hurt? I'm so tired of hurting people, Jay. And I sure as fuck don't want to hurt you."

"I'm not Melanie," he says. "Melanie didn't sign up for this. She married you before you went to war. Before you had issues. And what you had was bigger than either of you back then, but this…we can work through this. You're not the man you were back then. You're getting help now. You've made progress. And I've seen that it gets bad."

"You haven't seen how bad it can get. Even this isn't the worst."

"Then let me see. Let me decide for myself if I can handle it. Because I do love you, Reese. I didn't think it was possible for me to feel this way for another person…love you so much that even after you were a complete dick to me, it still wasn't over for me. Let me in. Don't shut me down now when we could be so happy together."

I hate myself right now because I want it so much. I want to be with him, but I'm still scared as shit that this'll blow up in both of our faces.

"And what will you do when a year from now…or five years from now…when you've had to coach me out of every panic attack, when you've

214

had to wake up time and time again to me nearly about to attack you in bed over some nightmare? Melanie couldn't even sleep in the same bed with me when it got really bad. Is that what you'll do? Or what about when I can't go out anywhere with you because I don't even want to leave the bed? How will you handle that?"

He approaches me, not breaking eye contact. Not even flinching. He takes my hand. "Why don't we find out together?"

The warmth of his touch offers me comfort, comfort I'm ashamed of accepting.

He places his other hand against my cheek, equally comforting.

"Let's do this together, Reese."

As he leans into me, I don't refuse him. I just kiss him. Kiss him because I want his lips on mine so badly. Because a night without him was already too much for me. Because even if I'm making the wrong decision here, even if I'm being selfish, I want him more than I can bear. Hearing him offer to do this with me is too much for me to resist. It's not that I don't want to be alone. It's that I don't want to be without Jay.

Not for another day. Not ever again.

40

Jay

Reese's kiss is as intoxicating as ever.

It's the sort of kiss that dissolves all the confusion from yesterday.

He wants me. He cares about me.

I came here thinking I could be wrong. An idiot who desperately wanted to believe in something that was never there to begin with. I'm so fucking glad Reese showed me how right I was.

He starts to break our kiss, but I slide my hand around his head and pull him back.

"I don't...want...to stop," I say between kisses. "I don't...want...it...to end."

We enjoy the moment. Embrace it. And I feel all the tension in him relax with the tension I've carried around since our fight last night.

When we finally catch our breath, Reese whispers, "I love you so much, Jay." He leans back. "I'm sorry for what I said. I really just wanted to do what was best for you. I don't want to make you unhappy. I look at you, so filled with life and energy, and I'm just horrified that I'm going to break you with everything that's broken me."

"Don't be arrogant assuming you're the only one who's broken," I say with a smirk.

He cracks a smile.

I see, finally, hope in his expression. Hope we might actually be able to make this work.

"I just haven't cared about anyone like this in so long, and that scares the fuck out of me."

"I love you, too, but if you ever pull any of that fucking shit like last night, you're gonna lose another appendage."

He laughs out loud, momentarily breaking the spell that he's been under.

I know it's not that easy for him, but it's nice to think that, even for a moment, he's able to shake off some of the burden he's been carrying around.

"I'm so fucking sorry."

As soon as he kisses me again, that's all the apology I need. His body against mine. His love. His affection.

I understand where he was coming from, especially now that I know what really happened with his ex-wife. Now that I know he pushed her away because he cared about her, and now that I know he was trying to protect me.

I feel a warm tear on my cheek as we kiss. I can't tell if it's his or mine because I've felt a few as we've shared this moment.

When we pull away from our kiss again, he looks into my eyes, and I see that his concern has returned. "I don't need you to be here for me, Jay," he says.

"I'm not here for you," I say. "I'm here for me. Because I want to be with you. Because I would rather be with you than anywhere else in the world. Because even the shittiest of moments with you is better than the best moment by myself...or with any of the guys I've ever been with."

We embrace again, kissing away all the worry and stress of the night without each other—the night where we both thought we might never see each other again.

I would have missed feeling his face against mine so much.

I would have missed feeling his breath against me. Feeling him inside me.

When we settle, we pull apart and just breathe together, holding each other. Not letting up our grips.

I gaze into those familiar blue eyes. Eyes that make me feel so special and important like that night we held each other, when he seemed to have the word "love" on his mind just as I did.

"I guess we have to get to work today," I say, knowing that I'm killing the moment, but also knowing that we need a little break after the emotional rollercoaster we've been on for the past twelve hours.

He smiles. "That sounds like a good idea. No more slacking off in the office like this."

My gaze settles on something I haven't forgotten. Something that's weighed on my mind since I saw it.

Melanie's letter.

He turns to it, his sad expression returning. "Can't we just enjoy this moment?"

I glare at him. He knows better.

"Aren't you tired of running from this?" I ask.

Releasing me, he approaches the desk and picks up the letter, which is even more crumpled up now that I had it in my clothes.

He tears it open and pulls out a four-by-six-inch photograph. It's the only thing inside.

The picture is of a woman—certainly Melanie—in her thirties with shoulder-length blonde hair and bright blue eyes. Beside her is a man with dark—nearly black—hair. They stand before a painting with a 1st prize blue ribbon on the side

Melanie cradles a baby in her arms, which is wrapped in a blue blanket. She has a bright smile on her face, her eyes glowing with light. This doesn't look like the woman Reese described. Jaded. Bitter. Destroyed. She's happy. A woman filled with life and zest and with the whole world ahead of her.

Reese's face trembles, and he bursts into a fit of tears, pressing his thumb into the picture so hard that it bends.

"It's okay, it's okay," I say, wrapping my arms around him for support. "I guess it'd be hard for anyone to see their wife moving on."

He shakes his head. "No, it's not that. It's just…I thought I'd ruined her life forever." He continues sobbing, fighting to speak through the tears. "And I'm so happy to see that she's smiling again. That no matter what happened, I didn't take that from her forever."

I study the painting behind her. It's just like the one in Reese's living room. A profile of a man staring off.

"It's that same painting she did before she left," he explains. "She had it in the garage. Hadn't shown it to me, and when I found it, I knew that it was over. That this was all she saw every day when she looked at me. And I knew that I had to save her."

"Looks like she turned that pain into something really productive," I say, acknowledging the honor she received for using that inspiration as she was moving on. "So you're clearly still her muse."

He nods as the tears continue rolling down his face.

He flips the photograph over, and on the back, a handwritten message reads, "I miss you. Please call me."

He drops the photograph and loses it in another fit of tears. He turns to me and wraps his arms around me, crying against me.

I hug him, holding him close, being there for him now the way I always want to be there for him.

"She's happy, Jay. She's really happy again."

I hear the relief in his words. How good it feels for him to know that he didn't kill her like he thought he had. And I'm so glad that I can be here for him once again. That I can share this moment of ease with him where he's free of a demon that has haunted him for so long.

"See," I say. "Even if you do totally ruin my life, I'll get better."

He laughs against me, and his sobbing transforms into a loud laugh as he pulls away from me, a bright smile across his red face.

He wipes at his eyes with the back of his hands. "You're awful," he says, but he's all smiles now. And I'm glad that I can be here for that.

As he stops wiping at the tears, he gazes at me again, his smile settling slightly.

"Thank you so much," he says. "You have no idea what it means to me that you came here today. That you didn't run when you could have. And the things that you said…that you're even willing to forgive me for being a total asshole."

"Whoa, whoa. I didn't say you were forgiven for that. You're just going to have to put in a lot of hours and work on this body to make up for it."

"You're fucking amazing," he says, leaning in and kissing me again.

We enjoy each other's affection until we calm down from the excitement of the morning. Then we part to do our jobs. But there's an ease as I work today. In knowing that, when I get back to Reese's place tonight, we're on the same page. That we both know how the other feels and where this is really going, and that he isn't going to try and pull some stunt like he did last night. It won't be easy. Nothing about being with Reese has been easy, but I'm not with him because I want it to be easy. I'm with him because I care about him so much, and because since he's come into my life, it's become so much better. Because he's made me a better person and made me want to be a better person.

And I just know there's so much more happiness in store for us…

Epilogue
Ten Years Later…

Reese

"Wait, wait," Jay says as he grabs the corn casserole we made out of the back seat.

He passes it to me and grabs the apple pie before closing the door.

I snatch his free hand and pull him to me, planting a kiss on his sweet lips.

His lips curl into a smile against my face. When I pull away, he says, "Well, wasn't that sweet?"

We walk side by side up the drive to Shelley and Tyler's new place, chatting about the wreck of a front lawn that Shelley will likely be putting in some long hours working on during the spring. Reminds me of my own garden—the one that Jay and I have expanded, the one we work on together now. I thought I had a green thumb, but Jay has a talent for bringing even the weakest of plants back to life. Just like he did with me.

As we reach the door, I'm reminded of the first time we visited their home all those years ago.

When Jay and I were so new…so scared of what we felt for each other.

Now I'm holding my husband's hand as we visit some of our best friends. The first people either of us really opened up to and started allowing into our lives.

I turn the knob and the door opens.

"Hey, hey, hey!" Jay announces.

The screaming kids upstairs assure us that Shelley and Tyler's kids are as healthy and energized as usual.

Michael, their youngest at six years old, rounds the corner at the top of the stairs. When he spots us, he calls out, "Uncle Reese and Uncle Jay are here!"

He races down and gives us hugs. His sister, now in her teens, follows shortly after him, acting far cooler than she used to act when we would babysit her and play hide-and-seek and dollhouse together. I hear she has a boyfriend now, so I'm sure she's way too cool for silly games now. Just a shame that her older brother Martin can't be here today because he has to work at his job up in Tennessee, where he's going to school.

We lead the kids into the kitchen, where Shelley squats before the stove, assessing the turkey.

Charlie sits at the kitchen table, sipping on a drink. "Why hello there," he says. We always invite Charlie to Thanksgiving dinner with Shelley and Tyler, and he's become a good friend of ours as well.

"Boys! I could hardly tell you were here," Tyler says, eyeing Michael as he enters from the living room.

We hug, and Jay sets the apple pie and casserole on the counter while I approach Charlie, greeting him and making small talk. Jay asks Shelley what she needs help with. We came a little early to make sure we could assist before the other members of her family and some of our mutual friends arrived.

Shelley and Tyler are two of the most welcoming people I've ever met, and I'm proud to be part of their circle. To have shared so many great memories with them from bingo nights to Saturdays at Six Flags with them and their kids.

While Jay, Shelley, and Tyler take charge of dinner, I tend to my responsibility, wrangling the kids. We play hide-and-seek, Michael screaming as loud as always every time I find him. I'm searching for them when the doorbell rings.

"I've got it!" I call since I'm already in the entryway, about to head up the stairs to find the kiddos.

I open the door, and there she is.

Melanie.

With her bright blonde hair and eyes sparkling as she smiles, she's as beautiful as I remember her being when we first met.

Her ten-year-old boy Jarod has his arms around her hip. And her husband Toby is at her side.

It's nice how relaxed I feel in this moment. It's not like back when I tried to avoid her calls.

She's back in my life, but this time, as a friend and confidant. After I opened the envelope with the picture she sent, Jay encouraged me to call her, and with the help of Jay and Laura, I eventually met up with her. It's taken years, but finally we've become close again, and I feel like I'm a better person because of it.

"Hi, Reese," she says, her voice a sweet melody on my ears. It's a voice filled with life and energy—something she lacked for so long when we were together.

"Aren't you going to say hey to Reese?" Toby asks Jarod. "Come on, be nice."

"Oh, I know he's shy," I say. I squat down until I'm eye-level with him. "Nothing wrong with being a little shy, is there?" I wink, and he smirks.

I guide them into the kitchen where we all chat. Tyler tells me about the last game he played with his softball league. I glance over and catch Jay picking up Michael and twirling him around in a circle, Michael screaming loudly again.

When he finishes, Jay glances at me.

We've talked about kids.

We keep talking about them. I know they're in our future, but we both want to wait until we're ready. And I think that time is coming sooner rather than later.

Jay winks at me, and a warm sensation fills my chest.

I never believed I could have fallen so deeply in love with someone. Not the way I have with Jay for all these years.

It's an amazing dinner. We chat and catch up with everyone and eat until we're stuffed.

Then when it ends, we head out, and I know now's the perfect time for my surprise.

"Before we go," I say. I reach into my pocket and retrieve an envelope. Hand it to him.

"What's this?"

I sing "Happy Birthday" to him, and he grins as my voice cracks straight through the song.

"It's not really my birthday yet," he says as I reach the end.

"Shut it. It's was the only way I could create a surprise out of it."

He opens the envelope and pulls out two tickets to the Rita Rudner stand-up show.

"Oh my God," he says. "I can't believe you got these. We're seriously going to her farewell tour?"

"Yup. We're going to Vegas! I already booked our flights."

"You shouldn't have done that."

"Well, considering my pay raise and your new job as supervisor, neither of us is hurting, so I figured we could indulge this year."

He hugs me.

He deserves this and so much more after ten years together. Ten years of friendship. Ten years of love.

As he pulls away, he kisses me. "Thank you. That was really sweet."

It's not the first stand-up show we've seen together, and it won't be the last. We've had a lot of laughs over the years.

Not to say it's always been easy.

In fact, some of the years were hard. I was right about the darkness. It came and consumed me the way it does every so often. There's no magic pill. The triggers don't fade. It wasn't five years ago when the depression got so bad that some days it was hard to breathe, but Jay stood by me and helped me get to my doctor's appointments, helped me through experimenting with new med combinations. He helped out at work when I needed time off, which is what led to his new position. He more than stepped up to the challenge. So while I was right about this terrible thing within me, this thing that will never leave me, I was wrong about Jay. I didn't kill him. If anything, he's only become stronger and someone I can't imagine living without. Not because I need him for what's wrong with me, but I need him because he makes me a better human being.

We head back to our house and stand in the bathroom after our shower, nude, getting ready for bed. I strap into my hands-free crutch.

Jay says, "I know we talk about kids, but…what do you think? We're about ready?"

I beam. I've been waiting for him to say this with such confidence.

"I'm more than ready," I say.

"I wouldn't mind a few. And you're great with them."

"A few?!" I ask with a laugh, but I'd be happy to raise a dozen kids with him.

No one else I'd rather raise kids with than my Jay.

"No, seriously this time," he says.

"Let's do it." I study his face.

"What are you looking at?"

"Just how beautiful you are?"

"Oh, the lines?" Jay asks as he runs his forefinger across his crow's feet.

"Yeah. How they sit just right on your face. How they complement it, even. Not like this old thing that you're stuck with."

"You mean this sexy silver fox." Jay runs his hands through my hair. "I could've done a lot worse."

I kiss him and push him back against the doorframe. I wrap my arm around him and press against the small of his back so that his abs meet mine.

And soon, we're groping and stroking each other's bodies, our stiff cocks rubbing against each other's pelvises.

I want his body more than ever.

We hurry into the bedroom in a frenzy, and I push him down onto the bed.

"Is this the fat dick you want inside you?" I ask him as I raise his legs and pull him back to the edge of the bed.

"Yes, Reese. Oh fucking God yes."

I spit on my cock and ease into him.

It takes more time like this, but it reminds me of the first time we ever fucked raw. When I got to come inside him and make him totally mine, and when he did the same to me. When we were set free of all those remaining boundaries between us and it was just love. *Our* love.

I remove the crutch, and we toss and turn, crawling around on the bed, shifting positions. He fucks me for a bit, and we swap again. He ends up on his back again, his favorite way to come. On my knees, I push into him, watching his expression, lines and all, as his eyes roll back in that familiar way that lets me know just how much he's enjoying what I'm giving him.

Sweat drips off my forehead and onto his tight body—the one he's earned through all his dedication at our local gym—memberships we both take full advantage of.

He starts to reach for his dick, but I snatch his wrist. Then I grab his other and push them back against the mattress. Pinning him down while I fuck him.

He gazes up at me, eagerness in his eyes, excited about what we share.

I shake my head. "Uh-uh. You're gonna come my favorite way.

The way I know how to make him come. The way I prefer it.

"Fuck yes, Reese," he says.

I can see the trust in his eyes—trust that I'm going to fulfill him in the way that's most satisfying to him—in the way that leaves him breathless.

I fuck him harder, and soon he's moaning. I glance down as the come shoots out of his cock and across his body.

"I did that," I say with pride.

Then I come inside him, and the explosion sends sharp, powerful sensations racing through me.

I collapse on him, resting in his seed and sweat, enjoying him being filled with me.

This is who we are. Totally together. Totally wrapped in each other's love.

Our life together is so much more than I could ever have hoped for. Could have even have dreamt for myself after I returned from the war.

"We're gonna need to get those panties out this weekend," Jay teases. "Whaddaya think?"

"I think I'm one lucky son of a bitch," I say. "Who would've thought all it would take was one asshole to shove me down at work…some asshole I can shove down every fucking day now."

Jay beams, and I imagine all the years to come. Years I'm so looking forward to.

THE END

About the Author

A good ole Southern boy, Devon McCormack grew up in the Georgia suburbs with his two younger brothers and an older sister. At a very young age, he spun tales the old fashioned way, lying to anyone and everyone he encountered. He claimed he was an orphan. He claimed to be a king from another planet. He claimed to have supernatural powers. He has since harnessed this penchant for tall tales by crafting worlds and characters that allow him to live out whatever fantasy he chooses. Devon is an out and proud gay man living with his partner in Atlanta, Georgia.

CPSIA information can be obtained
at www.ICGtesting.com
Printed in the USA
LVHW010041030919
629673LV00011B/380/P